REMEMBER
ME
TOMORROW

ALSO BY FARAH HERON

The Chai Factor

Accidentally Engaged

Tahira in Bloom

Kamila Knows Best

How to Win a Breakup

Jana Goes Wild

Just Playing House

REMEMBER ME TOMORROW

A NOVEL

FARAH HERON

SKYSCAPE

Published by Skyscape, Seattle

www.apub.com

Amazon, the Amazon logo, and Skyscape are trademarks of Amazon.com, Inc., or its affiliates.

ISBN-13: 9781662520518 (paperback)
ISBN-13: 9781662513015 (digital)

Cover design by Caroline Teagle Johnson
Cover image: © Ibai Acevedo / Stocksy United; © Westend61, © Tina Terras & Michael Walte, © kool99, © lingqi xie, © DebraLee Wiseberg / Getty

Printed in the United States of America

This book is for all the people who are thriving in places where other people think they don't belong.

ONE

For me, this story starts the day I realize I don't need my best friend anymore and move out of our shared university dorm room. But really, it started *before* that day. And also, *after* that day. I just don't know it yet.

"Aleeza, stop. You can't move out. We *need* to live here together all year," Mia, the aforementioned former *best friend forever*, says.

I snort at her using the words *need to*. Because she's wrong. I simply don't *need* Mia anymore.

As one of the only nonwhite kids in my hometown, years ago I developed a theory that there are two ways to survive socially when you're different. One—be like everyone else. In other words, make sure that my skin color is the only difference between me and my classmates. But I always knew that strategy would never work for me. Because I've always been . . . well, odd. Which was fine when I was a little kid living in Toronto, because being a weird Brown kid was pretty common in the city. But not in Alderville, the tiny town that my parents moved us to when I was seven. I realized then for the first time that my strangeness—not adorable quirkiness but uncool nerdiness—could be a problem for me.

Case in point. Many kids in my Alderville elementary school were into horses, or sometimes goats or sheep. (Which, fair. It's farm country.) And of course, lots of kids were into cats and dogs. But me? I was into octopuses. Obsessed with them, actually. Ever since I saw an enormous one in an aquarium when I was four, I've been fascinated by their big heads, nine brains, and unreal problem-solving skills.

Which brings me to the other weird thing about me. While other girls were into romances and fantasy books, I like old—like, practically ancient—mystery books. My mom's a librarian, and she always ordered Nancy Drew and other whodunit books for me, and I *inhaled* them. Movies too. I love old Agatha Christie films. I used to fanaticize that Alfred Hitchcock was my long-lost uncle.

Anyway, since being the weird, Brown new kid was making me a bit of a social pariah in Alderville, I put all my energy into my second strategy to survive—find a white friend as weird as I am.

Mia became that ride-or-die weird friend that all Brown girls living in small towns need. We became tight after noticing we were both obsessed with this kid-detective graphic novel series. Soon we were borrowing each other's books and movies. Mom started ordering Mia's favorites for the library—still mysteries, but Mia liked thrillers instead of classic whodunits. We had weekly movie nights in my living room dressed up as characters from whatever old movie we were watching. We daydreamed about opening a detective agency in New York City one day.

I thought our friendship was genuine. I honestly thought we'd be friends forever.

It took six months of higher education for me to realize that I didn't know a thing.

"Aleeza, seriously," Mia says again when I ignore her. "Stop packing."

I glance at her once, and keep shoving items into the box. I can't believe I was so dazzled to have a best friend who was popular and well liked and who loved all the same stuff as me (except octopuses), that I failed to notice Mia wasn't actually a very good friend at all. Because over and over, pretty much since the day we met, Mia has been pushing me aside whenever anyone she deems "cooler" is around.

And today is the absolute last time I'm putting up with it. After Mia once again ditched me for her boyfriend, Lance (or specifically, Lance's sister this time), I am not accepting her apologies and promises. This time I am walking away.

Apparently fed up with my packing, Mia comes toward me in our dorm living room. She takes a bright-orange octopus stuffy out of my box and throws it across the room. It lands legs up on the floor near the tiny sofa. "Tentacle Ted belongs in this room, remember?"

Of course I remember. And I knew she would claim custody of the orange stuffy we bought at a county fair near Alderville the day we found out we'd be rooming together, just like I knew she wouldn't let me leave without a fight. Because Mia hates feeling like the villain. She hates feeling like she's losing. It screws up her perfect mental image of herself. But I also know that despite her vow to stop standing me up and letting her boyfriend and his family get in our way *again*, Mia will eventually cave to one of their demands at my expense.

"I'm taking Ted," I say. "I bought him with *my* dollars. And octopuses are *my thing*, not yours." I cross the room to get poor Ted, brushing the dust from the cheap gray industrial carpeting off him.

"We said that Ted would be our first jointly owned dorm room accessory," Mia says, practically pouting.

"Since I'm moving out because of *your* actions, I'm entitled to keep the cephalopod that I paid for." I toss him back into the box.

Mia and I dreamed about moving to Toronto for school for years. I thought she would be better here, since we'd be making new friends together. She was always ahead of me—born and raised in Alderville, she knew all our friends first. But now that we've actually moved to the city, Mia is even worse than she was back home. She's like two different people. In our room, Mia and I talk about movies and books, and she seems to love my octopuses. Outside our dorm room, Mia ignores me. She's unreliable. She does whatever Lance or any of his friends want. In my opinion, she's trying way too hard to fit in with her new boyfriend's friends.

"You can't move out!" Mia says. "You're supposed to be my roommate all year!" She looks genuinely upset, but I know that's only because we're alone. If someone else were here—especially Lance or any of his crew—she'd be mocking me for my attachment to octopuses.

"Tell your precious Taylor to move in," I say. "I'm already gone." I'm not sure where my new bravery is coming from, but I am loving it right now. I hold up the university pass hanging around my neck. "This card won't open the building door anymore. My ResConnect profile is already updated. I am no longer your roommate." ResConnect is the campus residence app. I put in the room change request only hours ago, and I'm lucky they had a spot for me.

Mia shakes her head, her wavy brown hair falling out of its messy bun. She's always been pretty—her light-brown hair and big blue eyes give her a kind of girl-next-door vibe. She's dressed almost the same as me right now, in jeans and a sweatshirt. Hers has a Roots logo on it, while mine, of course, has an octopus.

"You're being stupid, Aleeza!" she says in the same voice she uses to yell at her dog. "You are not giving up years of friendship over a YouTube series!" She tries to snatch my favorite coffee mug—the one with a tentacle for a handle—but I beat her to it.

It's honestly a little bit surprising just how badly she's taking this. But I guess it makes sense—she's not used to me having a spine. I've been her doormat for years, but we're in the city now and I can make new friends. I don't need Mia anymore.

"No, Mia, *you* are throwing away years of friendship over a YouTube series! You're the one who replaced me with your boyfriend's sister!"

I pick up the top sheet of our campus newspaper to wrap the mug in. I'm a first-year journalism student and I wrote a film review in this edition, but it isn't on the front page. "We planned our *TCU Mysteries* web series for months," I say, not looking at my former friend. "We did market research, had a logo made, and bought a camera. One episode in and you want to replace me with your boyfriend's sister?"

"I don't want to replace you! I'm *adding* Taylor to the web series because she has a huge social presence; this will be great for our reach.

We could be huge! I thought you needed to do this for your media project?"

I blink. Yes, the web series was supposed to be my major project for my media class, but not all YouTube series are equal. Our series, *TCU Mysteries*, was supposed to be about mysteries associated with our school, Toronto City University. The first episode was about a student found dead in her apartment on Easter in the fifties, and we just started the research on our second episode, about this wealthy alumni who donated a ton of money to the school, then mysteriously drowned a few weeks later. But Taylor wants to change the entire focus of the series to be about skincare and makeup instead. I like a good face mask as much as the next person, but Mia *knows* my future goal is a career as an investigative journalist, not a beauty editor. My media project is supposed to align with my journalism career goals.

I look down, the picture in the newspaper catching my eye. It's that second-year student who disappeared off the face of the earth a few months ago. I wave the paper at Mia. "We were going to do an episode on this missing student! A TCU mystery that's literally happening right now! Maybe we could have found him!"

"There are already eight student podcasts about that missing guy," Mia says. "I know you're, like, *obsessed* with him, but I heard he was a huge asshole. He's not worth finding. And, he's been missing so long, he's totally dead. Just like our mystery web series is dead! Skincare is hot now! Taylor says we can leverage off her existing TikTok brand, and we'll have a hundred thousand subscribers in a month!"

I really don't want to have this discussion. If I let it go on too long, Mia will win. She always wins. This is a pattern, and patterns become cycles until someone breaks them, and I am in the mood to break things. But not this mug. I wrap the octopus mug in the newspaper.

Mia is finally silent, so I fold the flaps of the box closed, then put on my boots, parka, hat, and mittens. After I'm fully suited up to brave the snowy March weather, I look around the small living room of the apartment-style dorm room Mia and I have shared since September.

The sturdy wood furniture that is surprisingly comfortable. The K-pop posters we framed. This building, West Hall, is considered the best residence in our downtown university, and Mia and I cheered when we found out we got a room here. And now I'm willingly leaving it behind, just like I'm leaving behind my best friend of more than a decade. With a duffel bag hanging off each shoulder, a knapsack on my back, and the box in my arms, I leave the room without another word.

I should have walked away from this friendship a long time ago. Actually, I should have walked away from Mia when an octopus told me to five months ago. Ironically, it was the same night that Mia first met Lance.

~

Five months earlier—October 29

It was a mistake to wear a mustache to my first ever university party. A *fake* mustache, mind you. True, as a Brown girl, I do grow visible upper-lip hair, but my mom found me a threading aunty in Toronto even before frosh week. Fake or not, though, I am the only girl with a mustache at this party.

Actually, even before gluing the handlebar mustache to my upper lip, I made a mistake by *not* dressing like an octopus like I had for the last few Halloweens. Last year I was Ursula the sea witch, and the year before that Henry the Octopus from *The Wiggles*. But this year, Mia insisted that for our first *university* Halloween, we needed to match each other, and our costumes should be tied to our upcoming YouTube mystery series so we could create content for our socials. She would be Sherlock Holmes, and I would be Watson. My mom mail-ordered me a tweed jacket, a bowler hat, and a very realistic fake mustache, and I assumed Mia did the same.

But the moment I show Mia my Victorian physician costume, I know I miscalculated. Mia's costume isn't accurate to the period at all.

Instead, she got a cheap "sexy Sherlock" costume, complete with fishnets and a skirt short enough to make a Victorian faint.

I suppose her costume does what she actually wants it to do, because seconds after we walk into the campus pub, she catches the attention of some dude wearing a bad Spider-Man costume without a mask. He admires Mia's legs and makes fun of my mustache in the same breath. Mia laughs her fake, flirty giggle, and the dude orders her and all his friends (but not me) tequila shots. I head to the bar alone, yanking the bowler off my head. I didn't bother to put any product in my shoulder-length, curly hair since I figured it would be stuffed into a hat all night, and now frizzy strands fall into my eyes. I brush them away and keep walking. I can get my own damn tequila.

I order a shot from the mad scientist tending bar. I have to show my ID, of course. I'm nineteen—legal to drink here—but I look younger, even with the mustache. When I get my shot, I take a tiny sip instead of drinking it all at once. It tastes like turpentine.

"My dear Watson, is it? How do you do?" a deep voice next to me says.

I turn to see an octopus. Literally, an *octopus* is standing next to me at the bar. I frown. Is tequila supposed to cause hallucinations? I look closer, and it's not actually an octopus, but a guy wearing a cheap Party City Cthulhu mask. He's also got on a black T-shirt and jeans.

"How do you know I'm Watson?" I ask.

"The tweed," he says.

I frown, which makes my mustache tickle my cheeks. "Lots of characters wear tweed."

"True." He rubs his hands on his tentacle beard as if he's thinking. "Are you supposed to be Mr. Bean?"

I snort. The guy nods toward my drink. "What are you drinking?"

"Tequila." For some reason I don't want this octopus-man to think I'm as lame as I actually am, so I drink the rest of my shot in one gulp. It burns going down. I suppress a cough.

The octopus-person stares at me. I can't read his expression because of the mask, so I can't tell if he's impressed or laughing at me.

"Are you alone?" he asks. I wonder if he's trying to pick me up. Maybe he has a thing for mustached Victorian doctors?

I nod. "My friend ditched me for a superhero." I glance over to Mia, who has her arm around Spider-Man's waist while she talks to sexy Wednesday Addams.

The bartender takes my empty shot glass and asks me if I want another. I look at the list of drinks taped to the bar top.

"I'll have a Witch's Brew." I give the bartender a ten-dollar bill, and he hands me a can of blackberry vodka cooler.

"I'll take the same," Cthulhu guy says, giving the bartender money. The bartender hands him a can. The guy lifts the bottom of his latex mask to take a long sip of his drink. I can't make out what his face looks like from this distance. In fact, I doubt he's trying to pick me up, or he'd be standing closer. He pulls his mask back over his chin even before he puts his can down.

"Are you in hiding or something?" I ask.

He laughs again. "It's Halloween, the only time of the year I can wear a Lovecraftian mask and be normal."

Him using the word *Lovecraftian* proves he's *not* normal. He may even be as dorky as I am. "Honestly, I think *normal* is overrated," I say. "I wish I could wear a tweed jacket all year."

"Why can't you?"

I glance at Mia, who is laughing and talking to her new friends like she's known them for years. What would it be like to be so comfortable with new people? "You ever feel like the whole world is spinning five steps ahead of you?" I ask. "And by the time you catch up with them, they've already moved on?"

I turn back to the guy who's maybe trying to pick me up. I'm sure I've scared him off. No one wants philosophical introspection at a party like this. But again, with that mask on, I have no idea what he's thinking. He's still staring at me, which is disconcerting—those latex tentacles almost glow in the dim lights of the bar. Even with a few feet between us, I can smell him. Clean laundry detergent and a hint of . . . cinnamon? He has broad shoulders and strong arms.

He finally speaks again. "Three things, Watson. One, your life is going to get so much better once you step away from the people holding you back, because real friends don't forget friends when things don't go as planned. Two, I have a very strong suspicion that it's not *you* who has to catch up with the world, but the world that needs to catch up with you."

The Cthulhu man has a nice voice. And for some reason he's making the hair on the back of my neck stand up. Suspiciously, I narrow my eyes. "Are you flirting with me?"

"Are you drunk?"

"No," I lie. That tequila went straight to my head. "What's the third thing?"

"I'd like to try and catch up with you. Do you want to dance?"

The song playing is "Save Your Tears" by The Weeknd, and maybe it's an omen. I *should* be saving my tears. I could be dancing with this mysterious octopus instead of whining about my friend ditching me for Spider-Man.

I smile, then take a big gulp of my drink. "Sure, but keep your tentacles to yourself, okay?" I peel the mustache off my upper lip, taking all the natural hair I had there off too. Well, at least I don't need to see my threading aunty this month.

He laughs. "Agreed, my dear Watson. I'll keep you safe if you promise to keep me safe too."

I nod. "Deal."

TWO

My new residence, East House, is on the other side of campus, and walking there with three bags and a box is hellish. Actually, doing anything in Toronto winter is hellish, and this year has been particularly bad. Cold. Icy. Treacherous. I push through blistering wind and blowing snow on the narrow path snaking through campus, cursing past Aleeza for not agreeing with the campus-housing guy who suggested I wait and move out on the weekend because of the snowstorm. But once I made the decision to move, I knew I needed to leave Mia as soon as possible.

When I put in the request for a midyear room change, the guy in the office immediately warned me he probably wouldn't find me a vacant room, as a month into second term is a weird time to move. But I had a gut feeling that there would be something for me. The room he found wasn't anything to celebrate, though. East House is the oldest, smallest, and least desirable residence at school, and the room was described as . . . modest. But it would be fine. I would deal. This would be my fresh start.

"Do you need help?" a voice behind me asks.

I turn and see a person about my height wearing a gray wool hat, an enormous blue parka with the hood up, and an orange scarf pulled up over her nose. Her voice sounds familiar, but beneath all the winter gear, I can't see her face.

"Oh, it's fine. I got it." I smile, but then remember she can't see me under my scarf either. I turn down the less-maintained path that leads to East House.

I can barely see thanks to the blowing snow, and I can't feel my cheeks even with my scarf on by the time I get there. The muddy-brown building is old. Even . . . crumbling. It was originally an early 1900s mansion that the university converted into residences in the nineties. I frown as I stand in front of the main entrance. I have no clue how to scan my card to open the door with all this stuff in my hands.

"Now will you accept some help?" I hear from behind me. I turn. It's the girl in the blue parka from earlier. She sounds friendly and amused.

I nod. "Yeah. My card is around my neck. I'm just moving in." I don't want her to think I'm breaking in. With all my possessions. During a snowstorm.

"I got it. I live here too." She takes her pass from her pocket and taps it on the card reader. After opening the door, she takes the box from me. With my hands now free, I push my scarf off my face as I walk into the residence.

The entrance opens to a lobby common area with a few couches. Very few of the mansion's original features remain here, only white walls and gray industrial carpet. To the right of the front door is the mailroom, with a bulletin board absolutely packed with small pieces of paper, flyers, and even artwork. I have no idea how it's still attached to the wall with the weight of all that crap on it.

"Where are you heading?" the girl asks.

"Um . . . second floor?"

She turns back to look at me, and I can see her eyes still look amused. "You're moving to the second floor? That's only professor offices."

"Oh . . . it's supposed to be room 225."

The expression in the girl's eyes changes immediately, and all her friendliness drains away. She takes a step backward, as if I just told her I have lice.

"What's wrong?" I ask.

She shakes her head and walks toward a set of stairs across from the mailroom. After resting the box on a stair, she pushes her scarf down and looks at me. That's when I realize I do know this person. It's Gracie Song from my politics seminar. I think she's also in my Introduction to Journalism lecture. I'm pretty sure she's a first-year journalism student like me, but I've never spoken to her. "Room 225 is on the third floor," she says.

I shake my head. "That makes no sense."

Gracie shrugs and starts climbing the steps with my box.

Ugh. Meeting people is awkward. I don't know what to say. But I don't have Mia anymore, so I need to make an effort. "Um, thanks for taking my box," I say as I climb behind her.

"No worries."

"You live here too?" I ask. Dumb. She already told me she lives here.

I see the back of her head nod. I've never spoken to her before, but I've seen Gracie Song around enough to know that she's normally chatty. Social. But right now she seems like she'd rather be stuck on this staircase with a dead skunk instead of me.

My heart beats heavily. I have no idea why Gracie doesn't like me now when a few moments ago she asked if I needed help.

"What floor are you on?" I ask.

"Same as you." She still sounds pissed off.

Why does it bother her so much that we'll be living on the same floor?

When we get to the third floor, she turns right and sets the box down. She points to the first door. "That's you," she says. "The bathroom's down the hall." She disappears in the same direction, walking past my room.

Okay. That was weird.

I look at the door in question, and yes, the number 225 is on it. I unlock the door and drag my things into what will be my room for the rest of my first year of university.

Modest is an understatement. The room is *small*. There's a shallow closet on one side of the door and a window on the left wall. The furniture is old and looks more run-down than what I had in West Hall. There are two twin beds, two desks with wood chairs, and two small dressers. Why are there two of everything? The housing guy told me it was a single room. With all the furniture, it's incredibly cramped, especially compared to the apartment-style room Mia and I had in West Hall. I have no idea how anyone could share a room this small. If a person slept on each bed, they could hold hands.

But there's no sign of a roommate. Both mattresses are bare, and there's nothing on either desk. Alone, I could make this room work. Put up some posters and tapestries. Some octopuses. Make it my own.

I drop my box and bags on the floor and search for sheets to make up the beds. I'll use the bed near the window for sitting on, and sleep on the other one. After making both beds, I toss Tentacle Ted on the bed by the window and start putting my clothes away. Eventually, I run out of space in one of the small dressers. I have a lot of bulky sweatshirts, so I'll need to use both dressers.

But when I open the bottom drawer of the second dresser, it's not empty. I try the other drawers, and they're full too. A stack of black T-shirts (men's size medium), jeans, and a drawer full of boxer briefs. This room is supposed to be empty. Maybe I *do* have a roommate? But this looks like a male-identifying person's stuff. The dorms at the school are coed, but individual rooms are not.

The top drawer has some mail in it. I hate to snoop—but I need to know who, or what, I'm dealing with here.

The top letter is from the school registrar and is addressed to *Jay Hoque.*

My breath hitches. I know that name. Jay Hoque is the *missing* guy. The one who Mia thinks is most definitely *dead*. That's why Gracie looked at me like I was moving into a ghost's room. I am.

At that moment, my phone buzzes with a message. When I check it, I see that it's from the roommate-chatting feature on ResConnect.

It's probably Mia begging me to come back. I open the app, intending to tell her I'm not her roommate anymore.

But it's not Mia.

Jay: Hey I just got notice you're my new roommate. Don't get too comfortable. I'll be fighting this. They told me I'd be alone all year.

I stare at the phone, blinking. So . . . Jay is back? How did I miss that the guy finally turned up? Maybe that's what that newspaper article is about?

I don't write back. What am I supposed to say? *Yay, you're not dead*?

This means I've been assigned to a room with a person already living in it. A male person. And the school won't allow a female student to live with a male one, especially in such a tiny room. The housing guy said there's nothing else in the school. I'm going to be sent back to Mia's room.

Ugh. There goes my chance for a fresh start.

THREE

Unfortunately, the university housing office is in West Hall, the building I just moved out of. With wind stinging my face, I trudge back there, cursing the storm. The whole campus looks deserted. It's creepy with the blowing snow and wind whipping the tree branches around. It feels like the end of the world.

My heart is pounding when I get to West Hall. I go straight to the first-floor offices, still not really believing that this is happening. I mean, what are the chances? Not only is the *only* empty room in the entire university not really empty after all, but it's *Jay's* room. Jay Hoque.

I didn't know Jay Hoque, but I'd seen him around campus a lot before he disappeared. In the student center, in dining halls, even at campus events. I'm pretty sure I even crashed into him in the library once. Actually, before he disappeared, it felt like I saw Jay *everywhere*, and when I mentioned that to Mia, she claimed I was obsessed with him or something. She even said it was just like me to lust after an unattainable guy, which was ridiculous. I wasn't *lusting* after him; it was just hard not to notice Jay.

I'm sorry for what happened to him and all, but the dude *exuded* bad-boy vibes. If this were a teen movie, he'd be either the stoner or the mysterious guy no one knows who somehow ends up with the head cheerleader. He'd be Bender if this were *The Breakfast Club*. Patrick in *10 Things I Hate About You*. Or Logan, if this were the best TV show ever, *Veronica Mars*.

And now I've seen the guy's underwear. I have no idea how I'll be able to face him on campus.

The guy who assigned me to East House is still in the housing office. I march up to his desk and put my hands on my hips, hoping a power stance will give me some confidence. "You gave me a room that has someone living in it."

The guy looks up from his computer and frowns at me like he has no idea who I am.

I exhale. "Aleeza Kassam. I was here this morning. You gave me a room in East House, but there's a guy's stuff in it. It's against school policy to room me with a male student, isn't it?"

The housing guy shakes his head. "No, that room is empty." He does something on his computer, not even looking at me. "The previous resident isn't coming back."

"You should tell him that. He told me on ResConnect not to get too comfortable because he's not supposed to have a roommate."

The housing guy suddenly freezes. His face goes a little whiter than it already was. "What did you say?"

"He messaged me in ResConnect," I say. "The residence app?" Considering this guy works at campus housing, he should know about ResConnect, shouldn't he?

The guy still looks incredibly confused. "We've had this conversation before, haven't we?"

"Yeah, earlier today when you assigned me the room. But you told me it was empty."

"No, I mean about the room being taken."

I raise a brow. "It's Jay Hoque's room. The guy in second year who went missing? He just messaged me on ResConnect."

The housing guy shakes his head. "He's not returning to the school. This morning the registrar informed us that he's been unenrolled. That's why the room was available today. Maybe ResConnect hasn't updated your room assignment, and it was your former roommate messaging you. Let me check the system."

I wait for him to do his thing, but I know he's wrong. It wasn't Mia. The message clearly said it was from someone named Jay. After a few seconds, he looks up at me. "The system's fine. You are the only assigned resident to East House 225. Could've been a glitch—a leftover message from when he was in the room."

I pull out my phone and open the app. "I'll show you." When the chat opens, it's empty. No messages at all. Definitely not one from Jay Hoque. I frown. "I swear, the message was here."

"You're a first-year student, right?" the housing guy asks.

I nod.

"Moving away from home can be a challenging transition, and—"

"What does that have to do with the message on ResConnect?"

"You've had some recent interpersonal struggles too. Plus, talk of the missing student has affected many on campus."

I raise a brow, incredulous. "You think I'm making this up?"

His expression doesn't change. "The university has resources you can take advantage of. Individual counseling, plus support groups. I urge you to connect with the student life—"

"I'm not delusional. I *swear* there was a message from Jay here."

The guy shakes his head and points to his screen. "Jay Hoque hasn't been seen in months. I apologize for his things being left in the room. His mother hasn't returned calls to pick it up. But it's not possible that he messaged you in the app. Even if he's back, no one else is assigned to room 225 in the system, so no one can message you on ResConnect. The room-chat function only allows people assigned to the same room to communicate." He turns his monitor so I can see the room 225 information on his screen. "See? You're the only one in the room. It's a single room. Eliza Kassam."

I roll my eyes. "It's pronounced A-*lee*-za. Just like it's spelled." He doesn't say anything to that. "If it's a single room," I ask, "why are there two beds and two dressers?"

He turns his screen back to face him. "It used to be a double, but a few rooms in East House were redesignated as singles in September due to their size. If you want, I can have operations remove the extra furniture. Most students opt to keep it for storage."

This is ridiculous. I *saw* that message. But the housing guy is right about one thing . . . I *am* stressed. The whole Mia situation could be messing me up more than I realize.

"What do I do with his things?" I ask. "Can't someone come get it?"

He shrugs. "I'll put in a call, but campus security is a little short-staffed right now. Maybe you can box up his personal effects until we reach the next of kin?"

Personal effects. Next of kin. Just like Mia, the school is assuming the guy is dead. His poor mother.

"This can't be the only empty room in the whole school, can it? I don't mind a roommate. As long as it's a . . . you know. Girl."

He looks at his computer screen, shaking his head. "You were lucky to get that one."

~

I've missed all my classes today, thanks to this mess. And now I'm hungry. East House doesn't have its own dining hall since it's so small, so I go to the food hall in City Tower next door. The selection there is disappointing. Sigh. That's another thing I gave up—West Hall has the best food in the school. I grab a boring-looking grain bowl to go.

When I finally get back to East House, I check my new mailbox to find it empty, then climb the stairs to the third floor. Gracie Song is in the hallway, talking to another girl. Maybe this is my chance to fix things with her? I'll be living next to Gracie until the end of the term, and awkwardly sneaking past her whenever I see her would be annoying.

"Hi, Gracie! Thanks again for helping me with my box," I say. "Looks like we'll be neighbors!"

She blinks at me. The person she's talking to, a white girl with long brown hair in a ponytail and an expensive winter coat, looks at me with a strange expression. She turns back to Gracie. "Thanks for letting me hide out in your place."

She kisses Gracie briefly on the lips and then walks toward the stairs. As she passes me, she nods toward my door. "What kind of voodoo did you do to get his room? I think it's *so* tacky. The room is probably cursed—you might want to burn some sage or something." The girl disappears down the stairs.

I look back at Gracie, but she doesn't seem to want to explain what her girlfriend meant. "She seems nice!" I say. I'm probably laying it on too thick.

"Are you really moving into that room?" Gracie asks. She looks irritated.

Okay. Fine. We'll skip the small talk and get right to it. I nod. "It's the only free room in the school. I had to leave my last residence. Roommate issues."

"Do you know whose room it is?"

I nod. "Yeah, the missing guy, Jay. I only discovered that after I moved in. Were . . . are you friends with him?"

Gracie crosses her arms. "No."

Now that she's taken off all her winter gear, I see that Gracie is wearing a very cute red-and-yellow floral dress with a yellow cardigan and red lipstick. Her wavy black hair reaches just past her shoulders, and her bangs fall into her eyes. Gracie is East Asian, with a round face and huge smile. She's not smiling now, though.

"I think you're in my program," I say. "Journalism, first year. I'm Aleeza Kassam."

Gracie's expression softens a tiny bit. "I thought you looked familiar."

I smile. I want to ask her why she was so spooked when she found out I was moving into Jay's room, or why her girlfriend (or hookup?) said I should burn sage, but I'm afraid that will just annoy her again.

"You really didn't know this was Jay's room?" she asks.

"No, why?"

She gives me a look that tells me she doesn't believe me, then uses the key around her neck to open her door. "Welcome to East House," she says before she shuts it behind her.

I exhale and unlock my door. It will take some work, but I'm *determined* to make Gracie my friend this term. This is supposed to be my fresh start. New residence, new Aleeza.

I already know that Mia wouldn't like Gracie. She'd call her *quirky* with that dress-and-glasses combo. She'd say that no one wears red lipstick just for class, and Gracie is trying too hard. But Mia's judgments won't affect who I associate with anymore.

I open the blinds. The room isn't really that bad. With the setting sun shining into it, it's kind of nice. Small, though. I decide to keep the extra furniture. The extra bed can be like a couch/daybed, and I can definitely use the extra dresser.

After eating dinner while watching an episode of *Only Murders in the Building* on my laptop, I go back to my duffel and continue to unpack. I put away my school supplies, then stack my books on the extra desk. Finally, I take my now-empty box and start packing Jay Hoque's stuff, trying not to think too much about him while I'm doing it.

This whole situation is so weird. That ResConnect message, Gracie's strange reaction to me being in Jay's room. Even Gracie's girlfriend's comment that I did voodoo to get it.

Should I burn sage? I don't usually put any stock in that woo-woo mystical stuff. Tarot, crystals, and burning sage were all the rage in Alderville last year, but I didn't get involved. Those things are all based on pagan traditions or Christianity. My family is Muslim, and even though we don't really practice much, I don't want to screw up any possible afterlife by dipping my toes into something I shouldn't.

What happened to Jay is such a compelling mystery, though. A few weeks ago, I did a tiny bit of research on his disappearance, thinking I'd do an episode on his case. What I remember is that he apparently disappeared from his own room. This room. His ID card logged him coming into the building one night—and then never leaving it. Apparently, an eyewitness saw him in the mailroom on the ground floor. When campus police checked on him the next day, after his mother had said he wasn't returning her calls, he wasn't here.

There was no trace of him. He'd just *vanished*. And no one could figure out how, or why. It's not possible to leave through the room windows—they don't open more than a few inches. The front-door camera showed no sign of him leaving the building.

I suddenly remember that newspaper article I wrapped my octopus mug in. I grab it from the recycling bin.

Just under the headline—Jay Hoque's Final Days—is a picture of him. The caption says it was taken in November, days before his disappearance. I study it, even though I remember exactly what he looked like. Jay had wavy hair in the deepest black imaginable, pale-brown eyes with dark, curly lashes, and a square jaw on a narrow face. I have no idea what his ethnic background was, but he had an olive skin tone—almost faintly Mediterranean, or maybe Middle Eastern. With Jay, it was his mannerisms, his *vibe*, that made him as striking as his looks. He was a combination of aloof, rebellious, and *way too cool* for this place. And honestly? He was kind of hot. He wasn't particularly tall but had broad shoulders and a way of moving that said he didn't care if someone was in his way.

I look closer at the picture. I have seen Jay smile before—when I used to see him around campus. I remember thinking his smile looked too big for his face. But that wide smile is not in this picture. In fact, he's almost scowling. Looking straight at the camera with those haunting pale eyes. Did he know what was going to happen to him?

I skim the article. There isn't any new information in it. Mostly it goes over his last few days on campus, which were pretty normal. The writer interviewed professors in his engineering program and Emma Coffey, his ex-girlfriend (or, from what it sounds like, one of his many ex-girlfriends). Looking at her picture on the second page, I'm not sure I've seen her before. But then again, I am not sure I'd remember her if I had. There is nothing that stands out about her. She looks like any other white Canadian university student with long, honey-colored hair. Emma claims that she and Jay were together for a few months, and she saw him on campus the day before he went missing. She said he probably took off because he was caught dating too many girls at the same time.

I chuckle to myself. If I were investigating this case, Emma is where I would start—a woman scorned. I've seen enough crime shows to know that either love or money is the motive for most crimes. I also doubt that Jay Hoque, with his devil-may-care attitude, would run away because a girl discovered he was unfaithful. He was a known player, so why would he care?

I shake my head as I toss the paper back into the recycling bin. There's no reason to obsess over the guy because I'm in his old room. I have a tendency to overthink things that don't matter to me, which is actually a great trait for a journalist. But I don't want to get too fixated on Jay Hoque. The whole situation is weirding me out, and I'd like to be able to sleep in his room. *My* room.

After unpacking everything, I head to the bathroom to wash my face and brush my teeth. It sucks I don't have my own bathroom any-more. No one acknowledges me there, or in the hallway. I may as well be invisible.

Maybe moving was a mistake. At least I knew people in West Hall. I could have lived with Mia and not talked to her. Or maybe we could have worked it out. I hate this feeling of being all alone. I've been feeling it a lot since Mia met Lance. Even for Christmas—we both went home to Alderville, but Mia came back to Toronto early to be with Lance and his friends, and I spent New Year's Eve with my parents.

But I'm not going to fall into despair. This is my chance to start fresh . . . make new friends. Focus on me for a change.

When I get back to my room, my phone buzzes with a notification. It's late—past eleven o'clock. I leave my bathroom caddy on my desk and unlock my phone.

It's ResConnect. Jay Hoque is messaging me again.

Heart racing, I sit on my bed to read his message.

Jay: Why are you still here? Kegan says no one else is assigned to this room, but I just got home and you're on my ResConnect again.

Jay: If this is a prank, it's not working. Stop.

I stare at the message. What. *The hell.* Is going on?

Why is Jay Hoque messaging me? Why is he existing at all? And who the hell is Kegan?

I have to agree with Jay, though, or whoever it is. This is a terrible prank. And in very bad taste, too, because the person the prankster is impersonating is *literally* a missing person. Could it be Mia? Even *she* couldn't be this heartless. Maybe Lance? Or his sister, Taylor? I wouldn't put it past them.

Or maybe lines are crossed in the app, and even though the message says it's from Jay Hoque, it's actually someone else?

Aleeza: Who are you?

Jay: I'm the person who was fucking promised no one would be moving into this room. It's supposed to be a single now.

Aleeza: No, I mean what's your name? What room? I think ResConnect is glitching.

Jay: East House room 225. I'm Jay Hoque. It says your name is Aleeza. Why are you here?

I inhale sharply when I read the name Jay Hoque. This isn't crossed wires. Clearly, it's a prank.

Aleeza: Yes, I'm Aleeza Kassam. First Year Journalism. I had to leave my other room because of a bad roommate, and this was the only empty room in the school.

Jay: Well, it's not fucking empty. I'm right here. I was at the office today and Kegan told me no one else is assigned to this room.

Aleeza: Who's Kegan?

Jay: Kegan works at campus housing! He told me I have no roommate and yet I come back and you're listed as assigned to Room 225.

My breath hitches. What is going on? Is Kegan the guy I talked to in campus housing today? The one who had déjà vu when I told him that Jay had shown up on my ResConnect?

Also . . . where did Jay say he is right now?

Aleeza: Where are you? Like at this moment?

Jay: I already said I'm in room 225. You're going to have to stay in your bad roommate situation because you can't come here.

Aleeza: Like are you inside the room right now? East House, third floor, room 225?

Jay: You sure you're a journalism student? Reading comprehension doesn't seem to be your strong suit. Yes, I'm here right now, sitting on my bed under the window.

I stare straight in front of me at the bed under the window, which has nothing on it but Tentacle Ted. Jay Hoque is most definitely not there. His underwear is in a box in my closet, but not the guy himself.

Someone is either playing a very cruel joke or I'm officially losing my mind because of loneliness.

Or, hell, maybe Jay *is* dead, and I'm talking to a ghost.

I turn off my phone. Clearly, I need to get some sleep. Hopefully, this whole hallucination will go away in the morning. I do *not* have the bandwidth for this.

FOUR

The next morning, Gracie is on the stairs when I come out of my room. I rush to catch up to her. "You heading to politics?" I ask.

She nods but doesn't stop to wait for me.

"Did you do the readings?" I ask. "That textbook is so dry. I need to have, like, electronic music playing in the background, so I don't fall asleep reading it."

She doesn't say anything. Operation Make Gracie My Friend isn't going well. "Hey, can I ask you a question? Is your room a double?"

She shakes her head. "All the rooms on the floor are singles."

"But they used to be doubles, right?"

She nods.

"You ever have messages on the ResConnect chat even though you're in a single room?" I ask. This morning the chat log was empty again, and all the messages from Jay—or from whoever was pranking me—were gone.

Gracie turns to me and frowns. We're on the main floor now. "I thought the ResConnect chat was only for roommates?"

"Yeah, but I had some weird messages last night. They're gone now. Probably a glitch."

"If they're gone now, then don't worry about it."

She's right. I shouldn't be worrying about this. It probably won't happen again. There is no way that I was *actually* messaging with Jay Hoque.

"Hey, how well did you know Jay?" I ask Gracie as she walks toward the front door. "Did he ever mention weird things happening in the room?"

Gracie opens the front door. She looks at me before going outside, her expression annoyed. "Look, I don't know how you managed to convince the school to give you *that* room, but this whole thing is so disrespectful. Jay is a person, and he's missing. It's bad enough you bird-watcher weirdos are obsessed with him just because he was hot and broody, but inserting yourself into his personal life is ghoulish. Go touch grass or something." She turns and walks outside, closing the door before I can follow her.

Okaaay. What is she talking about? Why does she think I'm into bird-watching?

I wait a few seconds before going outside. I need to let this go. Gracie is right—I shouldn't be concerning myself with this glitch, or prank, or whatever. In fact, I should plant myself in the student housing office until Kegan finds me a new room . . . one without a missing bad boy attached to it.

Wait. *Kegan.* Is that really the housing guy's name? I don't think I heard it when I was in the office yesterday. The only reason I *think* his name is Kegan is because Jay told me that last night. Or my brain told me the name when it was having its little hallucination.

When I get to politics, I sit near the back of the lecture hall. Gracie arrives and picks a spot up front with the people she usually sits with. But of course, I can't go anywhere near her. She clearly wants nothing to do with me.

The professor has already begun, so I quickly open my laptop to take notes. When she takes a break, I open the campus housing office web page. After scrolling through the arbitration process for roommate conflicts and the process for requesting a room transfer, I see the contact listing at the bottom.

Kegan Butler, Office of the Campus Housing Authority.

Shit. His name *is* Kegan.

But this isn't necessarily proof that the conversation with Jay last night was real. My subconscious may have seen Kegan's name when I was in the office, even if my conscious mind didn't notice it.

I have media after politics. While I'm waiting for the professor to show, my mind wanders to that interaction with Gracie. I still don't get why she called me a bird-watcher.

Wait. *Jay Hoque.* Jay is a type of bird. And *Hoque* is pronounced like the word *hawk*—also a bird. Are Birdwatchers people who watch Jay?

None of this makes any sense. And to be honest, none of it has anything to do with me. I need to focus on school, and on meeting people. Maybe I should join a school club or volunteer for something. I can't let drama with Mia ruin the rest of the year, and I can't go back to Alderville after exams with literally no friends.

During my media seminar, the professor calls each person to her desk to chat about our independent project. This assignment is worth a huge portion of our grade and is intended to be used in our portfolios to help us get internships and co-op placements in our second year. My *TCU Mysteries* web series with Mia was supposed to be my project, but after Mia dropped me to do the skincare one with Taylor, now I need a new one.

My professor, Sarah, frowns when I tell her that my plans have changed. "I loved the sound of that series! Such a great connection to investigate mysteries associated with the school. May I ask why you changed your mind?"

"I had a falling-out with my cohost."

"Is there any reason why you can't do it alone? It doesn't need to be a video series—a solo podcast would be great." Sarah looks down at her notes. "If I remember correctly, you're hoping to specialize in investigative journalism, right?"

I nod.

"Hmm. While I love the concept of the *TCU Mysteries*, I do think covering a different mystery each episode probably wasn't the best way to demonstrate your investigation skills. It would be better to focus on *one* mystery. Investigate every avenue. Interview everyone you can. Do a real deep dive."

"So do the podcast alone with only one topic?"

Sarah shrugs. "It doesn't even need to be a podcast. A long-form piece or a documentary would work. Think about what you want to do, not just for your co-op term, but in your *career*. Are you dreaming of print media? Then do a long-form article. TV? Do a web series. Demonstrate your passion! And make it relevant. Find a personal connection to the subject matter, like a mystery associated with the university, or maybe a scandal in your family—or anything, really." She smiles. "A personal connection in an investigative piece makes it all the more compelling. Show me a first draft next week. I have faith you can do this!"

At least someone has faith in my ability. I certainly don't.

After my last class of the day, I head back to East House. I'm nervous, though. Is the mystery prankster going to message me again? Maybe I can just delete the ResConnect app from my phone. Would that stop the hallucinations, or would they find another way to torture me? I need the app, though, for residence announcements and for the daily menus for the dining halls. But I turn off notifications. When I get in my room, I grab Tentacle Ted from his resting place on the bed by the window (I refuse to think of it as Jay's bed), give him a hug, then toss him on my bed. I sit at my desk and open my laptop to find a topic for my media project.

When I was a kid, Dad and I used to listen to a weekly radio show on CBC about mysteries, and it would be a dream to do something like that one day. I am a realist, though; I know it's a long shot. The entire media landscape is nothing like it was then. But Sarah said my project should align with my passions, and doing a ton of research to solve a mystery is my passion. That, and good food. My stomach rumbles. I need to think about dinner soon.

After spending some time digging for a scandal or mystery connected to my own family and background, I give up. My family is the most boring immigrant family ever. My grandparents on both sides are Gujarati Indians who came from East Africa in the seventies, and they're all healthy and still living in Canada. My parents met in the nineties at their prayer hall in Toronto, got married when they were twenty-three, had my brother, and then had me. When they got tired of city living, they moved to Alderville. Dad's a tech consultant, Mom's a librarian. Neither is the scandal type.

I google *famous Toronto mysteries* and scan the hits. The irony of searching for a mystery to investigate while I'm actively avoiding a mystery of my own isn't lost on me. Maybe the obvious choice here *is* to investigate Jay's disappearance. Mia said there were already several student podcasts about the case. Why couldn't I be one of them? Even forgetting the mysterious messages on ResConnect, I'm literally living in his former room. That's about the closest personal connection I can think of without actually knowing the guy. And I have another advantage over all the other amateur sleuths—I have a box of his crap in my closet that I could search through for clues.

But even though Jay was quite rude when he messaged me yesterday (or my mind's construct of him was quite rude), I have no intention of violating the guy's privacy and going through his things. I want nothing to do with Jay, with bird-watching, with his several girlfriends, or with any other bizarre thing I've learned about him since moving into this room. It's unsettling enough to be living in a space where someone disappeared without a trace. Investigating it closely would only make the whole situation even creepier. No, I'm going with my original plan to ignore the existence of Jay Hoque. Hopefully someone will take his stuff soon, and I can pretend he was never in this room.

After reading about mysteries for a while, I narrow in on an old theater tycoon and playboy who disappeared in 1919 after depositing a million dollars into the bank and walking out of his apartment. True, a white millionaire man disappearing more than a hundred years ago has absolutely no relevance to me at all, but years after his disappearance, the man's family's home was sold to Toronto City University and turned into a student residence: East House. He wasn't living here when he disappeared, but the fact that I'm now living in his house is hopefully enough of a personal connection for the professor.

My stomach rumbles again. I really don't want to go to the Tower dining hall for dinner. After what happened this morning with Gracie, I don't want to see anyone from East House. Maybe I should go to another dining hall? Definitely not the one in my old building—it may be the best in the school, but I don't want to see Mia either. I know I'd feel even worse about myself sitting alone while my former friend ignores my existence.

I decide on the new Indian kiosk at the dining hall at the other end of campus. I have no idea why the school took so long to provide Indian food, but their chicken korma bowl is out of this world. They even make homemade roti almost as good as my grandmother's. But they don't make the korma every day.

I open ResConnect on my phone. As I'm searching for the menu for the Indian place, a message from the chat comes onto the screen. Damn it. There's no way to turn off notifications while you're *in* the app.

Jay: So now you're back. You need to fucking leave me alone. This isn't funny.

I stare at the phone, my heart racing in my chest. It's him again. And he's grumpy. It's bad enough that someone hacked into ResConnect to prank me, but does he have to be such a dick while doing it?

Jay: I have no idea how you're making all your information appear and disappear, but I'm taking screenshots this time so Kegan and the campus police will believe me. This is your last warning. Leave me alone. This is harassment.

My hackles go up.

Aleeza: You're the one harassing me, not the other way around. All I'm doing is sitting in my room trying to decide what to eat for dinner.

Jay: Good. Stay in your room. You've canceled the transfer to East House then? Maybe the system hasn't updated yet.

Aleeza: I'm IN East House. Like right now. Sitting in 225 with Ted, checking what curries the Indian kiosk in Central has tonight. Leave me alone, or I'm calling campus police.

There is no response for a while. Good. I finally have him scared. This joke has gone on long enough. I return to the dining hall menu and see that the Indian place is doing beef vindaloo tonight. Drat.

Jay: The Indian place in Central Dining isn't open yet. I petitioned student services last year to get them to add it. We have a lot of international students from the Indian subcontinent at TCU, I don't know why it's taking so long.

Maybe this *is* a hallucination, because it's no surprise that my subconscious brain would go on unnecessary tangents about food like my conscious brain always does.

Aleeza: Whoever you are, stop. You are not Jay Hoque, and you are not in room 225. You're impersonating a real person for shits and giggles. I'm taking my own screenshots to show campus police.

Jay: I AM JAY HOQUE. And I'm sitting right here in my room trying to figure out how you can also be in room 225 when I'm alone.

He's not letting up. In fact, he's only getting angrier. Is it possible this is really Jay? I mean, maybe I *am* talking to a ghost. But there are two problems with this theory. One, ghosts aren't real, and two, if he's a ghost, wouldn't he know that he's dead?

I freeze. An idea comes to me. It's as implausible as the ghost theory, but honestly, this might be the only logical solution, even if it's not logical at all.

Aleeza: Okay, confirm some things for me. You're Jay Hoque, right? Second year student, solo resident of room 225 in East House, Toronto City University, correct?

Jay: Yes.

Aleeza: And you are right now IN that room, true?

Jay: Yes.

Aleeza: Describe where you are in the room.

Jay: Propped up on a pillow on my bed, under the window. I'm listening to the Velvet Underground and wearing a black T-shirt. It stinks in here because my wool sweater got wet in the rain at the Engineering Alumni Scavenger Hunt last night. I'd open the window, but there's a thunderstorm out there.

I sigh. Of course my new ghost-roommate is a retro-style goth listening to the Velvet Underground. I look over at the bed in question. It's completely empty. Nothing at all on it but Tentacle Ted. It's not raining out; it's snowing. Also? TCU Alumni Month is in October, and this is March. I went to a journalism alumni mixer back then.

I take a deep breath. This prank is getting way too elaborate. Someone—and I can't imagine who—wants me to think I'm losing my mind, but I am not going to let them anymore. I take screenshots of our conversation, and head out of my room without saying goodbye to the ghost, or prankster, or construct of my subconscious brain.

I need food to figure out what's going on.

~

I walk to the Central dining hall for dinner. My heart's still racing, and I'm probably white as a ghost. Honestly, I half expect Mia or someone to jump out from behind a bush laughing about this joke they're playing on me.

I calm down a bit after getting my dinner. Good food always relaxes me. The beef vindaloo bowl is no chicken korma, but the warm spices and fragrant basmati rice clear my head enough to think. Who would pretend to be Jay to mess with me? Mia seems the obvious answer, but honestly, a joke like this isn't like her. Not that I don't think she'd do something nasty to me for leaving our dorm room, but this is just too . . . slick. Calculating. Mia would take revenge by making fun of me in public. I suppose her boyfriend, Lance, is a possibility, but he's never seemed anywhere close to smart enough to pull something like this off. And I don't think I've made any other enemies at TCU. I've barely made any friends.

I take out my phone and do some googling. First, I find a listing of all the alumni events from last October. There *was* an Engineering Scavenger Hunt. It was on the eighteenth of October—almost five months ago. I find a site that reports the weather anywhere in the world on any historical date and search for October 18. It was raining heavily in Toronto that night. And there were thunderstorms the next night, on October 19.

This can't be real. There is absolutely no way.

But what if it *is* real? What if I found some sort of time-skip that's letting me talk to Jay before he disappears? It's utterly preposterous. But I'm either stuck in a paranormal anomaly, or someone hates me enough to want me to *think* I am. Or I suppose a third option is that I've lost my mind. Or maybe this is a dream. I pinch myself. Hard. When I squeal in pain, a guy at a nearby table looks at me, concerned.

"Bit my tongue," I say. He turns back around, shrugging.

I exhale. Honestly, the first explanation—that I found a time loop—is the most palatable right now.

Instead of going back to the room after dinner, I go to the library to research this time thing to see if it's real. But after about ten minutes of reading about time travel and time anomalies, I remember why I dropped grade-twelve physics. The theory of relativity makes no sense to me, and I'm pretty sure there isn't a wormhole in my dorm room.

I am not a scientist. I'm an investigator. So I consider the problem like an investigator. How would Sherlock Holmes, Veronica Mars, or the Scooby Gang approach this? They would look at the facts and evidence. And so far, all the evidence I have—the screenshots of our conversation, the weather back in October, Kegan at the housing office, and the engineering alumni event—point to me and Jay being in different times. And even if I think that it's impossible, I should remember that many things mankind once thought was impossible turned out to be real. Like space travel, computers, and cell phones. Hell, there are people currently growing lab-created meat. Which, *gross*. But also, who am I to say what's possible or impossible? I never made it through physics.

I need more evidence before I accept this, though. And I think I know how to get it.

FIVE

I'm shaking when I get back to the room, still weirded out. I immediately open ResConnect and message Jay.

Aleeza: I just finished my dinner.

Jay: And? Did you find another room to move into?

Aleeza: Can you confirm some more things for me? What's the date today?

Jay: It's the 19th.

I feel dread in the pit of my stomach as I ask for more details.

Aleeza: What month?

Jay: October. Why are you asking these questions like I've lost my mind or something?

Aleeza: Because you said you're in room 225 right now, but I'm here right now, staring at your bed. The only thing on it is Tentacle Ted, my stuffed octopus.

Jay: Ted is a stuffed animal? I thought he was a boyfriend or something.

Aleeza: I don't have a boyfriend. Ted is a large orange octopus. We are the only ones in the room. One more question. What's on my Instagram story right now? My account is Aleeza_OctoGirl.

Jay: What kind of name is that? Are you an octuplet or something?

Aleeza: Just look it up—what's on my story?

He takes a few seconds to respond. I use the time to look up my Instagram archive and find October 19. It's the day I bought my octopus mug. Instagram stories disappear after twenty-four hours, and only I have access to my own archive. If this is a prank, the prankster would have had to hack my Instagram *and* hack my ResConnect, which seems too far-fetched.

Jay: It's a picture of a girl drinking from a mug with a tentacle handle. Is this you? You're cute.

I blow out a long puff of air. The only person who can see this picture *right now* is me. Which means Jay isn't in this *right now*.

Aleeza: This is proof.

Jay: Proof of what? You're not even in this room in that picture.

Aleeza: You're right. But I am in your room right now, just like you are in your room right now. But our right nows aren't the same. It's March 15 for me.

Jay: You're not making sense. Maybe you should stop hanging out with a stuffed octopus.

Aleeza: I know I'm not making sense, but it's the only explanation. We are both in the same place, but at different times.

It's completely preposterous, but I *know* it's true. Jay Hoque and I are stuck in a weird-ass time loop. We're five months apart.

He doesn't respond to my message. I don't blame him.

Aleeza: It's been snowing for a week straight. We're a month into second term.

Jay: You've completely lost your mind.

I need to figure out how to explain it to him.

Aleeza: You went to see Kegan, the housing guy, after you saw the message from me on ResConnect, and when he looked in the system, it showed that you're the only registered resident in the room, right? I did the same thing when I saw your message. When I was in the office, Kegan looked at me funny and said he was having déjà vu. Because he was remembering having the same conversation with you five months ago.

Jay: An overworked school administrator mixed up student conversations, so clearly we're living in a Keanu Reeves movie?

I frown.

Aleeza: Was there a time loop in The Matrix?

Jay: No, another movie. Okay, gimme a second.

Jay: Found something. There's a basketball game on right now. Raptors versus Celtics. Look it up. Who's going to win?

I don't want to close ResConnect to look it up on my phone—I don't trust this connection between us, and I don't want the chat to disappear again. So I google *October 19 Raptors game* on my laptop.

Aleeza: Raptors win. Final score 136 to 134. Why are basketball scores so high?

Jay: No idea. Not a sports person. Except water sports. In about half an hour we can verify if you're right. Should I put money on this game?

I make a face. I don't love the idea of Jay trying to profit off this bizarre situation. Not until we have a better idea of what's going on. Isn't that, like, the first rule of time travel? My mom and dad are big sci-fi nerds, and I swear *Star Trek* had an episode about not profiting off a time glitch. Then I remember that the person I'm talking to supposedly had several girlfriends at the same time. Ethics may not be his biggest concern.

Aleeza: We don't know what we're dealing with yet.

Jay: Send me more sports scores. Maybe another ten. There must be more sporting events today in the whole world, right? Bigger sample size to know if this is real.

I quickly google *All sporting Events October 19* and write out final scores for ten different games into the chat.

Jay: Now send me a picture of you in of the room right now to prove you're there.

Aleeza: You can't send pictures in the ResConnect chat. Text only.

Jay: Oh. I've never had a roommate, so I've never used it. Try texting my number. Maybe we can talk on other platforms too.

He sends me his phone number, and I text a selfie of me sitting on my bed, but the text fails to deliver. I then try calling the number, and a voice says the number is out of service.

Aleeza: It didn't work. The number is out of service.

Jay: That's weird. I've had this number for years. Does that mean I'll change it in the next five months? If you're in March, why aren't I still there? This room is supposed to be mine all year.

Fuck. Of course the phone is disconnected. This guy went *missing* in November, and he doesn't know it yet. I have to tell him. But . . . would that be the responsible thing to do? Telling Jay about his future *has* to be a violation of time-travel rules. What if it causes a . . . I don't know. Time disaster. What if it makes the room implode into a black hole? Or what if it does something bad to his psyche? It would have to mess a person up to find out he'll disappear off the face of the earth in less than a month, right? Saying something now could make this situation worse.

Aleeza: I don't know where you are now.

That's the truth, at least. No one knows where he is.

Jay: Maybe I got a better room instead of this shit hole. My buddy Jack was talking about renting an apartment second term. Can you find out where I am?

Aleeza: Let's try something first. Do something in the room. Something that I can see now to prove that this conversation is real. Write your name on the wall or something.

Jay: Don't you think the cleaners would clean that over the holiday break?

Aleeza: Hide it. In the closet or somewhere like that.

Jay: Okay give me a minute.

I can't help but feel like I'm playing with fire here. I still believe that this is real and we're in a time-skip or something, but I also have this weird feeling that danger is coming and I should be careful. But of course danger is coming. This guy is literally missing. There were search parties.

Jay: Okay, I wedged a note between the upper shelf and the back wall of the closet. Read it and tell me what it says.

Aleeza: How am I supposed to get it?

Jay: Use a chair! That's how I got up there.

Aleeza: Give me time. I'm going to have to move the box from in there.

Jay: Why is your stuff still in boxes. I thought you moved in?

The box is *his* stuff. But I can't tell him that.

It takes me a few minutes to empty the closet enough so I can put a chair in and get at the top shelf. My heart is racing the whole time. If I find something there, then I'm right and this is real. If there isn't, then someone is playing the most epic prank on me, and people—presumably Mia and her new friend group—hate me even more than I thought.

I reach across the top of the shelf to where it meets the wall behind it. There is nothing there. I check the whole closet shelf, running my hand around it. Nothing.

I'm an idiot. This *is* a prank. And I completely fell for it.

I climb down and go back to my phone.

Aleeza: There's nothing there. Fuck you and leave me alone—I'm reporting you to campus police.

I turn off my phone and go to bed.

SIX

I'm a bit of a mess the next morning. And it's no wonder. In the space of a few days, I lost my closest friend, moved to a new dorm room, and fell for an epic prank that I still can't imagine the purpose of. I cannot believe I actually thought that I was talking through time to Jay Hoque, a guy who's been missing for months. Maybe I should take Kegan's advice and make use of the campus mental health resources.

I consider taking the screenshots of my conversations with "Jay" straight to campus police, but in the end, I decide not to. Mostly because I don't want anyone to know that I fell for it. If Mia or Lance is behind this, they're probably laughing their asses off at me right now. And if I report them, they'd claim it was just a harmless joke. A group of white kids could probably convince people that they're harmless better than I—a weird Brown girl with no friends—could.

Best thing to do is put it out of my mind. Thankfully, when I wake up, ResConnect shows me as the only occupant of room 225. Jay's name isn't there. So clearly the person who hacked in has removed themselves.

I have a busy day, which distracts me from this whole mess. After my last class, I head home to do some online research on my media project. If Sarah wants to see a draft next week, I need to hustle to get it done. But my mind keeps wandering. Weirdly, researching this hundred-year-old mystery keeps reminding me of Jay. How did I not notice the similarities between the two cases? Both were known players with several girlfriends. Both disappeared with no trace. In the old case, money seemed to be the main motive. I don't know the motive in Jay's case, but it wouldn't surprise me if money were involved too. Love and money—the two motives for almost all crimes. Yesterday Jay said he wanted to bet on sports. Maybe he had a gambling problem?

But wait. *Jay* didn't say that yesterday. I was scammed. It wasn't actually him texting me. I exhale and pick up my phone. I still have ResConnect notifications silenced, so if *whoever* is messaging me again, I won't see it unless I open the app. Against my better judgment, I open it.

There are four messages from Jay. All sent in the last hour.

Jay: I can see you on ResConnect again, so I'll tell you what I said last night. The Celtics got a three pointer with thirty seconds left of the game. The Raptors lost 137 to 136. So you were wrong about the score.

Jay: But if it weren't for the last thirty seconds of the game, you'd be exactly right. That can't be random.

Jay: I did some calculations on the rest of the scores you sent me, and they are 85 percent right. It's not 100 percent accuracy, but those odds are higher than random. Like way, way higher.

Jay: The probability of you randomly giving me eleven sports scores and being 85 percent correct is pretty much zero. I promise . . . I swear on my mother's life, I am not pranking you. This is real, Roomie.

Shit. I don't even know what to say. Or think. I stare at the messages. I'm no math major, but even I know that it would be virtually impossible for me to tell him sports scores from the future that are 85 percent correct unless *something* is going on. But if this is real, then why aren't the scores 100 percent correct?

Aleeza: Why aren't the scores completely right, then?

Jay: Ever hear of the Butterfly effect?

Aleeza: Isn't that an Ashton Kutcher movie?

Jay: Yeah, about time travel. Basically, every little thing that he did could change the outcome in the future. Time isn't linear. There are an infinite number of parallel universes branching off each other.

Aleeza: Like Everything Everywhere all at Once.

Jay: Yeah, and Multiverse of Madness.

Aleeza: Are we only going to use movies to understand what's going on?

Jay: Everything I know about temporal physics is from Hollywood.

Aleeza: I don't know if I should believe you.

Jay: We're roommates. If you can't trust your roommate, who can you trust?

I exhale. The irony is I left Mia's room because I *couldn't* trust her. But maybe Jay's right. Maybe I should trust this . . . because clearly something is happening. All the evidence I've seen is pointing that way.

Aleeza: Okay, why wasn't your name on ResConnect when I woke up this morning?

Jay: I left the room at six for water polo practice. I think it has something to do with us being physically in the room.

That could be it. Yesterday after I left the room for dinner, all our conversations disappeared.

Aleeza: Let's try something. I'll walk out, you stay there. Let's see if we can still chat.

I take screenshots of our conversations in case they disappear again. Then we do a series of little experiments, each coming in and out of the room. It seems our link only works while we're *both* in 225. If either of us steps out, even just to the hallway, the link is gone, and the chat logs disappear. There is no way to leave messages for each other.

Jay: This is wild. I have a million questions for you. So, the Indian food place finally does open in Central dining hall?

Aleeza: Yes, a month ago. It's delicious.

Jay: I can't wait to try it. I'm going to push them to open a shawarma stand next. Hey, you need to find future me and get him to tell me what's on my civil engineering exam.

I can't do that because *that* Jay is gone. He didn't even take his exams in December. I don't know what to say. I do believe what's happening—that we're in different times, despite how implausible it sounds. We are living the impossible. Or at least I am right now living the impossible. Jay *was* living the impossible five months ago. But I have no idea if present-day Jay is even living at all.

It's a lot to wrap my head around. If there is an infinite number of parallel timelines, then it's possible that the Jay I'm chatting with will be fine and won't ever disappear. And it's possible that the Aleeza in his timeline won't have a best-friend breakup with her oldest friend and will stay in the West Hall dorm room all year like she's supposed to.

Aleeza: How do we figure how similar our timelines are?

Jay: You can send me more sports scores. But I think we can assume that we are at 85 percent similarity. That's why the note I left you wasn't there.

Aleeza: What did the note say? In case I find it somewhere else.

Jay: JAY IS HERE. ALEEZA WILL BE HERE. 100458008.

Aleeza: What do those numbers mean?

Jay: Don't worry about it. Send me some sports scores for tonight.

I send ten scores for games on October 20. I'm really hoping that none of the sports predictions come true. Or at least, fewer than 85 percent. Because that would mean the guy I'm chatting with lives in a parallel universe not like this one, and he won't go missing. It's funny—before this, when he disappeared, I think I felt terrible for him only because it hit close to home to have a student in my own university be all over the news. But Jay Hoque's disappearance was abstract to me. I may have seen him around campus, but I didn't *know* him. He was just a guy with a bit of a bad reputation who probably did something to upset someone and found out that karma could be a bitch.

But now, now *I know* Jay. And he doesn't seem to be that bad of a person. He clearly loves movies, like me. He likes Indian food and shawarma. He's smart enough to be able to talk to about this mindfuck of a situation. He trusts me. He doesn't deserve whatever bad thing is going to happen to him, and I want him to be okay.

Aleeza: I guess it's possible that the version of you in my time didn't have this conversation five months ago.

Jay: Yeah, maybe if you find me, don't mention it. There's no reason to freak the hell out of two Jay Hoques, right?

Aleeza: No, I suppose not.

Jay: I don't know much about temporal anomalies. I should ask my physics teacher about this—hey, are we keeping this between the two of us?

That's an excellent question. I have no idea . . . On one hand, yeah, we discovered something amazing here. Science should be shared, right? But also, who would believe us? And if they did, would that mean that the researchers would take over the room? Would we have to leave? Where would I go? Not back to Mia. Also, the fact that in my timeline Jay is *gone* complicates things. Would people think I manufactured all this because I'm obsessed with him like Gracie seems to think I am? Would telling people somehow make things worse for Jay?

Aleeza: Maybe let's not. We have no idea if this will keep happening.

Jay: It has happened for the last three days, so why wouldn't it?

Aleeza: If it doesn't then we'll look like idiots when we tell everyone about it.

Jay: I'm used to looking like an idiot, but okay. It's our secret, Roomie.

I smile at the nickname.

Aleeza: So now you're okay with me living in this room?

Jay: Yeah, it's all good. I get the good parts of having a roommate and none of the bad. I don't have to deal with your shit everywhere but have a friend to talk to when I don't want to talk to myself anymore. I can even tell you that I smoke weed in the room, and you can't get me in trouble for it because I don't even live there anymore. And you can talk to me instead of to an octopus.

I exhale. He wants to be friends, but I'm keeping something from him. Something *huge*. And also? Me and Jay Hoque, friends? I'm the dork who just lost her only friend and now has no one else. And Jay Hoque is cool. A real city guy. One who smokes weed and dates lots of girls and has people obsessed with him. Jay Hoque and I don't belong in the same orbit. Also, he might be dead.

I feel awkward, so I do what I always do when I feel like that. Plan an escape.

Aleeza: I'm going to go. I have to work on my media project. And get dinner.

Jay: Yeah, no worries. Hey, how did you end up in this room, anyway? March is a weird time to move into a new room.

Aleeza: I had a falling out with my roommate.

Jay: Are you a bad roommate or something? You should probably tell me. But I mean, I won't know if you leave a mess.

Aleeza: No, I'm not messy. My roommate was my old friend, and we were supposed to make this video series together for my media class. But she changed the topic and added her boyfriend's sister without asking me.

Jay: Ugh. That sucks. That's not a good friend. One more question, how do you pronounce your name? I want to make sure I say it right in my head.

This is weird.

Aleeza: It's said just like it's spelled. A-lee-za Kass-um.

Jay: Nice to meet you, Aleeza. I'm Jay Hoque. Pronounced like two birds. I should probably do my homework too. Chat later, Roomie.

Aleeza: One last thing, in case we don't talk again, if you can, stay away from the dorm on November 6.

Jay: Why, does East House flood or something?

Aleeza: Yeah, something like that. Good night.

There. Hopefully that advice saves him from disappearing that day. The chat is silent for the rest of the night.

~

I do some more research on my media project that night—but my mind wanders again. I resist the urge to read everything I can about temporal physics to figure out what's going on. It's possible the ResConnect chat won't even work tomorrow, and if it doesn't, then there isn't anything we can do about it. It could have been either a tech glitch or some sort of unexplainable magic far out of my scope. I'm not exactly skilled at complex physics, or technology, for that matter. Maybe Mia could do something with her Ouija board or crystals, but I doubt that would help me figure this out either. At least I warned him about the day he disappears. Maybe I saved him. Or maybe I made things worse—I could be messing up his timeline.

I exhale. This is all ridiculous. I should focus on my schoolwork.

In the morning when I check the app, Jay Hoque isn't showing as my roommate anymore, and the chat log is gone. And I have no way of knowing if it will be back.

When I leave class before lunch, my friend Amber stops me. Well, *friend* is a bit of an overstatement. She's an acquaintance—and the biggest gossip in West Hall.

"Did you hear about Mia's *Skintimately Yours* YouTube series?"

I frown. "She's already got it up?"

"Just a teaser. She's interviewing a Korean skincare expert—"

"Amber, why are you telling me this?"

Amber is totally the type to rub someone's misfortune in their face. That's why we're not really friends.

She gives me a smug smile. "Because I know she was supposed to do a series with you. How are you getting back at her?"

"I'm not getting back at her. I'm happy for her," I say, trying to get away from Amber, but she doesn't let me go.

"I heard you moved to the murder room," Amber says.

"What?"

"I heard you moved to the dead guy's room."

I shake my head. "Jay's missing. Not dead." At least . . . I assume. I feel nausea take hold in the pit of my stomach. "Is there . . . new news about him?" My voice cracks. I should have told him more last night.

"What? No." She looks around as if to check if anyone is listening to us. "I mean, the guy was a total ass. I heard there's a whole, like, underground club of girls he fucked and ghosted. One of them did something to him, for sure. It's sad, though. He was a douche, but he was a *person*, you know?"

"There isn't seriously an *organized club* of girls who hated him, is there?"

Amber nods. "Yup. Haven't you heard of Birdwatchers?"

Again with Birdwatchers. I frown. "Do you know these people?"

Amber looks at me blankly, then shrugs.

I slide my laptop in my bag. "I didn't know the guy. I'm just in his old room. That's it."

"I couldn't live there." She shudders. "It's got bad mojo or something. You should have the room cleansed. Get his ghost out of there."

"I gotta go, Amber." I put my backpack on. I never liked that girl.

SEVEN

I eat lunch alone in an empty student lounge, mostly so I won't see any of Mia's friends, but also because I want to call my mom. As a librarian, she's really well read. If something like this time-skip has ever happened before, Mom would know. She doesn't work Fridays, so she should be home. My dad answers her phone.

"Leeza-bear," he says.

I'm glad no one is hearing this. I'm nineteen—a little old for pet names. He must have seen my name on Mom's screen. He works from home and is probably on his lunch hour right now.

I realize Dad might be able to help me with this puzzle too.

"Hey, Dad. I wanted to talk to Mom, but can I ask you a question about software and computers first?"

"Yeah, of course. I'm on speaker and your mom's here too. My consulting fee is out of your budget, but since we pay your expenses, I'll just invoice myself. What's up?" My dad is a computer-systems consultant. He's devastated that I didn't want to follow in his footsteps in IT like my brother, who's a computer programmer out west.

I think about how to ask the question. I haven't told them yet that I moved out of Mia's room. I know they would ask hundreds of questions, then probably call Mia's parents. It isn't something I want to deal with right now.

"What do you know about time travel?" I ask.

"Um," Dad says. "Not a lot? Why?"

I bite my lip. Obviously, I can't tell them the truth. "I was thinking, can technology be used to talk to someone in the past?"

"Are you talking about science fiction, or reality?" Mom asks. They're both into science fiction, but Mom's a bit more hard-core.

"Reality. I'm actually wondering if it's possible for a computer program to go back in time. Like, could you use software to talk to someone in the past?"

"Of course not," Dad says. "That's completely in the realm of science fiction. But AI has gotten to the point where it could *simulate* it. If there is a good enough record of the era the program is emulating."

"Yes, like a wayback machine or something," Mom adds. "AI can fake conversations very well. If enough raw data is accessible, you could use a computer to talk to someone from the past. Why are you asking?"

"A friend and I are trying to figure something out. So, a computer couldn't really go back in time, but modern AI could simulate it believably."

"Yeah, exactly," Dad says.

Could my conversation with Jay be an AI simulation?

"Who's the friend?" Mom asks. "Someone from your classes?"

I know my parents won't let it go unless I tell them who. They are sometimes typical Indian overinvolved parents. "He's not in my program, but he lives in my building. His name is . . . his name is Robin." Dumb. My mind is stuck on bird names. But if I say Jay, she'll think about the missing student. She mentioned him to me many times while telling me to be careful walking around campus after dark. "We were talking about time-travel movies, and it got me thinking about technology and time travel."

"I'm so glad you're meeting nice boys," Mom says. "He likes time-travel movies!"

Mom is forever trying to butt into my love life. Romance is her second favorite book genre after sci-fi.

"It's not like that, Mom. We're friends. And I'm too busy with school."

"Don't forget to have fun, too, Aleeza," she says. "The nicest boy has been coming into the library all winter. He asked me for mystery recommendations. He would be so perfect for you! It's too bad you're not coming home anytime soon. Maybe I can ask if he'll be here—"

"Dad, tell her not to be a stereotypical Indian matchmaking mother." On second thought, maybe I *shouldn't* ask my mother too many questions. The longer I have her on the phone, the more she will meddle. I love my parents, but I went away for university because my mother tends to be a little too . . . involved in my life. I'd rather not let her know I'm struggling with anything right now, or Mom will get in the car and drive here immediately.

My father laughs. "She's right that university is supposed to be fun, though. In fact, I'll send you a list of my favorite time-travel movies!"

"Yes!" my mother says. "I'll send you book recs too!"

I groan. "Okay, fine. Anyway, I have class soon. Love you both."

"Love you, Aleeza!" They disconnect the call.

~

I can't dwell on the Jay mystery forever—I have an assignment to finish. Luckily the library gods are kind to me, and after class I find some great pieces on the missing 1919 playboy. He apparently pissed off a lot of people . . . which, fair. A millionaire playboy *would* have a lot of enemies. After reading accounts from people who wanted him dead, I can't help but think of Jay. It's reminding me of that article from the school paper the day I moved into our room. The one that said a lot of girls were mad that he was cheating on them.

When a person has *that* many enemies, how can anyone narrow them down? After taking a few pages of notes on the missing 1919 playboy, I give in to my curiosity again and look up Jay's disappearance. There are no recent articles since the one from the school paper a few days ago. I wonder if the case is losing steam and everyone is moving on. Maybe no one is even looking for him anymore.

I skim the school paper article again. It doesn't mention Birdwatchers, but two different people have mentioned them to me now, Gracie Song and Amber. Was there really an organized club of girls who stalked Jay? That seems a little extra.

Of course, a Google search of the word *Birdwatchers* results in thousands of hits—none of which have anything to do with Jay Hoque. I try every search combination: *Birdwatcher + Toronto City University*, *Birdwatcher + Jay Hoque, Birdwatcher + TCU,* even *Birdwatcher + Jay Hawk + Toronto*. That last search gives me a lot, but none of it is useful unless I want to find jays and hawks on campus. Is Jay short for something? ResConnect has his name as Jay, but students can register anything as their preferred name, not just their legal one. I try Jason Hoque and find nothing.

I have an advantage that no one else trying to find him has—even more than his box of things. I have access to the *victim* himself. Maybe. The connection might not be there anymore. In fact, with the whole butterfly effect theory, it's possible that talking to him yesterday could have been enough to change the timeline so that the ResConnect chat doesn't happen anymore.

Thinking about it makes my head hurt. My brain is not cut out for this temporal-physics crap.

But maybe Jay has already given me a clue about what happened to him? He didn't mention anything about his so-called haters when we talked. In fact, he didn't say anything that implied he knew people were out to get him. He was easygoing and cheerful, once he stopped thinking I was pranking him.

I open the screenshots from our chats the last two nights. There's nothing there about a girlfriend (or several girlfriends) or about any conflicts he was having. I read the part about him leaving me that note in the closet—the one I couldn't find. Is the note somewhere else in the room? Did the cleaners throw it away after he disappeared? Or did the police take it as a clue? I doubt that, because if the police had a note with my name on it, someone would have asked me about it. I'm pretty sure I'm the only Aleeza at TCU. But maybe the police aren't investigating his disappearance at all.

Jay is here. Aleeza will be here. 100458008.

What does that number mean? It has to be significant to Jay, right? I google the number with *Jay Hoque*, *Jay Hawk*, and *Birdwatchers* and find nothing. It doesn't look like a student number. Maybe a social insurance number? A little bit of research tells me that social insurance numbers starting with a 1 are issued in the Atlantic provinces. Is Jay from Newfoundland or Nova Scotia? But why would he give me his SIN anyway? It could be a date. Or at least the first four numbers could be: 1004 is the tenth of April. Less than a month away.

I sigh. There are two things I know for sure. One, I *have to* tell Jay about his disappearance if he shows up on ResConnect again. I need to warn him to avoid these Birdwatcher girls. And two, I need to step away from this mystery. I have to focus on school, and on making new friends who won't neglect me for their boyfriend, or their boyfriend's sister. Friends who aren't missing people only available to talk to when I'm in my room.

After my last class of the day, I grab dinner to-go again and go straight to East House. Hopefully Jay is there so I can come clean to him. If not . . . then I don't even know what I'll do.

When I get to the room, I check ResConnect, and his name isn't listed as a resident of 225. Maybe he's at dinner. After turning notifications for the app back on, I open my computer and start writing the script for my media project podcast while eating my poke bowl.

I keep checking ResConnect over the next few hours, but he's still not there. I look at Tentacle Ted, who is sitting alone on Jay's bed.

"Did I imagine the whole thing?" I ask the octopus.

Ted's wide purple eyes stare at me. This is ridiculous. Jay is right—I should stop talking to a stuffed animal.

My phone buzzes. It's ResConnect. The message appears on the screen.

Jay: Hey Roomie. We're still at about 85 percent continuity.

I quickly pick up my phone.

Aleeza: What are you talking about?

Jay: The sports scores. We can test a few more times before we start betting. We're about to make a KILLING. Should I leave your cut in my mattress? Even if only 85 percent of the money is there, we'll both be golden. 50/50 profits.

Aleeza: Wait. I don't think we should bet.

Jay: Don't wimp out on me now, Roomie, this time-glitch is happening to us for a reason. Maybe getting rich is the reason.

Jay's right. This *is* happening for a reason. But betting on sports isn't it.

Aleeza: Jay, there's something I need to tell you.

Jay: Lottery numbers! Do they publish old ones somewhere?

Aleeza: No wait. You're right, this is happening for a reason, but I don't think the reason is to get rich. I think it's happening so I can prevent something bad from happening to you.

Jay: What? What are you talking about?

Telling Jay this seems huge. He has no reason to believe me. Why would he? He knows nothing about me. He'll probably think I'm just another Birdwatcher trolling him. I take a breath and type quickly before I lose my nerve.

Aleeza: You're missing.

Jay: What do you mean, missing?

Aleeza: The Jay Hoque in my timeline has been a missing person for four months.

There is no response, so I keep typing. If he never speaks to me again after this, then so be it. I did my part.

Aleeza: There were search parties all over campus at first. And in the city. It was on the news a lot, but not as much anymore. On Saturday November 6, you were seen in East House in the evening, and you haven't been seen or heard from since.

He still doesn't respond, so I keep going.

Aleeza: There are no leads. No one has any idea what happened to you. That's why I'm here now. You were officially unenrolled from the university this week.

Finally, Jay responds.

Jay: Shit. That's why you told me to stay away from the dorm that day.

Aleeza: Yeah, I don't know how to prove it to you. I can't send you pictures or articles from the future on ResConnect. I can cut and paste the text from an article, but there's no way to prove that I didn't make it all up. But trust me, it's true.

There is no answer for a while.

Aleeza: Are you still there? I can cut and paste some articles.

Jay: I'm still here. Am I dead?

Aleeza: I don't know. I'm so sorry. No one knows where you are. You probably don't believe me.

Jay: Why wouldn't I believe you? You're my roommate. How

He doesn't finish the sentence.

Aleeza: You still there?

Jay: Yeah, how's my mom doing?

Aleeza: I don't know. I don't know any of your friends to ask.

Jay: Let me read the articles.

Into the chat, I cut and paste the text from several articles published right after he disappeared. It's going to take him a bit of time to read them. I feel terrible for Jay. When I first read them months ago, it all seemed so juicy—an actual student at my own school the subject of a huge mystery. But now, Jay is a real person who calls me "Roomie," and who insisted we'd split the profits from a sports-betting scheme. This is a hell of a thing for him to learn while alone in his room.

Our room. I am here with him, even if we can't see each other.

Aleeza: You okay, Jay?

Jay: This is all so wild. Like reading about something that happened to someone else, but it's me.

Aleeza: Do you know what could have happened? Or what will happen?

Jay: Someone must have done something to me. I wouldn't have run away. Not from my family.

Aleeza: I heard there's a group of girls who are stalking you.

Jay: Seriously?

Aleeza: Maybe. An ex of yours, Emma, might be one of them.

Jay: Emma Coffey?

Aleeza: Yes, she spoke to the school newspaper saying you were cheating on her.

Jay: I wasn't seriously dating her. We hooked up a few times.

Aleeza: Why did it end?

Jay: She was getting too serious, and I'm not really a commitment kind of guy.

I exhale. It's true—he's a fuckboy. But no matter his commitment habits, he deserves to know what's going to happen to him. He deserves to *live*.

Aleeza: Could someone you dated have wanted to hurt you?

He doesn't answer for a while.

Jay: There was this Tumblr last year that said some shit about me. It was a long time ago, though.

Aleeza: Who even reads Tumblr anymore?

Jay: You'd be surprised.

Aleeza: What did it say about you?

Jay: Bunch of lies. Like I cheated on exams, bought assignments, and lied to get into the school. None of it's true. I wouldn't even think of cheating on my schoolwork. My aunt would come at me with a sandal if I did, and that shit hurts. My mom works at a law office, she got a law clerk to write a stern letter and had it taken down.

Aleeza: Who was behind it?

Jay: No clue at all. It was all over by March last year. Haven't heard a peep about Birdwatcher since then.

Aleeza: Wait. That's what Birdwatcher is?

Jay: That was the name of the Tumblr.

Aleeza: A couple of people have mentioned Birdwatcher to me, but they implied it's a club of girls that you wronged. No one mentioned a Tumblr.

Jay: Weird. There wasn't anything about girls or relationships in the Tumblr. Just accusing me of being shady at school.

This is very strange. Gracie and Amber implied *Birdwatcher* is a current thing, not a thing from a year ago.

Aleeza: Maybe someone who hooked up with you resurrected it. And they're also behind your disappearance. What was the account name?

He tells me, and I search for it on Tumblr, but it's not there. I search for any mention of his name on the whole Tumblr site but find nothing.

Jay: Do you really think someone I hooked up with kidnapped me? A bit of online slander maybe, but this?

Aleeza: Can you think of someone else who might be out to get you?

He could have shady dealings that he's not telling me about. He jumped to betting on sports so quickly—maybe he wronged a bookie or something? Or hell, maybe he *did* bet on the sports scores I gave him, and the bookie was pissed that he won so much and went after him.

Jay: The black Corolla.

Aleeza: What?

Jay: Lately, like for the past month, I've been seeing a black Toyota Corolla a lot. I thought I was being paranoid, but I think it's following me.

Aleeza: Did you report it to anyone?

Jay: No, like I said, I thought it was in my head. It's a pretty common car. I mean, my mom drives a Corolla.

Aleeza: So does mine. Silver. Anyway, someone going after you isn't the only theory.

Jay: What else do they think?

Aleeza: Suicide.

Jay: No, I'm not suicidal.

But the disappearance is weeks away for him. Could someone become suicidal in a couple of weeks?

Aleeza: Things change.

Jay: I've never been suicidal in my life. Or depressed. I know what it looks like. My mom has depression. I suppose anything is possible, but I can't imagine I'd be willing to do that to my family. It would destroy my mom.

Aleeza: Is it just you and your mom?

Jay: Yeah, she raised me alone. It wasn't that bad . . . she has reoccurring depression, but she gets treatment. And my aunt and uncle, and Nani and Nana are close by. My grandparents.

Wait . . . that's what I call *my* grandparents.

Aleeza: Are you Indian?

Jay: My mom's from Bangladesh. I'm biracial South Asian.

Wow. I didn't know that. Now that I think about it, his racially ambiguous looks could totally be half–South Asian. I don't know why this changes anything for me. Growing up in an almost completely white town, I'm not used to having South Asian friends. Even here. Most of the friends I met with Mia are white, too, despite the school having a lot of South Asian students. But this is another connection Jay and I have.

Aleeza: I'm Indian. My family is Gujarati, but my grandparents are from Tanzania and Uganda.

Jay: Yeah, I figured you were Indian because of your name. You didn't recognize Hoque as a Bangladeshi name?

Aleeza: No.

Jay: Is there a way you can find out how my mom is doing? Fuck, I hope her depression isn't back.

Aleeza: I'll see what I can find out. I assume we still don't tell anyone all this, right?

Jay: Yeah, I think that's safest. I don't want to worry people more. And at least now that I know what will happen, I can avoid it. I'll go stay at Mom's that day so I'll be safe.

I think about that. Yes, in theory if he's not here to go missing out of the room, then he won't go missing at all. But what about *Birdwatcher*? What about Emma saying someone was bound to get him eventually? What about the black Corolla?

Aleeza: Okay, but without knowing what happened to you and why, how can we prevent it? Like if it's an accident or a random thing, then not being here that day might save you, but if this is targeted, then stopping the person from doing whatever on that day only means they'll try another day.

Jay: With all those infinite universes . . . it's possible that what happens to me in your timeline won't happen to me in mine.

Aleeza: True. But I don't know. I feel like we can't not take it seriously.

Jay: I agree. This is my life.

Aleeza: I feel like this is the reason why we can talk to each other now. We're supposed to figure out what happened or will happen to you. I want to be an investigative journalist. I'm good at mysteries. And I have something that no one else trying to solve this case has.

Jay: Me.

Aleeza: Exactly. Access to the victim. And because you're in the past, solving it in my timeline could keep you safe in yours.

Jay: Okay, but no one knows we know each other. If you go fishing around, people will wonder why. People might not talk to you. Or they'll question why you care so much.

Aleeza: What if I did it for my media project?

Jay: The one that you were supposed to do with your old roommate?

Aleeza: Yeah, I can do a true crime podcast about you instead.

Jay: That's perfect. We can piss off both whoever the fuck did this to me and your former friend.

Aleeza: And save your life.

Jay: Yeah, that too. My only requirement is that I must approve anything you say in the podcast.

That's fair, so I agree. I send a quick email to my professor to let her know what I'm planning for my project, and then Jay and I decide to meet here in the room the following night at eight again. Before that, we'll each make lists of suspects and everything we can find out about his disappearance. We both also take screenshots of our entire conversation, so we'll have a written record of it after we leave the room in the morning.

It's pretty late by the time I go to bed. But for the first time since I moved into room 225, I feel good about being here. I feel like I have purpose. Like everything will be okay again.

I have a new friend. And I'm going to do everything in my power to make sure he's safe.

EIGHT

On Saturday morning I get a phone call from Sarah, my media professor, who apparently doesn't believe in weekends. She got my message the night before about me changing my media project, and she loves the idea.

"I think a podcast on Jay Hoque's disappearance would be fantastic. This is exactly what I meant by a personal connection. I assume you knew him?"

"No, actually, I didn't. But I just moved into his former dorm room. Is that good for a personal connection?"

"Yeah, it's great. Even better than knowing him. Your investigation will be completely unbiased. An insider and outsider at the same time." She gives some examples of investigative journalism pieces where the author had a personal, but distant, connection with the victim. "A good starting point would be to speak to the student who wrote the recent article about him in the school paper. Maybe you can collaborate, even interview her for an episode."

"Oh, okay . . . who was it?" I don't remember looking at the byline when I read it.

"Gracie Song. She's in my Thursday class. I can ask her if she'll speak to you."

Of course it's Gracie. We have a bit of a truce now, but she doesn't trust me. When she finds out that I'm investigating Jay's disappearance, she'll definitely think I'm obsessed with him. But I don't have much of a choice. "I know Gracie. She lives in my residence. I'll ask her."

"Great. Talk to her and let me know your progress on Wednesday."

After running down to the dining hall to grab a smoothie bowl, I bring it back to the room to start on my homework. But I'm having trouble focusing. This is my first Saturday without Mia, and it seems so . . . quiet. Alone. Maybe I should work in the library? It's not like I'm not used to being alone. My dad travels a lot for work, and Mom always works on weekends. And my brother left Alderville a while ago. But this feels weird. I expected my Saturdays in university to be busier. I expected there would be more people around.

I open my Instagram and scroll for a while. There's nothing interesting going on. My ex-boyfriend, Chase, back in Alderville posted about some work he's doing on his car. I leave a comment saying it's looking good. Mia has a new post—pictures of her going out with Lance and his friends last night. I really should stop following her. I check, and she's still following me, too, but I haven't posted anything since I left West Hall. I thought I was being really mature by *not* deleting her from my socials when I left our room, but now I think I'm torturing myself. She's still got the boyfriend and all her new friends. All I have is a stuffed octopus, a neighbor who dislikes me, and a roommate who doesn't actually exist. I mute Mia's feed.

I'm going to have to get used to being alone, now that I don't have a roommate. Or at least now that I don't have a *conventional* roommate. I check ResConnect, and Jay isn't listed as a resident of the room, which means he's out. *Sigh.* I do have a ton of schoolwork, though. I pull out my politics text and start on the readings for Monday.

After finishing my politics readings, I go to my media project. It's time to start investigating what happened to Jay. I open a fresh Moleskine notebook—Dad bought me a bunch of these when I started school, saying all reporters needed black notebooks—and put headings on the first three pages: *Possible things that could have happened, People to talk to, Investigate Further*, and finally, *Suspects*. I add *Birdwatcher* to the suspect list, even though I have no idea who that is. I add *black Corolla* after it.

Jay claimed that, yes, he hooked up with a bunch of girls at TCU, but he didn't think he upset any of them enough for them to stalk him, or even hurt him. He said Emma is the only one who may have been upset, because she wanted a relationship when he didn't. I add *Emma* to the suspect list.

Of course, it's possible that Jay is the only one responsible for his disappearance. Maybe he needed to escape something big and bad, so he ran away? But if that were the case, wouldn't he know about the big bad thing less than a month before he leaves? It also could have been an accident. In fact, the leading causes of death for men his age are accidents and suicide. He could have gone for a walk on a dark road and been hit by a car. Or attacked by a bear.

Wait. I'm in the city now. No bears.

Surely there are more ways to get hurt in the city than out in the country. At least, according to my mother there are. I write down possibilities: *mugging, drug overdose, hit by a streetcar, drowning* . . .

I feel sick to my stomach. Poor Jay. I don't have a clue what, but I know *something* happened to him. I exhale, remembering what Sarah said. I need to stay unbiased and unconnected.

Despite what Jay said last night, I add *died by suicide* and *ran away* to the list. Jay was adamant that he could not be intentionally responsible for his disappearance, but a lot can happen in a few weeks.

Also, why am I so sure that Jay's being honest with me? Maybe he *is* depressed and doesn't want to admit it. Or maybe he's into some shady shit that put a target on him. Why would he tell a first-year that he's never met all about the messy bits of his life?

I look at Ted. How would an octopus solve this? Is it wise to trust Jay, or should I treat him like an unreliable narrator? But why would Jay lie to me? I am the *only* person he knows who can find out what happened to him. Or what *will* happen.

I have to believe him, even if he is a shady, commitment-phobic fuckboy. If I doubt Jay's honesty, I may as well give up completely, because I'll have nothing to work with.

I go back to my list of what could have happened. An accident of some sort seems the most likely, but also the hardest for me to solve. Jay *could* have somehow left the room that night without anyone noticing, and just about anything *could* have happened to him on the busy downtown Toronto streets. But if it was an accident, the police would have found him by now, wouldn't they? Even a hit and run leaves a body behind. Or if there were murderous animals terrorizing the city, there'd be more missing people, right? Or, you know, remains.

Local hospitals have already been checked. Hell, after his disappearance, there was a full search of the nearby parks and green spaces. I look around the room. The only ways in or out are through the door and, I suppose, the window near his bed. I check the window. There's nothing remarkable about it, and from what I can tell, there is no security alarm on it.

The window does open . . . but only about four inches because of a little metal thing stopping it, presumably to keep idiotic students from chucking something out the window. Or to keep students from jumping out. Removing the locking thing needs a key. I make a note to find out who has that key, but it seems very unlikely that Jay left through the window. Also, we're on the third floor. So he went out the door.

According to one of the articles about the case, Jay was seen on cameras in the stairwell going up the stairs at six, back down again at eight, and then up again a few minutes later. Someone also saw him in the lobby area on the first floor at eight. I make a note to find out who it was. Also, are the only security cameras in the building in the stairwell and at the front door?

There was no activity on his student card after he was logged coming into the building around six. No dining hall purchases, no library loans, no entry to any university building that requires a card swipe. The card readers only log when someone comes into a building, not when they leave it. In the *Investigate Further* column, I add *card readers* and *are there more cameras?*

I look at my mostly empty notebook. I hope Jay has more leads than this. I add *Gracie* to the list of people I need to talk to. But I need to tread carefully. I don't want to make things even more awkward with her.

Over the course of the day, I check ResConnect a few times, but Jay's name is never there. It's possible he'll never be there. Our timelines are only 85 percent the same—it's possible that in his timeline, he'll disappear before November 6.

But at eight o'clock sharp, a message comes through ResConnect.

Jay: Okay, just got in. What did you come up with?

I tell him we should start by figuring out how he got out of the room.

Jay: Probably the same way I always leave. Through the door, then the stairs. Didn't the stairwell camera catch me?

Aleeza: No, you were seen going up at six, then going down at eight, and up again a few minutes later. Could you have left through the window?

Jay: The window doesn't open all the way. And I'm not a huge fan of heights, I can't see me going out a three-story window.

Aleeza: Maybe you had no choice.

Jay: I would have caused a holy ruckus. I can scream loud. Believe me, it's unlikely.

I write *afraid of heights* in my notebook.

Jay: Can you try and see the camera footage?

Aleeza: Why?

Jay: I don't know. Maybe they missed something. Or you can describe it to me and I'll notice if I look strange.

Aleeza: Okay, I'll ask campus police on Monday. I also want to find out if there are any more cameras in East House.

Jay: Okay.

I'm realizing that there is little Jay can do to help me figure out how he got out of the building, since he hasn't actually done it yet. It makes more sense for him to help me with suspects and motive.

Aleeza: I'm going to try to talk to Gracie. You know her . . . she lives next door.

Jay: Yeah, I know her a little. Do you think she saw something?

Aleeza: Maybe. But she wrote that recent article about you in the school paper. She may be able to help.

Jay: Okay. I like Gracie. Do you have suspects yet?

Aleeza: My suspects are the Birdwatcher, the driver of the black Corolla, and Emma. But I doubt Emma's behind it because she's willingly talking to the press. I don't think she's that dumb. Were you cheating on her?

Jay: We were never exclusive.

Aleeza: Did she know that?

Jay: Of course. I don't lead anyone on. I keep things casual, and I make that clear.

This is so weird. Me. Aleeza Kassam. Talking to a guy about his hookup habits. But . . . I still feel uneasy. If I hooked up with someone like Jay, I'd probably want more than casual, too, right? But if he sent clear "casual" vibes, then I would make sure that's all I wanted before hopping into bed with him.

I don't have a ton of experience with guys. I've had only one boyfriend, my ex, Chase, who I dated for four months before I moved away from Alderville. We broke up when I left town because we both knew we weren't really into each other enough for long distance. We're still friends. Sort of.

But even someone like me who's not the hookup type, and who has barely dated, can see that Jay isn't—or wasn't—relationship material. Sexy, but not one to settle down. If Jay made his intentions clear, then why would any girl be upset at him enough to actually hurt him?

Maybe he's not being honest with me, though. Maybe he *did* promise more.

Aleeza: Is it possible someone thought they could change you or something? Maybe they all wanted to be the one to tame the wild rake.

Jay: Oh my god, did you call me a rake?

Aleeza: Yeah, like a libertine. A playboy.

Jay: I know what a rake is. It's HILARIOUS you're calling me one.

Aleeza: I can't tell if you're making fun of me.

Jay: I would never, Roomie. Okay, yeah that's possible, but I think I would've got that vibe from a girl in person, you know? I'm still pretty friendly with girls I hooked up with. Only Emma is weird, and she only got that way after we stopped talking.

I can't believe he's calling Emma weird because she was into him. I roll my eyes. This is why I steer clear of fuckboys.

Aleeza: How many girls are we talking about?

Jay: Not a huge number.

Aleeza: Numbers are relative. Some might say 25 isn't a huge number, but in this context . . .

Jay: Okay, four since I started uni. Hooked up with some of them more than once.

Four. It's more than my number of one, but not as many as I was assuming. I suddenly remember Jay saying I was cute when I told him to look at my Instagram. He was probably humoring me. I doubt short girls with frizzy hair are his type. Then again, I have no idea what the girls he slept with look like. Well, I've seen Emma in that newspaper article. She is . . . gorgeous. Is he being open with me precisely because I'm not the type of girl he normally goes for?

But four isn't really that big a number.

Aleeza: Did you really ghost Emma?

Jay: Definitely not. She ghosted me. I was the last one to text her. She kept it on read, but never responded. I figured that was it.

Aleeza: Is it possible that your recollection of the relationship isn't the same as hers?

Jay: It wasn't a relationship. I always wondered if she was more into my friends than me.

I clearly need to speak to Emma Coffey.

Aleeza: Who else might be the Birdwatcher? The other three girls maybe? What are their names?

After a few seconds, he sends me three names. I don't know any of them, but I jot them down in my notebook.

Aleeza: Why did you tell them you didn't want a commitment?

Jay: Are you asking me the actual reason I don't want a commitment, or the reason I told them?

Aleeza: The second one. Actually, both.

I don't know if I have the right to ask for the actual reason, but I want to understand him better. And . . . I'm curious.

Jay: I didn't give them a reason. It's not their business. I told them all—before sex by the way—that I wasn't looking for anything serious.

Aleeza: Has anyone ever backed out after you said it? Put their clothes back on and said all right, I'm out.

Jay: No.

That does not surprise me one bit. I wouldn't walk away. I have no idea why this is all annoying me so much. Or if he can tell how irritated I am at him. One thing is clear—Jay Hoque and I are from completely different worlds.

Aleeza: Okay what's the real reason? Why are you such a commitment-phobe?

Jay: I don't know. I don't think I'm a commitment-phobe. Like I'm not scared or anything. I'm just not wired that way.

Aleeza: You don't want to settle down with someone?

Jay: No, do you?

Aleeza: Well, not now, but yeah, eventually.

Jay: Husband, mortgage, and 2.5 kids. Or wife.

Aleeza: I'm straight. But isn't all that—a family and a home, what everyone wants? Isn't that the dream?

Jay: You're a little naive, Roomie. Where are you from anyway?

Aleeza: Why does that matter?

Jay: It doesn't. But we're roommates. We should know about each other, right?

Aleeza: I was born in Toronto, but I grew up in Alderville. It's a small town east of here on the Bay of Quinte.

Jay: I know it. Super white. My mom's boss loaned us her cottage about twenty minutes from Alderville once. Amazing food around there. What was it like growing up in a tourist town?

Aleeza: It was fine.

It wasn't always, but I don't want to get into it.

Jay: I think you'll change after you've been in the city longer. You have a boyfriend out there in your cute, small town?

Aleeza: I did. We broke up before I started university.

Jay: Proves my point.

Aleeza: What point does that prove? And what does a small town have to do with you being afraid of commitment?

Jay: My mom used to hang out in one of those all-white communities. Finding a happily ever after in a place you're not supposed to be in is nearly impossible.

Aleeza: Are you saying I wasn't supposed to be in Alderville, or you're not supposed to be here at TCU?

Jay: Both. Neither.

Aleeza: You make no sense. Anyway, my parents are still happily married. And in Alderville.

Jay: I'll bet they are. What do they do?

Aleeza: Mom's a librarian. Dad's an IT consultant.

Jay: Sounds idyllic.

I exhale. I don't know why talking to Jay makes me feel exactly like I did the first time I took the subway alone in Toronto. Like everyone knows the unwritten etiquette that I'm clueless about. It's probably not that necessary to get into all this personal stuff anyway.

Aleeza: I think I have enough to start with for now. I'll talk to campus police and Gracie and let you know what they say.

Jay: Okay. Should we meet here tomorrow at eight again?

Aleeza: Okay. That works.

Jay: Bye Roomie.

Aleeza: Good night, Jay.

NINE

The next morning I get dressed in all my winter gear, but I don't leave my room. I wait at my door with my eye on the peephole. When I hear Gracie's door open and see her walking to the stairs, I rush out.

"Gracie! Hi!" I say, catching up to her.

She doesn't look happy to see me. Yeah, this girl doesn't trust me.

"Aleeza, hey."

"Such great timing to bump into you! I was hoping to talk to you about something. Are you going next door for breakfast?"

Gracie clearly doesn't want to have a meal with me. Rightfully so—I'm awkward and being way too pushy, and she thinks I'm one of Jay's stalkers. I need an angle here . . . How would Nancy Drew get a suspect to speak to her? Should I trick her into talking about Jay?

But . . . Gracie isn't a suspect. And I'm trying to get her to trust me, not only because of this Jay project but also because I'm going to live next door to her for the next two months. "Professor Sarah said I should talk to you about my media project. I've had to restart it because . . . well, for the same reason I had to move in here. Also"—I hope I'm not rambling—"it would be nice to have someone to talk to in East House. I don't know anyone here."

I can see the moment Gracie's compassion convinces her to throw me a small friendship bone. Her shoulders relax as we get to the bottom of the stairs. "Yeah, okay. Let's talk over breakfast."

This is the first time I'm actually *eating* in the dining hall in City Tower instead of grabbing food to-go. The old hall is cramped with beaten-up wood tables and chairs, and walls that clearly used to be white but are now a graying beige with teal moldings. I get a buttered cinnamon bagel and a tea. Gracie gets a breakfast burrito and a smoothie. We sit near the window, where at least the view is less depressing since the sun is finally shining after so many days of nonstop flurries. The snow outside looks pretty, actually. On these clear, bright winter days, Mom and I used to go to this conservation park near Alderville for a winter hike or snowshoeing. Walking through the busy downtown Toronto streets wouldn't be the same. All my loneliness is making me homesick. Maybe I should go home to Alderville next weekend.

"Why is this dining hall always empty?" I ask while stirring my tea.

"People only eat here if they have nowhere better to go." Gracie shakes her bottled smoothie. She's in pants today—wide-legged black ones—with a turquoise button-up and a cream cardigan. And of course, her red lipstick. Her dark hair is in a ponytail, with her bangs and some front pieces framing her face. Gracie is pretty, but more than that, she has a kind face—when she's not annoyed with someone. And she always seems annoyed at me.

I take a bite of my bagel. It's actually quite tasty.

"So . . . what did you want to ask?" Gracie asks, getting right to it. Okay. No small talk, then.

I take a deep breath. "My media project. Since I'm living in Jay's old room, I'm doing an investigative podcast on his disappearance."

Gracie looks at me with no expression on her face.

"Because," I continue, "you know. I have a personal connection with him. Sarah said it will make me invested but not biased, since I didn't actually know him. I know you wrote an article in the school paper about him. Sarah said I should talk to you about it. You know . . . to figure out where to start. Maybe I could even interview you for my podcast."

"I knew it." Gracie shakes her head. She stands, picking up her tray. "I don't know why you vultures won't leave him alone. He's gone . . . Haven't you all done enough?"

"Wait," I say, putting my hand out. "I'm not stalking Jay. I honestly didn't know him. Please hear me out."

She blinks at me, then sits back down, expression still annoyed.

I exhale. "I need a new media project. I had to restart, and it's late."

"Why do you need to restart a month into the term?"

I sigh. I haven't really told anyone details of how my old friend ditched me. Except Jay, of course. I tell Gracie all about Mia, Lance, and Taylor. Her expression sours when I mention her new skincare YouTube channel.

"Wow. She changed the entire focus of your show without asking you? Even though it was for your school project? How long did you know this girl?"

"Since we were seven. We came here together from our hometown."

"Where's the hometown?"

"Alderville. It's on the Bay of Quinte. In Prince Edward County."

"Never heard of it. Sounds like good riddance, though. I hate it when a person's entire identity becomes about the person they're dating. She may have been your best friend, but you weren't hers."

I blink. Mia *was* my best friend. But . . . was it possible it had never been mutual? This isn't the first time she pushed me aside for a boy. And she knew I needed a good media project for my portfolio. Something that would demonstrate my passions. But she didn't care about that. All she cared about was YouTube views. And Lance.

"Is she in journalism too?"

"No, retail management."

Gracie shrugs. "I suppose the skincare thing makes a little bit of sense for her then. Why are you pivoting to a podcast instead of a web series?"

"If I'm alone, I'd rather not put my face on camera."

She frowns. "That's silly. You have a great face. Why investigate Jay's disappearance if you don't know him?"

"Sarah said I should pick something that's relevant to me instead of some random mystery because it makes it more compelling to the listeners. But she said it was good that I didn't know Jay because I'll be unbiased." Even though I *do* know Jay. I just didn't know him before he disappeared. And I can't tell Gracie that I know him now because she'd think I'm nuts.

"Okay, I get that. So you only want to cover Jay's case for the class credit?"

No, I also want to investigate it because Jay didn't deserve what happened to him. Because even if he's a player or an ass, he's also a funny guy and kind of my friend. But again, I can't tell Gracie that.

"I'm really into mysteries," I say. "And, I don't know, it's weird to be living in the room where he disappeared. I feel bad for him. He's a person, right? He couldn't have been all bad."

Gracie shakes her head. "He wasn't. I didn't know him that well, but I liked the guy. He was upbeat and a little silly. I could never reconcile the things people said about him with the person who lived next door to me. That's why I wanted to write that article. I wanted to show a different side of Jay than what everyone was saying. But hell, it was hard to find anyone who'd say something positive about him. Except his teachers. They all loved him."

Gracie saw the same thing in Jay that I see. A friendly, optimistic person. It makes me like her more. But also, this adds to the mystery of Jay. Why is he a fun, nice, friendly person to me and Gracie, and not to anyone else? Where Jay Hoque is concerned, I have more questions than answers.

"Yeah . . . that's kind of the angle I want to take," I say. "Unbiased and actually empathetic to the victim, which no one else seems to be." I've looked up the other student podcasts about his disappearance, and they're not exactly kind to him. One of them is actually called *Karma's a Bitch*.

"Okay . . . so what do you want from me?" Gracie asks.

I shrug. "Whatever you are willing to help me with. An interview about what it was like to live next to him. What you heard or saw on the day he disappeared. I'd love to be connected with that ex of his you spoke to—"

"Emma. Yeah, she's on my . . . friend's soccer team. Let me ask her." She picks up her phone and texts someone, then looks up at me. "Actually, Aster—she's the one who was outside my room the other day. She's in second year and knows a lot of people who know . . . *knew* Jay. People he hung out with last year. I can't promise anything, but yeah, I'll help you out." She looks at her phone for a bit, then back at me. "You ever get this feeling that someone is getting the short end of the stick all the time? I felt that about Jay even before he went missing."

I nod. I understand exactly what Gracie means. Jay said something like that, about how hard it is to have a happily ever after in a place you're not supposed to be.

Also, turns out the girl in the hallway isn't Gracie's girlfriend. Just a hookup? Friends with benefits?

Gracie's phone buzzes. She checks it. "Emma's in. Not surprised. Last time, I wouldn't let her ramble on about how terrible Jay was for as long as she wanted, so of course she's jumping at the chance to meet again. You know she tried to talk to the major media, too, but they wouldn't listen to her? She says five o'clock in the student center Starbucks. That work for you?"

I nod. I have nothing else to do today—until eight, when Jay and I are supposed to talk.

After spending most of the day doing coursework in the library, right before five I head across campus to the student center. It's not snowing anymore, but it's still cold. I reassess my desire to have something outdoorsy to do today, because I can't feel my cheeks at all. It's March—why is this winter being so cruel? Everyone told me that winters in Toronto would be better than Alderville, which is in the snow belt, but it's been brutal here. The chill goes all the way to my bones.

When I get to Starbucks, I see Gracie standing with two long-haired girls near the entrance to the cafe. They're both in winter gear, too, but not as heavily bundled as Gracie. As I get closer, I recognize the girl I saw in the hallway with her the day I moved in.

"It's really busy in there," Gracie says. "We'll have to sit in the student lounge. Did you want to get a drink first?" I shake my head. I have my water bottle with me. We find seats in the student lounge—a place that looks weirdly like a Tim Hortons coffee shop, except without a serving counter. Gracie formally introduces Aster, then Emma Coffey.

From far away, I wouldn't have been able to tell the difference between Emma and Aster. Both have long brown, highlighted hair and rosy cheeks. Both are wearing sweatshirts, and both have pink lipstick on. I wonder if this is the standard look for the school's soccer team. Up close, though, Aster has a warmer, friendlier smile and has less makeup on than Emma. She has visible freckles on her nose. Also, Aster has oversize, gold-rimmed aviator glasses on. I immediately notice the Gucci label on the side of them.

"I hope you don't mind Aster joining," Gracie says. "When I told her about your project, she squealed."

Aster nods vigorously. "Sorry I was being weird when we met. It's *so cool* that you're doing a podcast on Jay. I'm *obsessed* with true crime podcasts."

"Yeah, no worries," I say. Gracie said Aster knows a lot of Jay's friends, so she could be useful to the investigation.

Emma flips her hair over her shoulder. "Podcasts are dying. You should do a true crime TikTok series."

I shake my head. "I'm going to stick with a podcast." I put my phone on the table and open the voice recorder app. "Do I have your consent to record you? I might use some of this in the podcast, but if you don't want me to, that's fine."

Emma nods. "Definitely. Go ahead."

I hit "Start" on my phone's voice recorder. "If you say something that you want to retract, let me know." She nods. "Okay, how and when did you first meet Jay Hoque?"

"In the fall. I think it was, like, the first week of school. We met at the Wolfe." The Wolfe is a bar near campus that has a reputation for cheap drinks and not checking IDs. I went once with Mia in September—it played nineties house music too loud and smelled like a mix of beer and Lysol. I prefer another local bar, the BookShelf, because I'm a cliché who likes a literary theme. Now I wonder if Jay and Emma met the same night I was at the Wolfe.

"Did you approach him?" I really can't imagine my friend Jay with Emma.

Emma snorts. "Uh, *no*. I was *so* not looking to hook up that night. My friend had just had a nasty breakup and wanted to get tanked. Jay picked *me* up."

"What was your impression of him back then?"

Emma frowns. "I'd seen him around last year, you know? With Jack and that crew." She glances at Aster. I wonder if *that crew* means the people Aster knows. I remember Jay mentioning a friend named Jack.

"But you hadn't met him before then?"

She laughs a little self-consciously and sneaks a glance at Aster again. What is that about? Emma looks like she wants Aster's approval.

"Nah. I heard he was an ass. But he was *so hot*. He was on the water polo team, you know. You should have seen those pecs."

That checks out. Jay did mention water polo practice once.

"How long were you two . . . associating?" I don't want to say *together* because Jay said they never really were together. And saying *sleeping together* seems weird.

Emma doesn't seem to notice my awkward phrasing. "A couple of weeks? Until, like, end of September? He totally ghosted me. I mean, I should have known. Like they say, a giraffe can't change his stripes."

"Zebra," Gracie says, correcting Emma. She looks like she's holding in a laugh.

Emma waves a hand. "Whatever."

So it seems Emma wasn't talking to him anymore at least a month before he disappeared. I really don't want this interview to turn into a *Jay was terrible* session, so I guide the conversation forward.

"What else can you tell me about him? Was he close to his family? Did he have hobbies? What did you guys talk about?"

She shrugs. "I dunno. We didn't really talk that much. He's from Scarborough, if you can believe it. I guess living there makes you paranoid—he was *convinced* he was being followed. The guy was so strange—I have no clue how he ended up with Jack's crowd." She snorts. "Jay used to take the subway all the way to Scarborough just to get a sandwich." She makes a face. "I'm sorry, but no sandwich is worth getting potentially shot for."

Scarborough is a district in the east end of Toronto that has a reputation for being dangerous and full of crime. In reality, the crime rate is no worse than the rest of the city, but Scarborough has a lower average income, is underfunded, and is mostly full of immigrants and people of color. I follow a food blogger from the area, and the food there looks *incredible*. I'd be tempted to take a long subway ride for a sandwich that good.

Gracie scowls at Emma's elitist—and frankly, *racist*—comment. I can tell that Gracie doesn't like Emma, and that Emma doesn't notice or care. The only person here that Emma seems to care about is Aster. And Aster seems to be indifferent to Emma's fawning. She's mostly looking at Gracie.

What's the story with Aster, anyway? She has nothing to do with Jay or his disappearance, but there's something about her that I can't put my finger on.

"So, were you and Jay exclusive?" I ask.

She blinks. "I thought we were. But after he ghosted me, I found out that Jay Hoque doesn't do exclusive."

"Did he *say* you were exclusive?"

She doesn't answer that question. Between Jay and Emma, clearly Jay is the more trustworthy one. Even though I've never seen his body language.

But I still can't tell if Emma is capable of *hurting* Jay. Does she hate him enough for that? I ask another question.

"You said earlier that you knew he was an ass. Where did you hear that?"

"Oh, you know. Around." She giggles. "Everyone knows he was an asshole, right? It was all over *Birdwatcher*."

"Wasn't the *Birdwatcher* Tumblr taken down last spring?" I ask.

Gracie turns to me, surprised. She might have heard of Birdwatcher, but I don't think she knew about the Tumblr.

Emma looks around the student center, then leans close, as if she's talking only to Aster. "You haven't heard? Birdwatcher is *back*." I wonder if Gracie included Aster in this conversation because she knew Emma would be more likely to open up. Seems Gracie truly does want to help me.

Aster raises a brow. "It is?"

Emma nods, grinning. "On Instagram."

Instagram? I pick up my phone and do a quick search for Birdwatcher on Instagram. All the results have to do with actual birds. Not Jay.

"Who's behind the account?" Gracie asks.

Emma shakes her head. "No one knows. It's *anonymous*." She looks at Gracie. "I wanted to show it to you when you interviewed me, but the posts were all deleted when he disappeared."

I make a note in my black notebook to do a more detailed search for Birdwatcher on all social media. "What did they post on Instagram? Pictures of Jay?" I ask.

Emma shakes her head. "No. The grid was just, like, random pictures of birds, but the captions were full of all the horrible things that Jay did. Did you know he paid some Indian guy to do his final projects for him last year? Someone even said he *forged* his high school transcripts."

I frown. This is the same stuff Jay said was on Tumblr. He said none of it was true, and I believe him. I barely know Jay at all, but I don't think he's the type to do stuff like that.

Or is he?

He *did* ask me to ask his future self what would be on his engineering exam. And he did want to bet on sports to make millions.

"You told me Birdwatchers were girls who he cheated on. Not people accusing him of cheating at school," Gracie says.

Emma nods. "Yeah, they do both. So, like, in October they had this story up that said girls could DM them about things Jay did, and they'd post them anonymously. Lots of girls wrote in about what an ass he was to them. I wrote in too."

"Okay," I say. "Do I have this straight? Last school year there was a Tumblr blog about how terrible Jay was. Then it was taken down. But then this year, an Instagram account appeared under the same name saying the same stuff from Tumblr but also posting stuff girls sent in anonymously."

Emma nods, grinning. "I told you he was an ass."

"No, you told me that anonymous social media accounts said he was an ass," I say. "You do know that not everything online is true, don't you?"

Aster snort laughs at that, then grins at me. "I like you," she says.

Emma's forehead creases, but she doesn't say anything.

"When did the Instagram start?" I ask.

"Like, early this year. I saw it in September."

"Did anyone tell the police about it when they were searching for him?" I ask. "It's cyberbullying."

Emma shrugs. "I don't know. I assume someone said something. But is it bullying? Everyone knew he was bad news—"

Gracie interrupts again. "If you knew he was trouble, why did you date him?"

"I told you. He was, like . . . *chiseled*. Plus, you know." She looks at Aster. "His friends all still hung out with him, so I thought he was okay. But then I saw his true colors. He was always so *secretive*, disappearing every weekend. He said it was to see his family, but he never talked about them."

"How did you find out about the Instagram in the first place?" Gracie asks.

"Bailey Cressman showed it to me." I detect a touch of pride when Emma says that name. And for some reason, Aster snorts again.

"Who's that?" I ask.

Emma raises a brow. "You don't know Bailey? I thought *everyone* knew Bailey. I was at a party with her, and she showed me the whole thing." She giggles. "Bailey gets chatty when she's drunk. We're good friends, you know."

"Can you give me Bailey's contact info?"

Emma looks at me like I asked for her firstborn.

Aster waves her hand. "I can connect you to Bailey Cressman. We don't need Emma."

Emma looks at Aster, then frowns. "I can come when you talk to her. I mean, in case you want to ask me—"

"I really don't think that's necessary," Gracie says. "Aleeza, I think we're done with Emma. What do you think?"

"One more question," I say. "You said you saw Jay before he disappeared. Where and when?"

"It was, like . . . the day before, I think. He was being super creepy . . . like, hiding behind a tree in front of West Hall, staring at the door. When he saw me, he turned away. Like, he didn't even say hi. I told you he was super paranoid—it was like he didn't want anyone to know he was there."

I raise a brow. It's quite a leap to assume someone standing near a tree is clearly doing something wrong.

"I think I have enough," I say, turning off the voice recorder. I really don't want to spend any more time with this girl. "Here's my number." I write it on a Post-It note. "Call or text me if you want to add anything. Thanks for talking to us."

Emma pouts a little, then pulls some sunglasses out of her bag and puts them on. They are aviator-style, like Aster's eyeglasses, but there is no Gucci label on them. Emma says goodbye to Aster and walks away. Gracie and I barely get a nod from her. I have no idea why Emma looks so disappointed. What was she expecting from this meeting that she didn't get?

Gracie grins once Emma is gone. "She told us a ton, didn't she? I kept hearing about Birdwatcher—I had no idea it was a secret Instagram account." She picks up her phone. After a few seconds, she frowns. "I can't find it."

I try again on my own phone, searching the words *Birdwatcher + Jay Hoque* on the app. I find plenty of hits with pictures of birds. It would take me a while to find the right one. "I wonder if it's been deleted like the Tumblr." I shake my head. "She basically admitted that every evil thing she thinks about Jay is from that account." I look up Jay's name alone on Instagram and find his personal account, but it hasn't been updated in a while. And there are no birds on it.

"Doesn't surprise me," Aster says. "Emma Coffey doesn't have an original thought in her head."

After searching a few more seconds, I put my phone down. This would be easier on my computer later. It's strange. My gut feeling is still that Jay is more trustworthy than Emma, but at the same time, I've lost some respect for him now that I know he dated her. Or hooked up with her. Or whatever. She seems so . . . I don't know. Not like him. I don't know why I care, but I do. "Okay, so what do we do now?" I ask.

"I'll see if Bailey will talk to you," Aster says. "Warning, though . . . I'd take everything Bailey Cressman says with a grain of salt. She cares more about *status* than anything else."

I frown at Aster. Status. Emma seemed pretty status obsessed too. The comments she made about Jay's family left such a bad taste in my mouth.

I still can't figure out why Emma was acting weird about Aster, though. What's the deal there? I could just ask Aster. "I got a weird vibe from Emma. Like she wanted to impress you or something. Were you two . . . a thing or something?"

Aster snorts incredulously. "Yeah, *absolutely not*. I have no interest in *pick-me* straight girls."

Gracie laughs. "You're right, though. Emma definitely wants to impress Aster. She wants a ticket into Aster's world. Like everyone else does."

"Except you," Aster deadpans, looking right at Gracie.

Gracie looks away awkwardly. So, even if Gracie and Aster aren't girlfriends, there's something between them. I think Aster is into Gracie, but I can't read what Gracie feels for Aster.

And why does everyone (except Gracie, apparently) want a ticket into Aster's world?

Gracie finally explains. "Did you notice that Emma talked about Bailey the same way? She would love her name to be used in the same breath as Aster and Bailey. Because they're . . . rich."

That explains Aster's expensive glasses. "Emma wants to be friends with you because you have money?"

Gracie shakes her head. "These people aren't just wealthy; they're like . . . *stinking wealthy*. Like, one percenters. Socialites. Actual trust-fund kids. Aster here included."

"Yes, but you know that I'm a socialist hippie deep down." Aster gives Gracie a look of pure admiration. Yeah, she's totally into Gracie.

Gracie doesn't say anything to that. "Bailey's friends are all snooty as hell. Emma would *kill* to be one of them. Hell, I'll bet she only hooked up with Jay to get closer to them."

That surprises me. "Wait . . . Jay's rich too?" Nothing he told me about his family made me think they had extreme wealth.

Gracie shakes her head. "No, not that I know of."

"But he was friends with some of that crew," Aster says. "I used to see him at parties all the time last year. Not sure why. Anyway, I wouldn't put it past Emma to hook up with him to get into those parties. And then she lost interest when she realized he wasn't really partying with them much anymore." Aster looks at her smartwatch. "Shit. That's my mom." She looks at Gracie. "It's my weekly pilgrimage to the Bridle Path for Sunday dinner."

Wow. They weren't kidding about extreme wealth. The Bridle Path is the wealthiest neighborhood in the city. Actually, it's the wealthiest in all of Canada.

"I guess I'll start transcribing that interview," I say. "Thanks a bunch. Both of you." I know there is no way I would have gotten this far without them. But also, I don't feel any closer to learning what actually happened to Jay.

"No problem," Aster says, grinning. "I'd love to come along if you interview someone else. Oooh, should I get a lapel microphone?"

"Are you two . . . ," I stutter. "I mean, do you want to *keep* helping me?"

Gracie nods. "Yeah, I'm game. Jay deserves justice. I can also help with your podcast. I'm doing a documentary on the history of Toronto's Koreatown for my media project but working on yours, too, will look good on my résumé."

"Yeah, absolutely, that would be cool," I say. "And I can help you, too, if you need . . . anything."

"I've always wanted to be in a Scooby gang," Aster says. "I'm going to buy detective gear. Give me your number. I'll let you know what Bailey says."

I give Aster my phone number. I know this doesn't mean I have friends, but it's at least something. "Okay. Thanks for helping me."

"No problem! Bye!" Aster and Gracie leave the student center together.

I smile as I slip my notebook into my backpack. Apparently, I found myself a little mystery-solving gang.

TEN

I go back to the dining hall near East House for dinner. I'm honestly not sure why I've never actually eaten in here before today. They have the same grain bowls I used to get from West Hall, and it's a lot quieter. No one talks to me during the whole meal, which is fine because I have work to do. While I eat, I put my headphones in and transcribe the interview with Emma on my laptop.

It's seven thirty when I get back to my room after dinner. It's just enough time for a shower before my date with Jay. Well, not a date. A texting date. Sort of.

I get a buzz on my phone before I've even plugged in my laptop to charge.

Jay: There you are!

Aleeza: I just came from dinner. We're talking at eight, aren't we?

Jay: Yeah, I was excited to tell you something. I did some sleuthing all by myself!

I unwrap my scarf from my neck. The room is drafty, as usual, so I pull my wearable blanket over my head.

Jay: I saw a campus security guard in the building so I asked him some questions. I was all casual. You would have been so impressed. The perfect undercover investigator.

It's kind of adorable how excited he is about this.

Aleeza: What did you find out?

Jay: First of all, there are two cameras in the building. The stairwell one, and one in the lobby pointing at the front door. He even showed it to me. It's pretty hidden.

Aleeza: I assume that's the one that saw you come in, but not out again that night.

Jay: Yeah, but here's the weird thing. The stairwell camera is between the first and second floor. Cheap school doesn't have a camera on every floor. So, I realize, I could have taken the stairs to the second floor and the camera wouldn't see me.

The second floor has only professor offices.

Aleeza: Is there a way out of the building from the second floor?

Jay: Not that I know of. My Civil Engineering prof's office is there. I can ask her next time I see her.

I make a note to check the outside of the building to see if there's a door that could come from a second set of stairs.

Aleeza: If there is another way out of the building, the police would have checked that, wouldn't they have?

Jay: Yeah, I assume. I haven't exactly solved the case.

Aleeza: It's still excellent information. I had an eventful day too.

I text him a brief description of my meeting with Gracie, and then with Gracie, Aster, and Emma. I tell him I'll send him the transcript of the conversation when I'm done with it.

Jay: Holy crap. Your detective work today was better than mine. By the way, Emma is lying. She picked me up in the Wolfe—not the other way around.

Aleeza: Can't say I'm surprised about that.

Jay: Is there really an Instagram account specifically for people to complain about me?

Aleeza: Apparently. We couldn't find it, though. Emma said it's been taken down.

It's a lead that goes nowhere, just like most of the leads we'd found.

Jay: It's taken down in your time, but it should still be there in mine, right?

I'm an idiot. Why didn't I think of that?

Aleeza: Look for it.

He doesn't respond, so I assume he's looking. I take the opportunity to look up which professors have offices on the second floor here. Looks like they are all psychology or engineering professors. I jot down their names in my black notebook.

Jay: I found it.

Aleeza: What's it posting?

Jay: The pictures are all random shots of birds around the city. The captions are the same unsubstantiated BS from the old Tumblr posts. Also anonymous accounts of me being a dirty player. Like I'm dating three girls at once, or I'm a serial ghoster. One says I gave someone an STI. It's not true. This is defamation. Ugh. I should call my lawyer again.

Aleeza: I'm so sorry. What's the account?

Jay: Birdwatcher_City. I assume the city is for Toronto City University. Someone started it six weeks ago.

I look for the site on my end, and I do find it. It's empty, though. All the posts have been deleted. The profile picture is of a blue jay.

This is proof that Birdwatcher exists, at least. Unless this account is for, you know, actually watching birds.

Aleeza: Have you never noticed this account before?

Jay: I very rarely use social media. This is the first time I've logged on in weeks, except for when I checked your account a few days ago.

Aleeza: Who follows it?

Jay: 76 followers. No names I recognize. Wait. Emma and Bailey. And some others I know. No one else I hooked up with.

I check who's following the account on my end. It has about a hundred followers—none that I recognize after a brief scan, except Emma. It looks like a bunch of bots are following—there are some sketch names here. It doesn't surprise me. A bunch of bots follow my account too.

Aleeza: I don't recognize any of the followers.

Jay: I just followed it and put a notification on it so I'll see if it posts again.

Aleeza: Maybe they'll stop posting once they see that Jay Hoque is following them.

Jay: Give me some credit, Roomie. I set up a fake account. A fake account to stalk my stalker.

Aleeza: Good idea. Maybe Bailey Cressman will tell us who's behind it. I'm glad Gracie and Aster are helping me get access to her.

Jay: Yeah, I feel like I should go knock on Gracie's door and thank her for having my back in a few months.

Aleeza: She said you two weren't close.

Jay: Not really. We say hello in the hallway. Canadian polite acquaintances. I know Aster a little better. Still not really friends, though. Aster and Gracie have been attached at the hip since September. Are they dating?

Aleeza: I don't know what's going on between them. But Gracie's been protective of you since I moved in. At first, she actually thought I was your stalker.

Jay: Has she seen the Birdwatcher Instagram?

Aleeza: No. How does Bailey Cressman know you?

Jay: Same as Aster. I saw her at parties last year. I know what you're thinking, but no, I didn't hook up with her. Bailey seems . . . high maintenance.

Aleeza: Otherwise you would have hooked up with her?

Jay: No.

Aleeza: She doesn't hang with your friends anymore?

Jay: No, I don't hang out with that group very much anymore. Happens a lot in first year. Your friends in September will probably not be your friends forever.

I have no idea if Jay is talking about me when he says that. A couple of weeks ago, I would have denied it. Mia and I were going to be friends forever. But look how much my life has changed in a week.

Aleeza: Gracie says Bailey and Aster's group is rich and snobby.

Jay: Yep. You can see why I don't really fit in with them. I met them last year through water polo. Serves me right to pick such a bougie sport. So, what's our next step in the investigation?

Aleeza: I wait to see if Bailey Cressman will tell us more about Birdwatcher. And I need to actually start the podcast. I'm thinking episode one will be a little bit about you and the details of the disappearance. Like the time you were last seen and possible ways you could have gotten out of the building. I can use what you learned about the cameras. Then episode two can be a deeper dive into "Who is Jay Hoque." Can I ask you some questions for that now?

Jay: Um, I'm supposed to be missing? Who are you going to put down as your source for this information?

Good question.

Aleeza: We can keep it surface level. Just tell me things that would be easy for me to find out on my own. This will save me from having to actually do the research.

Jay: Okay. Hit me with your hard-hitting questions, Roomie.

Aleeza: What's your major?

Jay: Engineering. I want to be a structural engineer.

Aleeza: Why did you pick this university?

Jay: I got a scholarship here. And I like being close to home.

Aleeza: You grew up in Toronto, right?

Jay: Yep. Specifically, Scarborough.

Aleeza: Any siblings?

Jay: No.

Aleeza: Are you close with your dad too?

Jay: I don't have one. You don't need to mention a father.

Aleeza: Everyone has a father.

Jay: Yeah, and mine's not in the picture. It's not relevant. I've never met him. Don't mention him in the podcast.

This is weird. He doesn't want me to even say that his father isn't in his life? It's totally significant to who he is, right? Did his father abandon him? Is he dead? I can't tell if Jay truly doesn't think it's significant and has no feelings about his birth father, or if he's hiding something.

One thing I can safely assume is that Jay's father isn't from Bangladesh, like his mother. He said he's biracial, and he implied earlier that his mother used to be in an all-white community. Is that where she met his father? I make a note to find out what I can about Jay's father—without telling Jay, of course.

Aleeza: Maybe it would be better if I spoke to a family member. Do you think your mother would talk to me?

Jay: I'd rather you didn't. This is probably hard enough on her.

I remember he said his mother had depression. I hope she's doing okay. There must be a way I can check on her without upsetting her.

Aleeza: Can I speak to a cousin or something? You said you were close to your aunt and uncle. Do they have kids?

Jay: Yeah, Madhuri and Manal. I'm tight with both of them, but especially Manal. She's a student at OCAD. She's a year older than me.

Aleeza: Do you think she'd speak to me.

Jay: Don't know. I assume they're all desperate to find me. At least I hope they are. Next time I see Manal, I'll say I have a new friend who loves octopuses. She's always drawing underwater stuff so it will make sense. Then you can DM her and she won't think you're a stranger to me.

Aleeza: Hopefully that action will carry on to my timeline—85 percent, remember?

Jay: It's worth a shot.

Aleeza: Yeah, I guess so.

It feels a little like we're playing with fire. It's one thing to get information from past Jay to figure out where present Jay is, but to have past Jay make changes to his timeline based on things I tell him could increase the differences between our worlds. Or cause a temporal paradox so big we'll blow up the universe.

But changing the past is exactly what we're trying to do . . . Jay needs to change something in his timeline based on what we figure out in mine. He needs to *not* disappear.

I make a note to do a little more research on the physics of time. Maybe watch some movies from Dad's list.

Aleeza: Are you single right now?

Jay: Yeah, I told you. I don't do relationships.

Aleeza: Like ever?

Jay: I don't know. You putting this in the podcast?

Aleeza: Not if you don't want me to. But it's relevant since I'll be talking about Birdwatcher and Emma Coffey.

Jay: Okay fine. I don't think relationships are for me. Ever.

Aleeza: Maybe you haven't met the right person yet.

Jay: You ever been in love, Roomie?

I frown. What does that have to do with his disappearance?

Aleeza: Are we talking about you, or me?

Jay: I'm curious. If you get to know everything about me, I want to know something about you.

Aleeza: No I haven't been in love.

Jay: What about the Alderville boyfriend?

Aleeza: I liked Chase. But it was never going to move to love. For either of us.

Maybe love isn't for me either. Maybe I'm more like Jay than I'm willing to admit.

Jay: Okay, so maybe you're not as idealistic as I thought you were.

I don't know what he means, so I don't write back. On one hand, I kind of wish he were here—physically, I mean. I need to see his body language . . . to know if he *really* thinks I'm nothing but a naive child. But also, there's no way I could have this conversation with him face-to-face. I'm supposed to be investigating *him*, and instead I'm telling him things I don't normally tell anyone. But if I don't answer his questions, I'm not sure he'll talk.

Jay: I just looked at your Instagram again.

Farah Heron

Aleeza: Why?

Jay: We're roommates. I want to see what your life is like. You're cute. Wholesome.

He called me cute before. But not *wholesome*.

Aleeza: You're mocking me.

Jay: I'm not. Truthfully. I really do think you're cute. You're really into octopuses, aren't you? Your grid is full of them.

Aleeza: Yeah, I collect them.

Jay: Is the orange one in your pictures the one that lives on my bed?

Aleeza: Yeah, that's Tentacle Ted. Since I don't have Mia anymore, he's been keeping me company.

Jay: Mia's the friend that ditched you, right? I saw her in your pictures.

Aleeza: Yeah, she was my best friend since we were kids. We haven't spoken since I moved out Tuesday.

It's the longest I've gone without talking to Mia since we met. My chest tightens. I have no regrets about moving out, but I didn't expect this emptiness after losing that friendship.

Jay: Good riddance. I think you'll find out that you can be yourself now. And be a much better person without her.

That's . . . kind of him to say.

Aleeza: Can I ask you questions just to get to know you too? Not for the podcast.

Jay: Go ahead.

Aleeza: What's your favorite TV character?

Jay: The Swedish Chef and Nick Fury. What's yours?

Aleeza: Wait. Why the Swedish Chef? Like the Muppet?

Jay: Yes, the Muppet. He loves good food, and I love good food. Also, there's chaos whenever he's cooking and nothing ever works out right, but that doesn't stop him from trying again the next time. I like his commitment.

Aleeza: So you DO like commitment. ☺

Jay: I am very committed to excellent meals. What's yours?

Aleeza: Veronica Mars or Velma.

Jay: Velma from Scooby Doo. Of course. Teenage sleuths. Favorite type of food? Mine's sandwiches.

I chuckle, remembering when Emma said he would take transit to Scarborough just for a sandwich.

Aleeza: Samosas, but only my grandmother's homemade ones. That or bowls.

Jay: Bowls?

Aleeza: Burrito bowls, poke bowls, papri chat, curry bowls. I like a whole bunch of random things mixed in a bowl.

Jay: Were you the type of kid who mixed all the cereals together?

Aleeza: Yes, I still do.

Jay: We have the opposite taste in food. I like things neatly between bread, and you like them chaotically mixed. Ask me another question.

I do have another question for him. One that's a bit heavier. I'm a little afraid to ask it. But I do anyway.

Aleeza: Why aren't you more freaked out? About being missing, I mean. You seem to be taking it well.

Jay: I am freaking out. I'm freaking out so much that I went home yesterday for no reason and spent the whole day with my mother. But I have you, right? My own Veronica Mars to solve this case for me.

Emo bad-boy Jay Hoque is a huge optimist. And at the same time, a total pessimist. He's a mystery.

Aleeza: You mentioned earlier that this is like a Keanu Reeves movie, but not The Matrix. What movie were you talking about?

Jay: The Lake House.

Aleeza: Never heard of it.

Jay: It's a romance. It makes no sense, but I liked it. It's gentle and cozy. My mom's a big Keanu Reeves fan. I watched it with her.

Aleeza: My parents are really into science fiction. I asked them about time travel and technology, and my dad emailed me a list of all the best time-travel movies.

Jay: We should watch them together.

I frown. Did he want to spend time with me outside of our investigation?

Aleeza: How are we going to watch movies together if we're months apart?

Jay: We'll stream them at the same time and text each other while we're watching. It'll be fun. And it's research. Do you want to start tomorrow after our eight o'clock update on the case? The Lake House must be streaming somewhere.

Why not? It's not like I have anyone else to hang out with.

Aleeza: Sure. When are you going to talk to your cousin?

Jay: I'll text her. We have lunch together fairly often. I'll casually mention my new investigative reporter friend who's into bowls and octopuses.

Aleeza: Okay. I'll wait until you do before I contact her.

Jay: I'm heading to bed—I have water polo practice in the morning. Same time tomorrow?

Aleeza: Yep. Tomorrow we can start the scripts for the podcast too.

Jay: Good night! Say good night to the octopus for me.

"Jay says good night, Ted," I say aloud.

Aleeza: Done. Talk tomorrow.

~

On Monday, between my classes, I start drafting the first episode of the podcast. And after my last class, I go to the campus security main office to try to get access to the camera footage from East House.

"Not without a warrant," the guy at the desk says, barely looking at me.

"I'm doing an investigation on Jay's disappearance—"

"Not without a warrant," he says again, a smirk on his face. He looks like he's on a power trip. Which he probably is.

"I assume that footage was given to the police?"

"Of course."

"What about his student card logs? Did Jay use his card after—"

"Not without a—"

"A warrant. I know." There has to be something this guy will tell me. "One question: Are there any exits in East House from the second floor? Like a back stairwell or something?"

"How would I know?"

I sigh. "Okay, can you tell me if there is a back-door camera?"

"I'll throw you a bone. No, there isn't, but the alarm on the door is connected to the system. We'd know if someone opened it."

"Was it opened the night Jay Hoque disappeared?"

"Not telling you without a warrant," he says. He suddenly looks over my shoulder and smiles.

I sigh. This is clearly going nowhere. As I'm leaving the office, I almost crash into someone in the doorway. And ugh. It's Taylor. I wonder if this is who the security guy was smiling at. Mia once told me Taylor has a thing for cops.

"Hi, Taylor," I say.

She stares at me like she doesn't know who I am. Which is ridiculous because I was almost always there when she came by to see Mia.

I'm so not in the mood for this. I roll my eyes and walk out of the security office. I wonder if she's hooking up with the guy.

On my way back to my room, I get a text from Gracie that says Bailey isn't answering Aster's calls. Figures. Nothing seems to be working out for me. When I get to East House, I search around the building, looking for other exits, but I can't find one. Just the front door, and the fire escape door in the back. And Jay couldn't have left from it because it's alarmed.

Defeated, I head next door for dinner. Later, in my room at eight, Jay texts saying he made plans with his cousin for lunch on Thursday, so I should wait at least until then to speak to her. I paste the draft of podcast episode one in the chat. He reads through it and suggests some changes.

After we're done, we both cue up *The Lake House* on our laptops and press "Play" at the same moment. We text each other while we watch.

The movie is weird, but I like it. It's about a doctor and an architect who live in the same lake house two years apart and discover they can leave each other notes in the mailbox. It's oddly similar to what Jay and I are going through, but also very different, because in the movie what one does in one time *does* directly affect what happens in the later time. Like he plants trees in the past and they magically appear in front of her eyes two years later. It's strange and confusing. Also, the mailbox is inconvenient because they have to go all the way there and leave long letters for each other. I much prefer texting.

The house itself is beautiful, though.

Aleeza: The next time we find a time-skip, it should be in a beautiful lake house instead of this run-down old dorm room.

Jay: This room is crap, but East House is a cool building. Did you know the original architect who designed it, Ernest Tanner, built almost identical homes for each of his sons? There are two other old mansions in Toronto just like this one.

I guess that playboy who disappeared more than one hundred years ago was related to Ernest Tanner. I tell Jay about the research I did on that case before I decided to do the podcast on him.

Jay: Weird that two people have disappeared from this house.

Aleeza: That guy wasn't living here when he disappeared though. And even if the history of this house is cool, it's kinda falling apart.

Jay: I guess it would have been cool if we could only talk in a bar, or a fancy café instead of a dorm room. Or someplace iconic. Like the Toronto Reference Library, or the Art Gallery.

Aleeza: Even a West Hall dorm room would have been nicer than this.

Jay: Nah. You'll soon be glad you left there. Once you're here for a while, you'll see that it's not about the newness. It's the people that make a residence.

Aleeza: Maybe. But if we're talking hypotheticals, I wouldn't mind finding a time-skip with Keanu Reeves. Especially nineties-era Keanu. Yum. But current Keanu is hot too. He's from Toronto—maybe I can find a house he used to live in.

Jay: You're breaking my heart, Roomie. Are you saying I'm not as yummy as John Wick?

I laugh. Jay is fun to tease. And he's easily as good-looking as nineties Keanu. Better, actually. Or, rather, he was as good-looking. Sometimes I forget that my new friend is *actually gone*, and no one knows where he is. And when I remember, it makes this whole . . . *friendship* we've found seem fragile. It's barely been a week since I met him, and I already can't imagine losing him.

Is this why Jay has a whole disgruntled fan club? He's so easy to get attached to. Maybe it makes sense that so many people were upset that they couldn't have more of him than he was willing to give.

Or maybe those girls were smarter than me and knew not to get too emotionally invested. It's possible that I'm only this attached because I'm vulnerable now. Because I lost my oldest friend and I'm in a huge city all alone.

Aleeza: We've never really met, so I don't know? But then again, I haven't met Keanu either.

Jay: Well, I suspect you're a better catch than that lady though. All those pantsuits? No thank you. She seems emotionally unavailable.

Aleeza: How is she emotionally unavailable? She freaking fell in love with a guy after only a handful of rambling letters.

Jay: He's a fantasy. She's escaping her real life and her real feelings too.

I don't say anything to that. Because I'm too busy worrying if that's what I'm doing. Escaping my real life. Jay and I aren't real to each other. Just a fantasy. And we've grown emotionally attached.

Or at least I have. Jay is quiet for a while before he finally texts.

Jay: On second thought, I think her falling for someone she's never met IRL is pretty realistic. Shall we continue our study of time travel movies featuring Canadian actors with Back to the Future, starring Michael J. Fox?

~

On Tuesday I'm having lunch on campus when someone calls my name. I turn and see it's Gracie and Aster, who wave me over to join them.

After I sit, Aster immediately grins. "Bailey finally resurfaced," she says. "I was just telling Gracie about it."

I stir my chickpea and feta bowl. "Did you ask her if she'll talk to us about Jay?"

"I did," Aster says. "And not surprisingly, she said no. She practically snarled. I'm not Bailey's favorite person. But during a break in our psych lecture, I asked her if she knows who the Birdwatcher is. She turned the most interesting shade of white. Could have been the whitest person at her country club with that face."

"We think Bailey Cressman is the Birdwatcher," Gracie says, grinning. They are clearly excited about this deduction.

I'm not so sure, though. Jay told me he didn't hook up with Bailey. Why would she care? "Really? Just because she turned white after you asked her about it?"

"Body language is *everything*," Aster says. "She clearly doesn't think highly of Jay. She probably hooked up with him."

"Did you ask her if she did?"

"No, but it makes sense. She hooked up with him and discovered he was a fuckboy. And she was so pissed that she created this whole Instagram account to re-spew all the crap that the Tumblr said last year. Plus posting about him being a player." Aster grins.

It's actually kind of adorable how invested they are about this investigation.

"I agree. This is textbook mean-girl revenge," Gracie says. "People like Bailey are used to getting what they want."

Aster nods. "When I asked her, she said, 'Why would I care about someone who grew up in a townhouse in Scarborough with, like, three families?'"

"Jay told her that?" I ask.

Jay has been a bit secretive about his family life with me. I had no idea he and his mom lived with other families. Why would he have confided in Bailey Cressman? Maybe he sees me only as the person who can save him, not his friend. I mean, we haven't known each other long. Only a week. I exhale. My life has changed so much since then.

"So what do we do now?" I ask, mostly because I don't want to linger on questions about Jay that I don't want to think about.

"I say we look into Bailey more. What's her Instagram?" Gracie pulls out her phone.

After a few minutes of looking at her grid, we find nothing of use. Her pics are heavily curated, and most are just of her. Selfies. Bailey at the beach. Bailey shopping in Yorkville. Bailey posing with . . .

"Is that Justin Bieber?" I ask.

Aster snorts. "Looks like it."

"There are no pictures of friends here. Just random celebs."

I notice the red circle around her picture, which means she has an Instagram story. I open it.

It's a shot of Bailey in a store fitting room, wearing a tight, low-neckline, pale-pink dress. Her curling-iron waves reach down her back, and one hand rests on her hip. She's posted a poll for her followers. **This dress for Jack's party on Saturday? Yes/No.**

Her next story is also about Jack's party. **Y'all, no! I can't get anyone an invite to the party! Ask him yourself!**

An idea comes to me. "Hey, didn't Emma say that Bailey is loose-lipped when she's drunk?"

Gracie nods. "Yep."

"I've seen her drunk," Aster adds. "Bailey Cressman would be what one would call a messy drunk." She laughs to herself at the thought.

"Can we get an invitation to this Jack guy's party?" I ask.

Aster raises a brow. "Are you out of your mind? You seriously want to go to *Jack Gormley's* party?"

I frown. Should I know who he is? Is this the same Jack who Jay is still friends with?

Gracie shakes her head. "Jack's parties are *legendary*. They're like . . . rich-people debauchery."

"You've been?" Gracie doesn't seem the type to . . . well, do whatever "rich-people debauchery" is.

"No. Aster has, though," Gracie says.

"I've known him for years." Aster frowns. I get the impression that she doesn't like this Jack guy much. "Jack Gormley is, like, a professional student. Lord knows how many years he's been working on his BA. His parents bought him a boat last year, and I think he lived on it all summer. Jack's family is . . . Toronto old money. He throws these enormous ragers for only the poshest of the posh. Bailey's whole crew will be there."

I frown. I can't believe this is the same guy who Jay said he was thinking of moving in with. "Hey, was Jay ever at one of Jack's parties?"

It's hard to reconcile the guy I watched an old romance movie with last night and this *rich-people debauchery*.

Aster nods while taking a bite of her burger. After chewing, she says, "Yep. He and Jack used to be really tight. Actually, to be perfectly honest, I think you should investigate Jack too. I don't trust him."

"Why? I thought the people posting on Birdwatcher were all *girls* who Jay had . . . wronged. Wasn't Jack Jay's friend?"

Aster shrugs. "There's something about Jack. I don't know. He got into trouble last year for being behind this other secret whistler Instagram account that aired all these rich people's dirty laundry. My parents were spared, but he ruffled a lot of feathers. The Birdwatcher Instagram thing sounds like something Jack would do."

Hmm . . . maybe the fact that Jack is the only one from this group who Jay has even mentioned to me means Jack *was* involved somehow. Because, as I'd recently learned, your closest friends are sometimes the ones who betray you the most. I pull out my notebook and add Jack Gormley to the list of suspects.

"So, can you get us an invite to this party?" I ask.

Aster squeezes her lips together, uncomfortable. Why is she reluctant about this? From what I've figured out about Gracie and Aster, they are not a couple, but Aster clearly wishes they were. Maybe Aster doesn't want Gracie to see what her life is really like with all the rich kids? But I need to go to this party. Jack, Bailey, and Jay's former friends will all be there. "It would be really cool if you could swing it. Maybe mention it to Jack?"

Aster sighs. "He'll say yes if I ask him."

"Will you ask?" Gracie asks.

"Yeah, all right. I'll get back to you on it."

Gracie looks at her watch. "I need to run to class. Hey, Aleeza, a bunch of us from East House are going to watch a movie in the common room tonight. You should come."

I shake my head. "Sorry. I have . . . plans." Jay and I are watching *Back to the Future* tonight.

She shrugs as she stands and picks up her food tray.

"Wait," I say. "Can you ask around to find out who the anonymous witness who saw Jay that night was?"

Gracie looks at me blankly, then nods. "Sure."

ELEVEN

J ay is not on ResConnect at eight o'clock like he said he'd be. Part of me is a little worried—I mean, he's just weeks away from disappearing, so I know he's in danger. Probably. I wish we could leave messages for each other somehow.

I tackle my schoolwork and try not to check ResConnect too many times to see if his name pops up. But I do check it a lot. He's never there. I want to ask him about Jack Gormley, and if he thinks going to this party is a good idea, or if Bailey Cressman could be the Birdwatcher. So far this mystery has more questions than answers, and I feel like I'm trying to travel upstream without a paddle. And strangely, the only person really keeping me on course—Jay—isn't even here.

But the biggest question plaguing me today is why the Jay I know, the slightly goofy, considerate, and nice person, doesn't match the picture I'm getting from almost everyone else. Maybe the Jay I know from his universe and the Jay everyone else knows from my universe aren't the same person. The universes are 85 percent similar. *Universes.* Jesus Christ, what has happened to my life?

I get in bed at around ten thirty, and the moment I turn my lights off, my phone buzzes. Finally.

But it's not Jay.

Gracie: We're in! Aster got the three of us invites for Jack Gormley's party on Saturday night.

Aleeza: That's great. Thank Aster for me.

Gracie: This will be a whole other kind of crowd. I have no idea what I'll wear. We should get ready together.

I have no idea what I'll wear either. In fact, I have no clue what rich Toronto people wear to parties. Hell, I don't know what *non*-rich Toronto people wear to parties. The only party I've been to here was that Halloween party, and somehow, I don't think a tweed jacket and bowler hat will be appropriate this time. But I don't want Gracie to think I don't know what I'm doing.

Aleeza: Nah, it's fine. I'm not concerned.

I am very, very concerned.

Gracie: We'll talk later to figure out how we'll get there. I'm excited. Jack's place is apparently unreal.

I'm not excited. I'm terrified. But I am *determined* too. I look over at Tentacle Ted. The person who hurt Jay could be at that party. I don't know if it was Bailey Cressman, or Jack Gormley, or one of the other trust-fund kids. Jay said that it's hard to find a happily ever after in a place you're not supposed to be. And from what I know about Jay and this crowd, he was never supposed to be one of them.

And I know I'm not supposed to be one of them either.

~

When I wake up the next morning, the first thing I do, even before checking my email or socials, is check ResConnect. When I see Jay's name as one of the two registered residents of room 225, I breathe a sigh of relief. I didn't realize how afraid I was when I didn't hear from him yesterday. Just because he disappears in November in my timeline doesn't mean that's when he'll go missing in *his* timeline. Ugh. This time-skip is giving me a headache.

But his name on my phone screen means Jay is okay. It means he's in this room now. Well, not now. *Then.*

I look over to Jay's empty bed, and Tentacle Ted stares back at me. Is Jay there sleeping right now? Or maybe he's awake and looking at his phone? Is he covered with a warm duvet, or a thin sheet? Is he wearing a shirt? And where was he last night? Did he have one of his no-commitment hookups?

I exhale. Mia was right. I do have to stop lusting after unavailable guys.

My phone buzzes. It's ResConnect.

Jay: You awake?

Aleeza: Yes.

I don't want to ask him where he was last night, because it's none of my business. But I don't know what to say. So I say nothing, because I'm awkward.

Jay: Sorry I bailed out on Back to the Future last night. I ended up meeting up with my cousin for dinner instead of lunch and stayed late.

I smile. He didn't ditch me. He was working on our investigation.

Aleeza: Can I ask her if she'll talk to me now?

Jay: Yep. I told her all about the new friend I met on campus. She's delighted with you already. She even painted you a little octopus. I'll figure out how to get it to you. Or even better—I'll give it to you in person when I'm safe and sound.

That's the first time either of us mentioned the possibility of Jay and me meeting in person one day. I smile. He sends me his cousin Manal's Instagram account and tells me to contact her there.

Jay: Fair warning, though. I'm pretty sure she thinks you and I are secretly dating, or I have a major crush on you. I had to tell her how much I trust you and value our friendship, and of course she jumped to conclusions. She was relieved when she found out you're Indian. And you being from a Muslim family was the cherry on the sundae.

I exhale. How am I going to talk to this person who thinks I'm *dating* Jay? As soon as she meets me, she'll see that I'm nothing like those perfect, tall, wavy-haired girls.

Aleeza: I'm not religious, though.

Jay: Neither am I. But my family is, and Manal knows now they'll approve of you.

I don't know what to say about any of this, so I change the subject.

Aleeza: Aster managed to get us an invitation to Jack Gormley's party on Saturday.

Jay: Seriously? You're going to a party at Jack's house?

Aleeza: Yeah, it's the only way we can get close to Bailey Cressman. The person who did this to you could be there. What's the story with Jack? Aster said he's a bit shady. You two are friends?

Jay: Jack's an interesting one. But yeah, we're good friends. It's just . . . Jack's parties are . . . a lot.

Aleeza: Sex, drugs, and rock n roll?

Jay: Minus the rock n roll. It won't be your scene.

For some reason, him assuming I'm too naive for this party bothers me.

Aleeza: Aster said this Birdwatching thing is something Jack would do.

Jay: It is his style, but I don't think he'd do that to me. Then again maybe he would. Jack's a bit of an enigma. He has his demons too.

This isn't making sense. Jay seems to be telling me to stay away from Jack while acknowledging that Jack may be involved in his disappearance.

Aleeza: So you don't think I should go to the party?

Jay: Honestly, I would consider anyone who would turn up at Jack's party a suspect. But there has got to be a better way to get access to them.

Aleeza: I'll be fine. Gracie and Aster are coming too. Emma said Bailey talks a lot when she's drunk, and she knows who the Birdwatcher is. It's the best place to get her to confess.

Jay: I don't like the idea of you being there.

Aleeza: Why? I've been to huge parties before. I went to a party at the campus pub for Halloween dressed as Dr. Watson, and people laughed at me, and Mia ditched me and yet I survived.

I close my eyes. I do actually care what people think of me. I hated being the object of ridicule that night. I try not to think about that Halloween party too much. The memory is . . . unsettling. It was the beginning of the end for me and Mia.

Jay: The crowd at Jack's are vultures. You're sweet and small town, and you love books and octopuses. You're too pure for their world.

Aleeza: You think I'm a naive child.

Jay: I don't think you're a child at all. I don't mean that you're too pure in a bad way. Far from it. You're

He doesn't finish that sentence.

Aleeza: You don't even know me. And don't forget, I'm going to this party for YOU. I'm trying to save you.

He doesn't write back for a while. I get ready for class—I'm not going to miss my politics lecture because my roommate decides to go all overprotective of me. Outside of our conversations, he doesn't know a thing about me. I'm the one investigating him, not the other way around.

Jay: I DO know you. We're talking right now. We've met.

Aleeza: I mean in the real world. In the same time.

Jay: I saw you yesterday.

My butt falls heavily back on my bed.

Aleeza: What? When?

Jay: I was in the library looking for books on temporal paradoxes and the Novikov self-consistency principle, and when I turned a corner, I full-on crashed into a very cute girl wearing an octopus sweatshirt. You dropped your notebook.

My breath hitches. I *remember* that. It happened. I remember him smiling at me when he apologized for the collision, and I remember thinking that his smile looked too big for his face. I even remember thinking that I didn't have a lot of meet-cutes, and bumping into someone in a library should have been my meet-cute. But I was too scared to say anything and ran away.

Jay: You turned the cutest shade of pink. I'd seen your Instagram, but you're different in person. If I said something more than "sorry" to you, I thought I'd blow up the universe or something.

Aleeza: I remember that. It happened.

Jay: Really? So sometimes what I do does happen for you too. I'm flattered you remember me. You probably bump into a lot of people. Why do you look down when someone talks to you?

This is awkward and weird.

Aleeza: I don't with everyone, but you're cool and good looking and I was afraid to look at your face after coming into physical contact with you.

I can't believe I said that. Why don't I have a filter on ResConnect? It takes him a bit of time to respond.

Jay: You think I'm good looking?

Aleeza: You know you're good looking. And I can't believe I admitted that. Can I retract a message across time?

Jay: You're cute, too, but also kind of sexy in your tentacle wear. Like . . . I kinda get it now. All those arms. The suction cups.

Aleeza: JAY . . .

Jay: Right. Your interest in octopuses is totally G-rated. We're not even going to acknowledge the existence of tentacle erotica.

If he thought I was cute when I turned red in the library, he'd think I was downright adorable right now.

And also, what am I doing? Flirting with Jay Hoque across time? I need to change the subject.

Aleeza: What are temporal paradoxes and Novikov whatever?

Jay: Time travel physics. Didn't understand any of it.

Aleeza: But if you were in the library looking up this anomaly, then how could I remember bumping into you in my timeline? In my timeline, we'd never spoken before. So you wouldn't be researching time travel physics in the library.

Jay: Yeah, it's weird. I was kind of hoping you wouldn't remember us meeting in the library. That would mean that our timelines are different enough that it would be safe for me to ask out past Aleeza, since you, current-Aleeza, wouldn't remember it at all.

I exhale. Is he real? Is all this real?

Aleeza: Are you making fun of me again?

It takes him a while to write back.

Jay: No, I'm not making fun of you. I mean it. Meeting you has me wondering if I've been drawn to the wrong kind of girl this whole time.

I don't know what to do with the fact that Jay Hoque thought about asking me on a date.

Aleeza: You're about to disappear, and you're analyzing your relationship preferences?

Jay: The fact that I'm about to disappear is WHY I'm overthinking everything, wondering if I made the right choices with my life.

His impending doom is really messing him up. It would certainly mess me up. And it's not like he can go to therapy or anything. I'm the only one he can talk to.

Aleeza: I get it. I know that it's nothing like what you're going through, but I was terrified last night when you weren't here.

He doesn't respond. I put my hands over my face. Jay's never going to speak to me again. We're only friends. How can I expect him to tell me where he is all the time? I'm being clingy.

But every time his name isn't there on ResConnect, I worry it will never be there again. All day I'm talking to people about him being kidnapped or hurting himself or running away. Or being killed.

The only time I know he's fine, that he's safe, is when we're in this room together.

Jay: I wish there was a way for us to keep in contact when we're out in the world.

Aleeza: Me too. Who knows? Things could happen differently for you. You could disappear on a different day. Or not at all.

Jay: And something bad could go down at Jack's party. And neither of us would know what happened.

Aleeza: I have to go to Jack's. I'll be okay.

It's the only way. Because even if I can't save Jay in my timeline, I have to save him in his.

Jay: I know. Promise me one thing though . . . Come home after the party and message me right away. No matter what time it is. Don't spend the night there.

Aleeza: I'm not interested in spending the night at a sketchy, snobby party.

Jay: Promise me anyway. And we'll talk before you go about what you can expect. Jack is . . . a lot. Deep down, he's a good guy, but you have to get through a lot of not good to see it.

Aleeza: Okay.

Jay: I wish I could come with you.

Aleeza: To protect me?

I know I'm not supposed to *like* the fact that he's going all caveman possessive on me, but when was the last time a friend actually cared about what happens to me?

Jay: Yes, and also, you'll probably be the most interesting person there.

I exhale. I have no idea what's going on with us today.

Aleeza: I have politics in an hour, and I need breakfast.

Jay: Okay. One more thing. If something happens to me when I'm not in the room, I'll leave you a message.

Aleeza: How?

Jay: I'll find a way. Back to the Future tonight? Eight o'clock?

Aleeza: Yes, absolutely. Looking forward to it.

Jay: Me too.

TWELVE

At breakfast I think about that conversation with Jay this morning. Yeah, I'd totally realized that I'd caught feelings for my unconventional new roommate—I mean, how could I not? This is *Jay Hoque*. But the stuff he said to me this morning makes me wonder if he's feeling something *real* for me too. It's completely preposterous, but he literally said he wanted to ask me out.

After everything people have said about him, and even what he's said about himself, how can I possibly take him seriously? Maybe this morning's flirting was Jay being Jay—a player. But what would be the point of him angling for a no-commitment fling? We don't even have a way to actually, you know, see each other in person.

Maybe we're both feeling things we wouldn't normally feel because we're going through hard things right now. I mean, I'm super lonely and had an epic friend-breakup, and Jay, well, Jay just learned that he's about to disappear off the face of the earth. We're both vulnerable. If Jay and I met in normal circumstances, when both of our lives were going well, none of this would have happened.

I search Jay's other three hookups on Instagram. One is white, one is South Asian, and one is East Asian. All are conventionally attractive. And all seem to have active social lives. None of them have octopuses on their grid. My self-esteem is fine, most of the time, but I know that I'm a little strange. Compared to these girls, I'm a lot strange.

But also . . . these three girls aren't really like Emma Coffey either. I can't put my finger on it, but they seem more down to earth. Emma is clearly a social climber, and her Instagram is all designer clothes and gorgeous selfies, while these others have food and city pics, and more casual shots. I don't know if I should bother reaching out to them. Something tells me they haven't commented on Birdwatcher.

Instead, I check out Jay's cousin Manal's Instagram. Pictures of her watercolor art dominate her whole feed. She is *very* talented. She has gorgeous realistic paintings of animals, but also some very cool, almost abstract pieces. Like you have to squint to recognize the thing you're looking at, but when you do, it's all you can see. She mostly works in warm colors—reds, yellows, and oranges—which gives her work a fiery quality. There's also something vaguely familiar about it. I open her DMs and write a message, saying that I'm a friend of Jay's and would love to speak to her for a podcast I'm doing about his disappearance. She doesn't respond.

Later, in politics, I check my Instagram while the professor is taking a break. But I can't see Manal's account this time.

"She blocked me!" I say, shocked.

Gracie, who is sitting next to me, raises a brow. "Who?"

I show her my screen. "Jay's cousin. I wanted to interview her for the podcast, but she blocked me after I DMed her."

Gracie pulls out her own phone and brings up the account. "Oh wow, she's talented. She's probably had a lot of people contacting her for interviews. I don't blame her for setting boundaries."

Yeah, but this is different. Jay *told* her to trust me. But I can't tell Gracie that.

"Yeah, I guess . . . but I . . ." I sigh. "I need to talk to *someone* from his family, don't I?"

"Lemme try," Gracie says. "I'm pretty sure I met her once when she was visiting Jay. Maybe she'll agree to see me."

Gracie sends her a DM. By the end of politics, she doesn't have an answer either. But at least she's not blocked.

~

The rest of the week is pretty uneventful, at least with regard to our investigation. Professor Sarah goes over my first draft of episode one and gives me great feedback. I record the episode with Gracie's help in one of the soundproof booths in the library. Gracie doesn't hear back from Manal. When I tell Jay that his cousin doesn't seem to want to talk to me, he says to give her space, and that Manal can be a private person. He's convinced we shouldn't bother his family—they're probably having a hard enough time. Since Bailey Cressman and Jack Gormley are our only suspects at this point, there isn't much we can do until Jack's party.

Jay and I watch all three *Back to the Future* movies on Wednesday and Thursday nights, and the movies are way better than I remember. Or maybe they seem better because watching movies with Jay is a ton of fun. His commentary is hilarious, and my eyes stay glued to our chat log more than the actual movie. We even break off into a tangent about food, and he tells me about all the best sandwiches in the city. Apparently, his all-time favorite is the beef shawarma from a place called Shawarma Delight near his house that he and his mother are both obsessed with. I make a note of the restaurant. I tell him about my favorite sandwich from this fancy teahouse in Alderville that makes everything from scratch.

The more time I spend with Jay, the more I think this connection we have, this easy friendship, isn't happening randomly. And it's not *only* so I can save him. He's sort of saving me too. Just when I lose my closest friend, someone else comes along, and I don't feel so alone anymore.

On Saturday, Aster and I get ready for Jack's party in Gracie's room. I finally agreed to let them pick out my clothes, because when I suggested I wear my red-and-green pleated skirt with my fuzzy white sweater, Gracie said there was no way anyone at the party would talk to me dressed like a Hallmark Christmas movie. Apparently, I need to look like one of the trust-fund kids. Or look like I *want* to be one of them.

The dress Aster loans me isn't my normal style. It's fancier than my prom dress. It's definitely tighter. I yank on the hem of the dark-mauve, sleeveless minidress, eyeing the deep halter neckline in Gracie's mirror. How am I supposed to sit in this without showing everyone my underwear? I'm not even wearing normal underwear, just this tight girdle thing to hold in my stomach and a halter push-up bra. They're incredibly uncomfortable.

"Your boobs look phenomenal in that," Gracie says, looking at me in the mirror. I frown. I don't think my boobs have ever been this high. And my hair—I used a YouTube tutorial to make my curls defined and voluminous instead of frizzy, and Aster made me wear a lipstick the exact color of my dress. Gracie is wearing an outfit that's a cross between a blazer and a dress with sequined lapels. She says it's her sister's, who works at Saks Fifth Avenue. She's also slicked her bangs back into a tight ponytail, which accentuates her cheekbones, and has on nude lipstick and dark eyeliner. She looks stunning, but she doesn't look like Gracie.

Aster's yellow dress is even shorter and tighter than mine, and her hair falls loose in soft waves. She's wearing contacts instead of her over-size Gucci glasses, and makeup covers her freckles. Since I've only seen Aster in jeans before, she also looks strange. And gorgeous. I frown at the three of us, reflected in the mirror on Gracie's closet door. Two journalism nerds and a girl-jock dressed like Kardashians. This is going to be an interesting night.

I throw a sweatshirt over my dress before my coat in case it's cold. The weather's still being so weird. Like it didn't get the memo that spring should be here by now.

We split an Uber to the party. It's late, past ten o'clock, but Aster says these parties don't pick up until this hour or later. The Gormleys live in the posh Forest Hill neighborhood—a part of the city I've never been to. The car drops us off in front of an enormous gray brick house with black window frames and doors. It looks to be about eight times the size of my parents' house in Alderville.

"Holy shit," I say as we get out of the car. "This house looks bigger than East House." I tighten my coat around my shoulders.

Aster nods. "It probably is. Jack says his parents are in Prague right now. The house is fucking nuts—careful you don't get lost. Stay in Jack's wing and you'll be fine. I'll tell Nat we're here." She pulls out her phone and texts someone.

Gracie glances at Aster, irritated.

We don't knock on the double doors—but someone opens them anyway. It's a tiny girl a bit younger than us with a short blonde pixie haircut. She's dressed in wide-legged light-blue jeans and a cropped purple crocheted tank. When she sees us, her face lights up, and she throws herself around Aster in a hug. Gracie blinks at them.

The entryway of the house is about the size of my living room at home. The floors and the curved staircase are dark wood, and a huge chandelier hangs from the high ceiling. There doesn't seem to be anyone else around, but a low beat drifts through the house.

Aster introduces the girl with the pixie as Nat and tells us she grew up with Jack. Nat nods and says he's practically her little brother. My eyes widen at that. Nat isn't a clone of Emma or Bailey, and she's not dressed how Aster told me I'd have to dress for this party. She seems out of place. When I look at her closely, I wonder if she's actually older than I thought. She clearly knows Aster really well.

I start to unzip my coat. Nat points to a formal-looking sitting room off the entrance hallway of the house. "You can throw your coats there, in that room. Don't leave any valuables in it. Jack wanted to hire a coat-check girl, but he's always a bit extra."

After we drop our things in the pile of coats, Nat loops her arm through Aster's. "I am so glad you came. You *never* hang out anymore."

As she guides Aster past the stairwell, Gracie and I follow, and I can feel Gracie's annoyance at this girl radiating off her. What exactly is going on here? At some point I have to get Gracie to explain the status of her "relationship" with Aster.

As we walk toward a huge kitchen, long hallways branch out on both sides. Nat takes us down the left hallway, and we pass several rooms—a gym, a library, and what looks like a locker room. The hallway ends with large double doors. This is where all the noise is coming from.

Nat opens the doors with a flourish. "We need to keep the doors closed so the housekeeper doesn't complain."

I do a bit of a double take once I see the actual party room. It doesn't look like it belongs in this formal house—it actually looks more like a quirky nightclub or an industrial loft. The lighting in the space is dim, but pale twinkle lights glow everywhere—around the windows, lining a bar area, even hanging from the ceiling. The flooring is gray tile, but there are several plush white area rugs scattered around.

An enormous screen covering one wall shows an old cartoon— something I don't recognize. The furniture in the room is modern— steel and leather—and mostly clustered on one side of the room. There are about fifty people or more here, which is fewer than I expected. Some lounge on couches, others sit on those cushy white rugs, and many stand near the bar. Everyone is in club clothes—we're not over-dressed at all.

My eyes are drawn to a guy wearing a three-piece white suit with a pink scarf around his neck lying in the middle of the floor, not even on a rug, with his eyes closed.

"I'm not in Alderville anymore," I say softly.

Gracie takes my forearm and squeezes.

"Natasha, tell me the sushi is here," the guy lying on the floor says, his eyes still closed. He's a stereotype of a rich white boy—impeccable features, shiny blond hair, bored voice. I assume this is Jack.

"Get off the floor, Jack," Nat says, kicking his leg. "Aster and her friends are here." She's still holding on to Aster's arm.

He snorts. "I thought Aster only cared about plebeians now."

"Hi, Jack, great to see you too," Aster deadpans. "Get up and meet my friends."

He groans with annoyance. "I cannot possibly be introduced to new people right now. My brain is *full* of people. Any more and they will drown out the much-needed voices." Suddenly, he rolls himself onto his side, crossing his legs and propping himself on his elbow. He squints at us. "Oh, it's you. I liked you better in a suit."

I frown. Who is he talking to?

Nat shakes her head. "Don't mind him. He's already wasted. Let's get you some drinks."

She steps over Jack's legs and heads to the bar area. I step around him. As we walk away, he mumbles something about glorious backsides.

We're introduced to several people at the bar area, which is really more of a small kitchen with a huge stone countertop and silvery gray cabinets. I don't recognize any of the people, and none of them are Bailey. The girls are all dressed like we are—in short, tight dresses. Some are shiny or glittery. The guys are more varied—some in jeans and T-shirts. A few in polo shirts, and at least one guy in sweatpants. There is a ton of untouched food on the counter—including a few trays of sushi. "I don't know why Jack always orders so much food," Nat says. "No one ever eats." She waves her hand. "Wine? Or there's beer, cider . . . and I think Travis was mixing cocktails somewhere." She turns around and walks away, yelling, "Travis, where's the vodka?"

Gracie takes this opportunity to slide next to Aster. Staking her claim? Who even knows. They go through the stacks of bottles and cans in the fridge. Gracie chooses something called a Spritz for herself, gets a small can of sparkling pink wine for Aster, then asks me what I want.

Although I've had alcohol before, I'm a total lightweight, so I don't drink very often. In fact, the last time I did was Halloween, and I way overdid it that night. I don't even remember a huge chunk of that party. When I hesitate, Aster grins. "You should have a Lavender Mule to match that dress." She opens a bottled cocktail in a deep-purple color and hands it to me.

I take a slow sip of the drink, doing my best not to make a face. It's strong, but also floral and gingery. I should probably stick to one drink all night so I can keep my wits to gather clues. Gracie and Aster chat with some of the nearby girls while I look around the room.

It's not hard to imagine Jay at a party like this. Even if he's not as wealthy, he's as attractive as they are. And he seems like the type who belongs anywhere. But one of these people could have hurt him. Maybe.

I'm not the only person of color here—of course I came with Gracie, and I can see at least one other Brown person and even a few Black and East Asian people. But it's a mostly white crowd. I feel like a bunny at a dog show.

From the other side of the room, Nat scream-laughs, and I turn to see some big guy in shorts and a polo shirt holding her over his shoulder so her butt is next to his face. Another new group of people come in through the double doors and walk around the still-screaming Nat.

"Nat is not what I expected," Gracie says.

Aster frowns. "Okay. What did you expect?"

Gracie shrugs. I don't know what's going on, but it's clear this is a continuation of a conversation they've had before.

"Let's not forget why we're here," Gracie says. "Do you see Bailey?"

Aster shakes her head. "She might not be here yet. Should we ask around about Jay?"

I squeeze my drink. Maybe I should have listened to him. Something is telling me that coming to this party was a mistake. But that could just be my anxiety.

"There's Tamara," Aster says. "She's tight with Bailey. She'll know if she's here."

Tamara is with a group of girls and guys near the window. After Aster introduces us, a girl asks Gracie and me if we're from Toronto. Which, weird question, but okay.

Gracie nods, but I shake my head. "I'm from Alderville," I say. "It's on the Bay of Quinte."

"Oh!" she says, chuckling. "Good. Thought you were international students."

Tamara rolls her eyes and asks me about Alderville. Apparently, her family has vacationed there several times. She's pretty, with dark-brown skin and long curls.

After some small talk, and thankfully no more microaggressions, Aster asks Tamara if she knows if Bailey will be here.

Tamara looks around, frowning. "She *was* here. Where'd they all go?"

"A bunch of people went to the wine cellar in the basement," one of the guys responds.

"Did you need Bailey for something?" Tamara asks. I like Tamara. She doesn't seem as snobby as the others. But I'm not sure how we'll answer that question. We can't exactly say we want to ask her about the secret Instagram account that was stalking a now-missing student.

But Aster appears to be two steps ahead of us. "I think we switched cleats after indoor soccer today." She smiles at the rest of us. "We do this all the time."

That leads to a conversation about the indoor soccer dome that Aster plays in and what other sports are held there. Someone, hilariously, laments that it's too bad they don't play polo there. Like horse polo.

"No one cares about equestrian sports in this city," a popped-collar-shirt-wearing guy says. "Now, water polo, on the other hand . . . I'm still mourning the end of the last season. Sigh."

"Dude, one of your players *disappeared*," another guy says. "Of course it affected the team morale. Have a heart."

Jay. They're talking about Jay. Gracie looks at me.

"I barely knew the guy, but it really sucks what happened to Jay," Aster says, not skipping a beat. "So wild he hasn't been found yet. You were tight with him, right, Alex?"

Popped Collar nods. "Yeah, from water polo. Jay was my *bro.* Wicked player. It's no wonder we couldn't make it through the semis without him." He shakes his head. He does look genuinely sad for Jay. "Dude was kind of weird sometimes." He snorts. "I kept telling him to cut the umbilical cord. But he was cool too. Like a mama's boy, but also not a mama's boy."

"What about all the gossip about him?" I ask. "I heard he was a . . . *player with girls* . . ."

Alex high-fives one of the other guys. "You mean he was a *baller*!"

Tamara rolls her eyes. "I don't believe that shit about Jay. He was in my program. He was one of the only engineering students who never talked down to me. He wasn't nearly as sexist as most of the guys his age." She side-eyes the guys she's with.

"I lived next door to him," Gracie adds. "And I'm with you. He was a chill, respectful dude. What do you think happened to him?"

Popped Collar shrugs. "Either someone wanted him gone or he wanted himself gone." He shakes his head, and there is real compassion on his face. "I didn't see it coming, though. Honestly, Jay was the most *together* guy on the team. Coach used to call him Yoda because he was, like, wise, you know?"

My stomach clenched. I know exactly what this guy means. I remember what Jay said when I told him about Mia.

"Looks like they hit the jackpot in the wine cellar!" one of the guys says. "How much you wanna bet they already drank a bottle downstairs?"

As the others continue talking, Gracie, Aster, and I move away from the group. Aster points to someone.

"That's Bailey," she says. "Over by the fireplace. The redhead."

I look over in that direction. In a group of girls with long, straight hair parted in the center, there's one whose vibrant red color doesn't look natural.

"Do we just approach her?" Gracie asks.

Aster shakes her head. "Not after she blew me off yesterday. Is there someone else with her that any of us know? We need an in."

I scan the largish crowd with Bailey. Several girls hold wine bottles and drink straight from them. And . . . fuck. There *is* someone I know in the group. Someone I know very, very well.

"Shit. Mia." I squeeze my bottle.

"Who's Mia?" Aster asks.

I take a long gulp of my drink. I'm going to need it.

THIRTEEN

I cannot believe Mia is here. *Mia.* My former *best friend forever.* I haven't seen her in almost two weeks, the longest I've gone without seeing her since my parents took my brother and me on a safari in Tanzania when I was fifteen.

So much has happened since I moved out of the room we shared at West Hall. I feel like a completely different person. It's weird seeing her now, my old roommate, while I'm secretly investigating the disappearance of my new roommate. My worlds are colliding. And it's making me nauseous.

Mia is wearing a dress I've never seen before, a royal-blue bodycon thing. She looks as strange in it as I look in mine. And her hair. Instead of her normal unruly waves, her hair's now pin straight and parted in the middle like the rest of the girls in her group. No wonder I didn't notice her right away.

"Mia's my ex–best friend," I say. "My supposed BFF."

Gracie's brows raise, and her hand shoots to her mouth. "The one who ditched your web series for skincare?"

I nod. Gracie knows Mia is the last person I want to see now. But this is our best opportunity to talk to Bailey Cressman. I scan the rest of the group.

Mia is with Taylor, because of course she's with Taylor. Which means Lance is probably here somewhere too. Bailey says something that makes Taylor laugh loudly, holding on to Bailey's arm with one hand as her whole body shakes. It's a fake laugh. The tall glass of bright-orange liquid in Taylor's grip sloshes onto the floor, and no one makes any effort to clean it.

Mia's head falls back, also laughing. I know Mia and her body language. She's drunk. And Bailey probably is too.

This is our best opportunity.

I gulp down the rest of my drink, put the empty bottle on the counter, and steel my nerves. "Okay. Let's do this."

With totally not-wobbly legs, I walk up to the group of girls. They're all still talking and laughing, and the three of us stand on the perimeter of the group for several long moments with no one acknowledging us, or even noticing us. I can't tell what they're talking about. Maybe horses? Why is every conversation I infiltrate about horses?

"I want to ride a camel one day," Mia says. "Total bucket list, right?"

"You have," I say.

Mia finally notices me. And she stares at me for several long seconds before speaking. "What are *you* doing here?"

"Hi yourself, old friend," I say. "We rode a camel together when we went to the Toronto Zoo when we were ten. You said it smelled like your grandma's breath." My head is spinning, and I can hear the blood sloshing in my ears. I shouldn't have drunk that Lavender Mule in one sip. But I wouldn't have had the courage to do this if I hadn't.

"Okaaay . . . ," Taylor says, looking at me suspiciously. "So, hi, Aleeza. Who are you here with?"

"They're with me," Aster says. I can't tell if Taylor's frown is because she doesn't like Aster, or because she's annoyed that Aster brought us to the party.

Gracie loops her arm in mine. "Mia, right? I'm Gracie. Aleeza lives next door to me now, and we've become so close."

Mia is still glaring at me, and Taylor doesn't look very happy that I'm here. I don't get it. When I left Mia's dorm room, she begged me not to go, and now she acts like I've been her antagonist for years. And Taylor . . . I have no idea why Taylor seems to hate me.

I look at Taylor, then smile at Mia. "I didn't expect to see you here!" I'm at this party for Jay, and letting these people know how much I dislike Mia and Taylor isn't the way to get them to talk to me.

"Taylor's known Jack forever," Mia says.

Seems everyone has known Jack forever. At that, Jack himself saunters into the fold of our group. He puts a loose arm around my shoulders and one around the straight-haired girl standing closest to me. "This is where all the ladies are."

Jack smells like old beer and expensive cologne. I don't know what I expected a rich person to smell like, but it isn't this. The other girl giggles. I do not. Gracie, who's still holding my other arm, pulls me away from physical contact with Jack.

He suddenly turns and looks right at me, his face inches from mine. The vodka bubbles in my stomach, and the smell of him is making me sick. Jack looks exactly like Harry Styles, except blond and tan. It's March. Is it a spray tan? Or from a holiday in Cabo?

His eyelids droop as he looks me over. "Where *exactly* did you come from?" I'm not sure whether that's a pickup line or a racial microaggression. He squints. "Are you one of Natasha's lesbian friends? I hope so. Lesbians are *fantastic* in bed."

Mia snorts at that.

"Um, no," I say. "I'm not a lesbian, I mean. But I am Nat's friend. Or, I should say, a friend of a friend."

"Right," Jack says. "Aster's friend. I remember."

"Jack," Aster herself says. "Leave Aleeza alone. Stop trying to corrupt anyone new."

"Oh, she's not new," he says, taking half a step away from me. He pouts. "She'd be the one corrupting me. She's exquisite, this one. I see his fascination."

Before I can figure out what the hell he's talking about, Mia literally laughs out loud at Jack.

"You're making Aleeza uncomfortable," Taylor says. Which is a surprise. Why is Taylor coming to my rescue?

With a bored expression, Jack looks over to the other side of the room. "Looks like Lance is making a move on Tamara again."

Mia's Lance? I look at her, one brow raised, but her head whips over to where Tamara is standing. Why is Mia's boyfriend making a move on another girl? Jack looks at me again. "Lesson one: *never* trust us, new girl." He shrugs and walks away.

Mia is still glaring at Tamara. The more I think about it, the more it makes sense that Lance and Taylor are here. I knew they came from a wealthy family, and Lance has this rich–frat boy quality—of course he'd be buddies with the trust-fund group. I wonder if these are the same people who were laughing at me at the Halloween party. I don't remember anyone specific from that night, except Lance, because I was drunk and they were in costumes. But this might not be my first interaction with the TCU one percenters.

I exhale. At least Jack is gone. I understand Jay's warnings now. Jack seems . . . *dangerous*. And not just because his flirting made me uncomfortable, although that was the first time anyone has ever called me exquisite. There's something about him that's both compelling and off-putting, and I can't put my finger on it.

Actually, *both compelling and off-putting* is the best way to describe this whole party.

"Don't mind Jack. He's coked out of his mind," Bailey says. Then she giggles.

Coked like as in cocaine? I am *really, really* not in Alderville anymore.

"Here," Nat says, coming toward us and handing me, Gracie, and Aster new bottles of premixed cocktails. "Mai tais. You'll love them. Doesn't taste like alcohol at all."

"Oh, I—" My head's spinning from my first drink. I'm not sure I should have a second.

Mia snorts. "Careful, Aleeza. That's a big-girl drink." Her voice drips with condescension.

I look at Mia. Two weeks ago, she was begging me not to end our friendship. But Mia has always been a different person when others are around. She always ignored me in favor of whoever seemed cooler.

"Oh, I love mai tais! I have them all the time!" I smile at Mia. I have to fit in with these people. The first sip is actually delicious. But strong. I immediately cough.

This is a disaster. Everyone here can probably see that I am an awkward idiot. Thankfully, Gracie is much better at peopling than I am and gets the conversation where we need it once Nat leaves.

"Aleeza and I have been having cocktail nights in my room. Did you know she moved into Jay Hoque's old dorm room?"

Taylor's eyes suddenly go very wide. Like, I'm actually surprised she doesn't spit out her drink.

Bailey's eyes are wide too. "They seriously moved someone into Jay's old room? I'd turn to drinking if I had to live in a dead guy's room."

"Jay's not dead," Gracie says.

"Oh, he's totally dead," Bailey says. "They'll find his body soon. Mark my words."

"I don't think so," I say, shaking my head. "I think he'll be found alive." Of course, I have no idea if he's alive or dead. It could be wishful thinking since I have a massive crush on him.

Ugh. I totally have a massive crush on him, don't I?

"Don't mind Aleeza," Mia says. "She's all into murder mysteries and, like, Sherlock Holmes and shit." She laughs, and it looks like she's expecting everyone to laugh with her.

No one does. Taylor's eyes are still bugged out. She looks quickly at Mia, then walks away.

Okaaay, that was weird. I wonder if Taylor is the Birdwatcher?

I take another gulp of the mai tai. It's so tasty. I have a new favorite drink. I want to be sipping mai tais on a beach somewhere instead of this awkward party with terrible people. Maybe that's where present-day Jay is—on a beach. I want to be there with him, not here. I take another long sip.

"Did you know Jay well?" Gracie asks Bailey.

Bailey shakes her head. "He was really tight with Jack before . . . you know." She looks at Mia. "Didn't Taylor have a thing with Jay?"

I frown. Did Jay hook up with Taylor? She wasn't on his list. The thought that the girl my best friend replaced me with hooked up with the guy who I've moved in with—sort of—and who I'm trying to save is a bit too much of a coincidence. I strain to remember if Jay ever mentioned Taylor or Lance to me, but my brain isn't working right. Probably the mai tai.

"Did you hear about that secret Instagram about Jay?" Aster says. Thank god for Aster and Gracie because I'm pretty useless tonight. "It apparently listed all the girls he ghosted in first year."

Bailey nods. "It was *amazing*," she says. "Seriously . . . *epic*. The guy was such a dick . . . I think he ran away from school because he was about to get caught for that engineering cheating ring. I don't know why he wasn't kicked out last year."

"I heard about that cheating thing," I say. "Was there any evidence?"

The girl with Bailey shakes her head. "The school's probably still investigating, but like, I seriously doubt they'd publicize that now while he's missing."

"It's all so tragic," a girl says. "You know he grew up, like, *poor*? Lived in a basement apartment in Scarborough. His mom came from India or something."

"Bangladesh," I say.

"Yeah, really *tragic*." Bailey giggles, taking a sip of her drink. I have no idea why she's laughing. "He *did* have privilege. Taylor told me he wasn't even paying his own tuition."

What? How would *Taylor* know that?

Mia turns to look at something to her right. It's Lance and Taylor coming back toward us. Lance immediately puts his arm around Mia. I can't decipher Mia's expression.

Lance nods at me. "Eliza, right?"

"*Aleeza*," I say. "With an *A*."

He shrugs, then looks me up and down in my tight dress, impressed. Gross. Mia puts her arm around his waist.

Across the room, Nat laughs loudly again, then calls Aster over. Aster grins and heads her way, and Gracie follows, which leaves me alone with Bailey, Mia, Taylor, Lance, and two other girls. I grip my drink.

"You said you're living in Jay Hoque's room, right?" Taylor asks.

I nod.

"Is there anything of his still in there?" Lance asks. "I mean . . . his family probably came to pick his crap up. I should have offered to bring it to them. I met them a few times—even went on a date with his cousin once." He whistles low. "She was a nutcase."

Mia looks surprised to hear all this. I am too. Mia and Lance started dating right before Halloween—a few weeks before Jay went missing. If Lance was tight with the guy who was all over the news, he would have mentioned that to Mia, wouldn't he have?

I look at Mia. "Did you know Lance and Jay were friends?"

"Of course I knew," Mia snaps. "Don't mind Aleeza," she says to the others. "She *hates* it when her friends have friends of their own. And she only wants to do things that *she's* into. I had to do a whole mystery YouTube because of her." She snorts. "Obsessed with mysteries and octopuses. What a weirdo."

I stare at Mia. This is the same person who bought me a Christopher Pike box set off eBay for my eleventh birthday. Who took the train into Toronto with me when we were sixteen so we could go to three escape rooms in one day. She was as much into mysteries as I was.

She's always pushed me aside when she has a boyfriend, but she's never been this cruel. I want to blame Lance and Taylor's influence, but really the blame should be on Mia only. This is the first time I've walked away from her, and she's being petty because of it. Actually, the blame should be on me for putting up with her for so long.

But I'm done. I'm done being Mia's sidekick, punching bag, or whatever. In the two weeks that I haven't been at her side, I feel like I am finally becoming someone. Becoming *myself.*

I made friends. A cute boy flirted with me (two, if I count Jack), and I found a purpose that could actually make a difference for someone.

It's time to cut the tether between me and Mia for good.

I glare at her. "Why are you doing this, Mia? You're even more exhausting when we're *not* friends than when we were."

She snarls. "What are you talking about, Aleeza? You're the one who abandoned me, remember?"

"Yeah, because I was tired of seeing you transform into a whole new person every time a cute guy looks at you. I'd rather have my own personality than be someone's clone, thank you very much. I'm going to find my actual, *real* friends."

At that, I walk away. I don't look back, and I don't say anything. No doubt they are all laughing at me. Just like they were when I was dressed as Dr. Watson at that damn Halloween party.

I can't see Gracie and Aster, and the room is spinning a bit, so I go in search of a bathroom. I leave through the double doors, which are now wide open, and head down the long hallway toward the entryway. My head pounds, and the lights in the hallway feel like they are flashing through my veins. I feel . . . wrung out. And alone. At a party with dozens of people, I feel alone.

Why did I even come here? Being around this crowd makes me feel so small. Unimportant. A country bumpkin obsessed with octopuses who has fallen for the most unavailable person possible. I deserve the ridicule.

But Jay has never once thought I was ridiculous. And he's the reason I'm here. He's the reason for it all. The reason I'm feeling both alone and valued for the first time. And he isn't even real.

Only one door in the hallway is closed. When I push it open, I find a bedroom, not a bathroom. A very messy bedroom. I wonder if this is Jack's room. It feels wrong to snoop, but I'm supposed to be gathering evidence tonight. Maybe there are some clues in here that he's the Birdwatcher? An open laptop or something logged in to the Instagram account?

But when I walk in, I see the room isn't really that messy. Only the bed is unmade. There's no desk, but an iPad sits on a chair. I try to turn it on, but the screen is locked. Nothing else here seems like a clue. There is an open door to a bathroom, though. I shrug, go in, and close the door behind me.

I look in the mirror, and I'm surprised at what I see looking back at me. I feel emotional, angry, and sad all at the same time. But that's not how I look. I actually look good. My hair is behaving, my curls still defined. My eyes look bigger with the mascara Gracie put on me. And the dress . . . the dress I thought made me look like a stuffed sausage is actually quite pretty on me. My lipstick isn't even smudged. And yes, my boobs look fantastic.

I *do* look like I belong here. I *look* like I fit in, even though I don't feel like it. Is this why Mia was so angry at me? Two weeks without her and I look like I fit into her new crowd? I shake my head, smiling. I wish Jay could see me now.

I exhale, because Jay can never see me. Everything between us is an illusion. Or maybe a delusion. Lately, I've stopped questioning if he's real. Watching movies together, talking about food, and flirting makes it real enough. But . . . never seeing him, and never talking to anyone about our connection, makes it seem like it's all in my head.

The letter he left in the closet wasn't there. He said he told his cousin about me, but that cousin won't talk to me. I know it's not just a fantasy, but it feels like one.

Nothing is real. Even the cute girl in the mirror isn't real. I'm Aleeza. Not this person.

I sigh and leave the bathroom, but jump a bit when I see that there's someone sitting on the unmade bed. It's Jack. The door to the hallway is wide open.

"It's you," he says.

"Oh, sorry," I say. "I needed a bathroom. I'll go—"

"No, it's okay. Don't worry," he says, putting his hands in front of him. "I'm not going to come on to you again. I can take a hint." He smiles, and I can see a bit of sadness in his eyes. "You know, you're like a water lily in the plastic swamp."

"Plastic swamp?" I raise a brow at him. He chuckles. Jack's face looks different now. Softened. Like he's not holding on to that determined boredom anymore.

He gestures toward the door. "They're the swamp." I can still hear the party. Nat is still laughing. "Sit and talk a second?" he asks. "I'll behave. You look sad. Did your friends do something?"

"Oh, no. I'm fine. I don't know why I came to this party." I bite my lip, remembering that he's the *host*. I sit on the bed next to him, several feet away.

"I don't know why I did either. Oh wait, it's because it's my fucking house."

"Isn't it your parents' house?"

He waves his hands, indicating everything around him. "It'll all be mine one day. It's equal parts curse and blessing."

Jack is . . . unexpected. Now that he's not flirting, he seems oddly wise. Like . . . Jay, actually. Twin Yodas. Maybe this is why they're friends?

"Hey, Jack, how well did you know Jay Hoque? I heard he used to come to your parties."

Jack looks at me, blinking a few times. Then he reaches into the bedside table and pulls out a joint. He wordlessly offers it to me.

I shouldn't. I've never mixed weed and alcohol, and those two (or three?) drinks are still making my head spin. But it feels like Jack's looking for an ally right now, and if this is what I need to do to make him talk to me, then I'll do it. Also, I can easily imagine what Mia would say to the others if she heard I said no. In fact, I want Mia to know that I'm sharing a joint with this incredibly hot and incredibly rich guy.

I also remember Jay's warning. I shouldn't be alone with Jack for too long. In his bedroom.

"Yeah, but . . . out there?" I indicate toward the party.

He nods. "I get it. Safety first." He stands and reaches out to help me up. I take his hand. It's warm and soft.

Back in the party, we sit on a lone sofa far from the others. He pulls a silver lighter from his pocket and flicks it open. I put the joint between my lips. As he holds the flickering flame in front of the joint, I inhale. I do my best not to cough . . . then hand it to him.

After he takes a long drag, he nods. His expression is blank. "Yeah, I knew Jay. He was also a wildflower . . . not a water lily, though. Jay was a thistle, or a forget-me-not." Jack makes no sense. I wonder if he really is on cocaine, like Bailey said.

"Are you into flowers or something?"

He shrugs, staring out into the distance. "Jay wasn't the first or the last person absorbed by this gilded swamp. He might be the most unfortunate, though." He hands me the joint again. I take it, enjoying the buzzy feeling moving through me.

"Were you close?" I ask.

He suddenly looks at me. "Why all the questions?"

"Just curious. Coincidentally, I'm living in his old room at East House."

Jack's eyes are hooded, but he stares at me with an unfocused gaze. I take another hit of the joint, then hand it back to him. Feeling floaty and unfocused, too, I have no idea how I'll remember anything Jack tells me now. He isn't saying anything important, is he? Would it be weird if I recorded him? He takes a long pull of the joint until it's pretty much done, then puts out the smoldering end on a plate of half-eaten sushi.

"Jay was different, you know? He was always drawn to unexpected bursts of light. He'd dance with the water lily and make it bloom. He didn't come from the swamp . . . he could see right through the murk." He sighs, sinking deeper into the sofa. "He could have been the best of us . . . he *should* have been. The swamp flowed through his veins, too, you know. But it's not right. He didn't sign up for any of it. Wanderlust shouldn't hurt anyone. It's a gift."

I nod, like any of this makes sense. I do know Jay. Sort of. And Jack's right. Jay *is* different. I try to imagine him here . . . He'd fit in, but also stand out. People would notice him. Be drawn to him.

Not like me. The only person paying attention to me is a high-as-a-kite trust-fund kid who talks in riddles that I can't understand.

A dull nausea builds in my stomach. My heart beats heavily in my ears. I close my eyes.

"I miss him," Jack says softly. "When I see him in the lagoon, I'll tell him that the water lily is in his room now. He'll be so happy to see you again."

Aster and Gracie are suddenly next to me on the sofa. "Jack, I told you to leave her alone," Aster says. She gives me an apologetic smile. "I don't think he's been sober since Halloween."

"After that," Jack says.

"We're going," Gracie tells me. "I've called an Uber." She looks at me for several long seconds. "What are you on?"

"She's high on life," Jack says, his voice changing again to bored rich kid. "Aster, you have to stop bringing civilians to my parties. We can't keep corrupting good people."

He's talking about Jay. Jay, who is . . . *was* a good person, but then got caught up with this crowd. And now he's gone. I look at Jack, my eyes welling up with tears.

"C'mon, Aleeza. Let's get you home," Gracie says.

I stand, but everything spins. I try to clear my head and focus only on Gracie as she gets our coats and hands me mine.

When we get outside, the car's already there. On the drive back to the school, I rest my head on Gracie's shoulder. "Where's Aster?" I ask, my words slurred, only then noticing that she's not with us anymore.

"She's staying. Nat needed her."

I can't tell how Gracie feels about that. I want to tell Gracie that she shouldn't let her girlfriend stay at the party, and that Jack said it's the swamp, and eventually they'll all get sucked in. That Aster will disappear, too, like the Mia I knew disappeared, and Jay vanished . . . that Aster might not be bright enough to see inside the swamp. But I don't say it because I am pretty sure that I'm not making sense. Also, if I talk, I'm afraid I'll throw up.

After the car drops us off in front of East House, Gracie helps me walk up to the door and props me up against the wall.

"Shit," she says. "I left my ID card in Aster's purse."

"Aleeza to the rescue," I slur, trying to open my purse. I don't quite manage it, but Gracie helps. Eventually, using my card, she gets us into the building. When we get up to the third floor, Gracie helps me into my room. I feel a little better—well, not really better. I'm still pretty sure I'm going to throw up, but being in the room weirdly clears my head a little bit. I'm happy to be here. I feel better in this room than anywhere else in the world.

"My key is with my pass-card," Gracie says as I sit on my bed. "I'll call the residence don to let me into my room." She looks at me carefully. "Or maybe it's a better idea to stay here with you tonight? You okay? I can sleep here."

My eyes widen. I haven't checked ResConnect yet, but this is Jay's room—I can't let someone sleep in his bed. "You sleep in my bed," I blurt out, standing quickly. "Because . . . I mean . . . I just changed the sheets on my bed. I'll take . . . the other bed." I open a drawer, straining to focus, and pull out a pair of plaid flannel pants and a T-shirt for Gracie, and my purple octopus pajamas for me.

She frowns like she's considering whether it's worth it to argue with a drunk girl about something that really doesn't matter. "Okay."

I leave her pajamas on my bed and take mine to the bathroom along with my bathroom caddy.

While I'm in there, I do throw up a little bit. And I have a big glass of water. I still feel like shit, though. After struggling out of the dress, I fold it the best I can, put on my pajamas, and brush my teeth. When I come out, I put the folded dress on a chair.

"Thanks for letting me stay," she says.

I nod. "I'm never drinking again."

"You did more than drink. I'm surprised you trusted Jack enough to smoke with him."

"He sees more than you think. He called his parties a gilded swamp."

Gracie shrugs. "Well, the siren call of all that gold certainly pulled Aster back in."

I frown. "Why is she staying there?"

"For Nat, of course. The two of them go back a long time. Eventually, Nat always says jump, and Aster asks how high." She yawns. Gracie looks sad and tired. "I'm glad I'm here tonight. I don't really want to be alone."

I nod, sitting on Jay's bed and hugging Tentacle Ted close. "I'm never alone in here." I feel my eyes well with tears again, so I turn away.

Gracie takes my key and goes to the bathroom to change. I find my spare blanket and pillow, and crawl into Jay's bed. It's my bedsheets, and my blankets, so it's easy not to think about who slept in this bed last. But it's also hard *not* to think about it. The bed's warm, with a faint scent that's not mine. A familiar scent.

I had way, way too much to drink tonight.

Is it true what Jack said? That Jay should have been the best of them? And who was *them*, anyway? The rich kids? I learned so many things at that party, but the whole picture is still out of focus.

Gracie comes back into the room and gets into my bed. "Good night, Aleeza."

"Good night." I flick off the lamp.

I lie on my back for a while, trying to stop the room from spinning. My eyes are still watering, and I don't know why. I don't know why the night made me feel like both a complete outsider and a brand-new person.

I *am* a new person. I'm not the same Aleeza I was when I left West Hall. Being alone, breaking free from Mia's influence, changed me. And also, Jay changed me. But I still don't know where he is. What happened to him. I don't know if he left on his own, or if someone hurt him. Or if he's still hurting somewhere. There's a lot more to this than I ever imagined. I hug Ted. "Tell me he's safe," I whisper into my stuffed animal.

My phone, which I left on the bedside table, buzzes. I grab it before it wakes Gracie. It's Jay, of course. I notice the time. It's past 2:00 a.m.

Jay: You didn't let me know you were home safe.

Aleeza: Sorry. My brain's not working right. I figured you were sleeping. Or out.

Jay: I was out. But I'm home now.

Aleeza: Where did you go?

Jay: I'll tell you about it another day. How was Jay's party?

I exhale. It was hard, and illuminating, and scary and wondrous. Most of all, it was lonely.

Aleeza: How were you friends with those people?

Jay: Did they do anything to you? Are you okay?

Aleeza: I'm drunk and stoned and

Jay: And what?

Aleeza: Tired. I did learn a lot, but I'm having trouble making sense of it now.

Jay: Drunk and stoned? My roommate has a wild side. I wish I could have seen it.

I silently snort.

Aleeza: I wish you were there too. Mia was there.

Jay: Your ex-friend? I'm not surprised. What did she do to you?

Aleeza: Nothing. I told her off. I'll tell you about it tomorrow.

Jay: Good for you. Get some sleep, Roomie.

Aleeza: Good night. Jay?

Jay: Yes Aleeza?

I'm not sure what I want to ask him. Or tell him.

Aleeza: Do you ever feel alone in a roomful of people?

Jay: It's just because the world needs to catch up with you.

I lie on my back, clutching Tentacle Ted to my chest. I close my eyes. My phone vibrates again.

Jay: Where exactly are you in our room?

Why is he asking that? He's never asked me that question before. I almost don't tell him because it's weird . . . I'm sleeping in his bed. But it's not his bed anymore. And we aren't even here at the same time anyway.

Aleeza: Why?

Jay: You're in my bed, aren't you?

My hands are shaking. How could he know that?

The same way I know he's here too.

Aleeza: Yes, Gracie is in my bed . . . she forgot her key in Aster's purse.

Again, the phone is silent for a while. Finally, he writes.

Jay: Are you crying?

Aleeza: It's been a tough night. I don't want to be alone.

Jay: Turn so your back's to the wall.

Aleeza: Okay.

I turn. And almost immediately, I'm engulfed in the most comforting warmth I've felt all night. I stop shaking. I can't feel him pressed against me, or even hear his breathing, but I feel warmth, comfort, and closeness.

Jay: I've got you. Get some sleep.

I close my eyes, relishing in cozy warmth surrounding me. I feel . . . protected. Accepted. *Wanted.* Not alone.

I fall asleep with Jay's arms around me, and I sleep better than I have all year.

~

"Aleeza! Aleeza, wake up!"

I have the headache to end all headaches. And Gracie is shaking me awake. She's got her phone in her hand and is sitting on the edge of Jay's bed. She looks like she's seen a ghost. I check the time on my watch—it's past noon on Sunday.

"I'm up, I'm up. What is it?" My brain feels like it's pounding on my skull.

"It's Jay."

I sit up quickly. They found him. "He's okay?"

But Gracie shakes her head. "His coat, phone, and wallet were found washed up on Woodbine Beach last night."

I blink, confused. "What?"

"Aleeza, they had a press conference. They're ending the search. Jay Hoque is now presumed dead."

FOURTEEN

I make Gracie repeat it a few times because I can't believe it's true. She finally climbs into Jay's bed with me and opens a news clip on her phone.

The steady-voiced news anchor looks straight at the camera as she speaks.

"The personal effects of nineteen-year-old Toronto student Jayesh Hoque were found washed up on Woodbine Beach Saturday. Jayesh, a second-year engineering student at Toronto City University, went missing in November from his dorm room. An extensive search in the fall uncovered nothing about his disappearance, but police are now presuming Jayesh lost his life to suicide in Lake Ontario after his coat, containing his wallet and phone, was found on the beach. The family has declined to comment and are asking for privacy at this difficult time."

A picture, clearly Jay's high school graduation picture, stays on the screen while the news anchor talks. I haven't seen the photo before, and it doesn't match the Jay in my head. Or the Jay I saw around campus last year.

He looks so . . . *normal* in the picture. Young. Slightly nerdy, but in a cute way. Glasses and shorter hair than I'm used to. None of that swagger, that certain something that drew everyone to him. Jay not looking like the Jay in my head makes it harder to grasp that this is true. That he's gone. Even his name is different—Jayesh.

But it's Jay. My *Jay*. The one who last night somehow had his arms around me across time and space.

Jay is dead. A ghost held me as I cried myself to sleep last night.

Or maybe no one did. Maybe my Jay doesn't exist at all. Just the echo of his consciousness left here in this room after his heart stopped beating.

I squeeze my eyes shut. There is no way to save Jay.

"Aleeza, are you okay?" Gracie has her hand on my arm.

I have to remember that everyone thinks I've never met the guy. "Just hit me kind of hard. Poor guy. I mean, we're sitting on his bed."

Gracie nods. "It's so sad. I wish I'd known him better . . . I feel like I failed him. Do you agree that this was a suicide?"

I shake my head, even though I really don't know. The Jay I know, the one who assured me that he'd never want to hurt himself, might not exist. The Jay from this timeline could be a completely different person. I can't check ResConnect now to see if Jay is there. Not with Gracie right beside me. "Should we still investigate his disappearance?" I ask.

Gracie nods. "Absolutely. We don't know what happened. Your missing-person podcast might actually be a murder podcast."

I sigh, slouching. "It feels exploitative now."

"Of course it's exploitative! It's always been exploitative. We were using Jay's life, his *misfortune*, for our gain. All true crime media is exploitative. But if we can help the case, maybe help give his parents peace, it'll be worth it, right?"

Just his mother. Not *parents*. But also his aunt, uncle, cousins, Nani, and Nana. All the people who love him. I decide then that even if I never hear from Jay on ResConnect again, I will still finish this. I will find out what happened to him. Because Jay's family deserves to know.

"And anyway, I think Jay would be okay with us doing this," Gracie says. "He'd like that people he knew have his back and will tell his story without leaving out his humanity. Well, one person he knew. And you. Where are we now? What do we do next after the party?"

I think about it. My mind is foggy, and Jay's the first person I want to talk to about the party. But also, there are two people we should be looking at.

"I honestly didn't trust anyone there. Any of them could have been bullying Jay. Bailey's definitely a possibility, but I want to look closer at Taylor and Jack. I think Taylor might be the Birdwatcher."

"Taylor? Why?" Gracie asks.

I don't even know how to explain it. "She . . . she had such a weird reaction when she found out I'm living in his room."

"That's not much to go on." Gracie frowns. "Are you sure . . . your history with Taylor isn't clouding your judgment?"

I think about that. True, I don't like Taylor. And she doesn't like me. But still, her reaction was so strange. "I'm not saying she's *definitely* the Birdwatcher, just that I want to look into it more."

"Okay. And why Jack? Not that I disagree with you . . . but you two were mighty cozy last night."

I don't know the answer to that question either. My gut tells me that he knows a lot more than he was letting on last night. "He was so . . . cryptic. When I was in his room, he—"

"You were in his room?"

I exhale. "Nothing happened. But he was talking in riddles. I want to talk to him sober . . . to see if I can make sense of him."

"You sober or him sober?"

"Both, ideally." I almost ask Gracie if we should call Aster to get Jack's number, but I still don't know what happened last night between them. And it doesn't seem like Gracie wants to talk about it. "But not yet. I need to recover from last night."

Gracie nods, then gets up and stretches. "I texted the don for a spare key. I need to shower, then have some readings to finish today. I'll give you back your pajamas after I do laundry later. Thanks for letting me crash here."

The moment Gracie is out of my room, I check ResConnect. I fully expect that Jay's name won't be there . . . but it is. Jay Hoque. I breathe a sigh of relief and message him.

Aleeza: Are you up? We need to talk.

He doesn't respond. He could be sleeping.

After brushing my teeth and taking some Advil for my killer headache, I boot up my computer and read everything about Jay I can on news sites. Basically, Jay's jacket was found washed up on the beach by someone on a walk. His phone and his wallet with his TCU ID card were in the jacket pocket. The person who found them turned them over to the local police station after googling the name on the driver's license. All articles state that the family won't be making a statement and ask for privacy.

But why aren't they making a statement? I look back at some earlier articles that mention Jay's family. Soon after he first went missing, Jay's mother made a plea in a press conference for his return. And his cousin had a post on her Instagram linking to an article, begging the public for any information, but they've been silent since then. Manal still has me blocked on Instagram. Is it possible that Jay's family is hiding something? I can't ask Jay about it—he's so protective of them. Especially his mother. But maybe I can snoop around without telling him.

My phone buzzes. Jay. *Finally.*

Jay: We spend one night in the same bed and already I'm getting a "we need to talk"?

What? Oh. He thinks I want to talk about us sleeping in each other's arms last night. Which I still don't understand.

I have no idea how to tell him what's happened.

Aleeza: You were on the news today. Gracie woke me up to show me.

Jay: What? Why?

Aleeza: They found your coat washed up at Woodbine Beach. Your wallet and phone were in the pocket. The police are now presuming you are deceased.

Jay: Show me.

I copy the text from a news article and paste it in ResConnect. While he reads, I go back to the research on my computer. I find his mother's name on one of those older articles and google *Salma Hoque*. There is a Facebook account with that name that has a few public comments on some Toronto community pages. She hasn't posted anything since the disappearance, though.

Which, fair. She's grieving.

Jay: This is surreal. Now they think I'm dead?

Aleeza: There is no mention of them searching for a body. There might be more that the police aren't saying. Something that's leading them to believe this.

Jay: Yeah, because finding just my coat doesn't mean a lot.

Aleeza: Your coat, phone, and wallet. Do you lose your phone and wallet often?

Jay: No, I've never lost them. I use my debit card for everything. I can't imagine going long without it.

Aleeza: I assume they've checked your banking activity and it hasn't been used since then.

Jay: Yeah, I assume. This is . . . wow.

Aleeza: Jay, do you want me to stop investigating this? Cancel the podcast? I feel like we're exploiting your misfortune for our own gain.

Jay: No, the fuck you are. You're not exploiting anything. You're trying to SAVE me. Maybe the Jay from your timeline is dead, but I'm not. Don't let me go, Aleeza.

I bite my lip. He's right. This is now about saving his life, not about getting him back. The Jay in my timeline isn't coming back. He's gone. But I can still save the Jay I know—the one from five months ago.

Jay: Besides, this news story tells me one thing loud and clear—I didn't jump into the water. Or go in intentionally in any way.

Aleeza: How do you know?

Jay: My fall coat. It's a vintage wool duffel coat. I'm an excellent swimmer—but not with a waterlogged wool coat on. I wouldn't have had it on if I went for a late swim.

Aleeza: That's a good point. What about shoes? What do you think you would have been wearing?

Jay: Unless I'm working out, I'm always wearing my eight-hole Doc Martens. I can't swim in those either. Did they find my boots?

Aleeza: Not that I've heard.

They could still be on his body, wherever it is. I feel nausea in my stomach.

Jay: What did you find out at Jack's? Or do you remember it at all?

Aleeza: I remember a lot.

Jay: How much did you drink, anyway?

Aleeza: About three drinks. I'm a lightweight. And I shared a joint with Jack.

Jay: And knowing Jack, it was probably laced with something.

I cringe at the thought of that.

Aleeza: How well do you know Jack? He said some cryptic things about you.

Jay: Jack is an interesting one. I would say he's the only one in that group I'm still friends with. He's both the most and the least trustworthy one of them.

Aleeza: Is he an addict?

Jay: I have no idea. Probably. He's tortured, that's for sure. I really don't know why. He's rich as fuck.

Aleeza: Someone said he hasn't been sober since the fall.

Jay: He certainly wasn't sober last night. What else did you learn?

Aleeza: I think Taylor might be the Birdwatcher.

Jay: Taylor, like Lance's little sister?

Aleeza: You know Lance well?

Jay: Yeah, Lance and I used to be tight. He was my first friend at TCU. He's the one who told me to join water polo when he found out I was on the swim team in high school. He introduced me to that whole crowd.

That's interesting.

Aleeza: Did you know that Lance is Mia's boyfriend?

Jay: That explains why she was at the party. What are the chances?

It does seem strange that after a falling-out with my friend because she ditched me for a boyfriend, I randomly move into the boyfriend's ex-friend's room. But it has to be a coincidence. Jay being gone was the reason this room was available in the first place.

Aleeza: It kind of sucked to see her again.

Jay: Did she do something to you last night?

Aleeza: She made me feel . . . small. Like a country nothing in the big city party. She made fun of me for feeling buzzed after two drinks and for liking mysteries.

Jay: Not a very good friend.

Aleeza: We're not friends anymore. She was being super weird. She hasn't always been this toxic. She's ditched me for guys before, but she was never this mean, or passive aggressive. When Jack called me exquisite, she literally laughed. It was humiliating.

Jay: Jack called you exquisite?

Aleeza: He was drunk.

Jay: What were you wearing?

Aleeza: This short tight dress of Aster's. Not my usual thing.

Jay: I really wish I could have seen it. You show up at a party at Mia's rich boyfriend's even richer friend's house looking like a snack. She's not used to being upstaged by her sidekick.

Aleeza: I wasn't upstaging her. And how do you know I looked like a snack?

Jay: Because I saw you two days ago in the library, and you looked like a snack then. All dressed up for a party? You totally turned every head there. And Jack has impeccable taste.

I have no idea what to say to that. Jay thought I looked like a snack in the library in my octopus sweatshirt?

Jay: Anything happen between you and Jack?

Aleeza: Are you jealous?

He doesn't respond right away.

Jay: Yes, I admit I am. Useless to be jealous, though. I'm just a ghost.

I still have no idea what to say. I suddenly remember something Jack said last night.

Aleeza: Last night Jack said YOU had impeccable taste.

Jay: Of course he did. This is strange. All of this.

Aleeza: Extremely.

The chat is silent for a while. This is proof that the complicated feelings I have brewing for my roommate are mutual, and I don't know what to do about that. To find out on the same day that a guy likes me and is also dead is a lot. Talk about a doomed crush.

But guys like Jay Hoque don't fall for Aleeza Kassam. Hell, guys like Jack don't flirt with Aleeza Kassam either. But then, Aleeza Kassam doesn't go to posh parties in the city wearing a short dress and drinking mai tais. She doesn't clap back when people make passive-aggressive comments.

Maybe Aleeza Kassam isn't the person I think she is.

But beyond how strange everything feels lately, I can't ignore that the only time I feel like I'm where I'm supposed to be, or *who* I'm supposed to be, is when I'm here in this room with Jay. Chatting with him. Watching movies with him. Or sleeping in his bed with the echo of his arms around me.

But since Jay isn't real, then the feelings aren't real either. There's no point in dwelling, or pining, or even thinking about it. Jay is gone. In this timeline, the person I have a crush on doesn't exist.

Aleeza: Jay, a question for you. Do you know why your mother or your family hasn't spoken to the media much after your disappearance?

Jay: How would I know that? I haven't even disappeared yet.

Aleeza: Well, you do know your family. Even your cousin ignored my DMs and blocked me on Instagram.

Jay: I assume they're upset? Did they ever talk to the media?

Aleeza: Your mother and uncle spoke at a press conference urging for any information from the public a few days after your disappearance. But nothing since then. Even Kegan from the housing office said your mother isn't returning calls.

Jay: I don't know what to tell you. I mentioned you to both my cousin and my mother, so they've heard of you. Maybe.

Yeah, maybe. Everything was a maybe. Our universes might not be the same.

Aleeza: Are you still saving all the screenshots of our conversations on your phone?

Jay: Yes. Shit. If my phone washed up on a beach then the police have my phone now. They could be reading this conversation right now.

Aleeza: I assume it's been underwater a long time. The data probably isn't recoverable. If it is, then I'm sure the police will knock on my door. I'm the only Aleeza at TCU.

My phone buzzes. It's not a ResConnect message, though, but an Instagram DM.

Jack: **This is Jack Gormley. I asked around, and Mia said the octopus sweatshirt someone left at my house is probably yours.**

Aleeza: **Oh yes. Thanks.**

Jack: **I'm going to be on campus later this evening. I can bring it.**

Well, that's fortuitous. I want to talk to Jack, and an opportunity to do that drops into my lap. I agree and arrange to meet him in front of the library at seven. I tell Jay that I'm meeting Jack.

Jay: Let me know what happens. And be careful.

Aleeza: I'm always careful. And I'm not going to give up on you, Jay. I'll never let you go, okay?

Jay: Okay. Thank you. You're all I've got.

FIFTEEN

I find Jack on the library steps at seven, sitting alone with his head in his hands. He's wearing the same suit he had on at his party, and my balled-up sweatshirt is next to him. I approach him slowly, not sure if he's asleep.

"Hi, Jack," I say.

His head shoots up. He blinks a few times, like he's not sure who I am. Which, fair. I'm back in my own clothes: jeans and my father's old sweater. My parka's on, but it's unzipped because it's finally warming up. Also, no more girdle.

"I'm Aleeza?" I say. "You have my sweatshirt?"

He shakes his head. "Of course. Octopuses can change their colors. Never the same look twice." He hands me the sweatshirt, then starts to get up. His eyes are bloodshot with dark circles under them.

"Do you have a minute?" I ask. "I was wondering—"

He shakes his head, then runs his hand over his hair. "The party is over. There's a shower with my name on it."

I raise a brow. "Have you slept at all since your party?"

He shrugs. "I quite honestly don't know."

He still might be high. I doubt I'll get any answers out of him like this. "Okay then, can I ask you one thing? What do you know about the Birdwatcher Instagram account?"

He snorts. "Ah. That's what this is about. You're looking for a place to air your grievances."

I shake my head. "No. I mean, I don't want to post on it or any-thing . . . I'm wondering, do you know who was behind it?"

He looks at me for a long time. "You really don't know?"

"No, that's why I'm asking you."

He snorts, then walks down the stairs away from me. "I can't read you, octopus girl. Are you the mastermind, or the sidekick? If you don't know who Birdwatcher is, what hope do the rest of us have of figuring it out? Follow the money. It always talks."

Yeah, he's still on something. Jack Gormley can't tell me a thing. Or maybe . . .

"When's the last time you talked to Jay Hoque?" I ask, rushing down the stairs to keep up with him.

"Why?"

"I'm doing a true crime podcast about him."

Jack turns to me, and the bored look I saw on his face last night is back. "The last time . . . I don't know. Memories are so fragile; how can I be expected to keep them whole for that long? I believe it started with a phone call. No, wait, a text. A picture on a text. Goodbye."

~

On Monday after classes, Gracie and I record the second episode of the podcast in the library. It feels a little strange, since the script covers the interview with Emma as well as some statements from his profs, his neighbors—and Gracie's account of living next to him. Emma's inter-view, of course, alludes to Bailey Cressman's involvement, but that's as far as the episode goes. The next episode will be more about his wealthy friend group and about Birdwatcher.

After we're finished recording, we talk a bit about how my editing of episode one is going, and how the script for episode three is coming along. I plan to end that episode with the news report about Jay's per-sonal effects being found at the beach.

"Have you decided if you're going to make the podcast public after you turn it in to Sarah?"

I shrug. I don't love the idea of exploiting Jay even more, but a popular public podcast would be utterly amazing for my co-op applications. "That depends. I imagine if we don't solve the case, the people we're accusing might be pissed off."

Gracie shrugs. "Let them be pissed off. I'm not going to have any compassion for anyone from that party."

It's quite clear that Gracie and Aster haven't worked out their issues. Gracie hasn't mentioned Aster once since the party. I'm not sure if I should say anything.

But I don't need to say anything, because Gracie does. "I can't believe Aster gave in to Nat's demands yet again. That girl is like a bad rash that never really goes away."

"They used to date?"

Gracie nods. "They have a lot of history."

"Aster should've left with us, though. I mean . . . if your date leaves the party, you go with them. Basic etiquette."

Gracie raises a brow. "What? We weren't on a date. We've never dated."

I give Gracie a look. "Okay, then what is going on with you two?"

Gracie looks down, fidgeting with the yellow highlighter on the table. "We're friends. That's it. We hooked up once . . ."

"That day I moved into East House?"

She nods. "Yeah, but we decided we were better as friends."

"You both decided or *you* decided?" Because seeing them together, it's quite clear that Aster wants more than a friendship.

"Someone like Aster isn't going to stay long term with someone like me," Gracie says. "She hooks up with me one night, then runs back to Nat the next."

My eyes go wide. "Did she hook up with Nat at Jack's?"

Gracie sighs. "No. Well, I mean, she says she didn't. She said Nat was on something that she shouldn't have taken, and Aster wanted to make sure she was okay."

"Oh." It sounds a little codependent.

Gracie takes the cap off the yellow highlighter. "Seeing those people, Aster's other friends, I don't know. Why would I want to get sucked into that world? Look what happened to Jay after he became friends with them."

"Jack called it the gilded swamp."

She snorts. "And he's their king. Anyway, it doesn't matter." Gracie gives me a look that tells me that she doesn't want to talk about this anymore, so I shrug and let it go. I suspect a lot of this is Gracie's insecurity after seeing those beautiful people, and I get that. Hell, I *felt* a truckload of insecurity at that party.

I open my notebook to the investigation notes. "Okay, let's get back to Jay. The way I see it, we're answering three main questions here. One, who killed Jay?" I swallow. It feels weird to say *killed*, because to me, Jay is very much alive. "Two, how did they do it? And three, why? If we solve any of these questions, then the other two will be clear too."

"For the who, you're still not entertaining the suicide theory or that he ran away?"

No, I'm not. But I can't tell Gracie that I know Jay, and that I trust he wouldn't do that. "Yeah, I suppose it's a possibility, but the *how* and the *why* still need to be answered."

"Who's on your suspect list?"

I list the names. "Emma, Bailey, Taylor, and Jack. And of course, the Birdwatcher. Who might be one of those people."

She shakes her head. "I think we can safely cross Emma off the list. It was clear that her only interest in Jay was using him to get closer to Bailey and her friends. Did you hear anything on Saturday that implicated anyone else?"

A lot of Saturday night is a blur. I shrug. "Jack said a lot of cryptic stuff. I'll bet he knows more than he's saying, but I have no idea if what he knows is relevant." I can't forget what Jay said about Jack—that he's both the most and least trustworthy person in the group. "When he gave me back my sweatshirt, he said he believed it started with a picture on a text, whatever that means."

"He texted Jay the night he disappeared? Why?"

I shrug. "He didn't say. Talking to Jack is like talking to a ghost." Except, not really. The ghost I talk to all the time, Jay, is way clearer than Jack.

"We should probably talk to him when he's sober," Gracie says. "What about Taylor? Why is she on your list?"

"There was something off about her expression when she found out I'm living in Jay's room."

"That doesn't really tell us much."

"No, not really."

"Okay, what about motive?"

And there I was at a loss too. True, I was a little blinded by my serious crush on Jay Hoque, but the reality was, none of the rumors about him were awful enough to motivate someone to commit murder. Some people thought he was a player, but not more than any of the other guys in that crowd. Others said he was aloof, yet he had a circle of friends. He ended up in a rich, snobby crowd for a while, then got out of it when he discovered they were fake as hell.

I go over what his professors told Gracie about Jay. None of them believe he actually cheated on his schoolwork. His professors all liked him. He was doing well in his classes. And he was close to his family. He wasn't the bad boy everyone thought he was. He was actually kind of sweet.

"Love or money," I say.

Gracie raises a brow.

"It's the root cause of all crime."

Gracie exhales. "Yeah, I have to agree."

"We can set aside the love motive for now. I don't think he dated anyone seriously enough to cause that, despite what that Instagram said."

"But we don't know for sure. He could still have a romantic stalker."

"True. But we should think about money as a motive. Even Jack told me to follow the money."

I squeeze my lips together. Suddenly I remember something from Jack's party. A random memory that somehow survived the vast amount of alcohol I consumed. And the marijuana.

"Gracie, was Jay's scholarship an *academic* scholarship?" I ask.

Gracie frowns. "He had a scholarship?"

I shrug, realizing it was Jay who told me about the scholarship, so I'm not supposed to know about it. "Yeah, at the party, Bailey said some racist crap about Jay's mother being an immigrant, and then said Taylor said Jay did have privilege. Said he didn't even have to pay tuition. Do you know if Jay's family has money?"

"No, he told me that he and his mom lived in his uncle's house . . . with six other people."

He hadn't told me that. "I need to learn more about the Hoque family. There's something off there. Why haven't they said anything for months? Why won't Manal speak to us?"

"I met Jay's mother once," Gracie says. "She was here visiting Jay. She was *young*. Gorgeous too. Like, I'd guess a decade younger than my mother."

"So, like, a teen mom, you think?" Jay never mentioned how old his mother was when she had him. Only that she lived in Scarborough, and his father wasn't in the picture.

Gracie nods. "I'd believe it. We chatted a bit. Jay's mom asked me about my hometown, and I remember her saying she still lived in the neighborhood she grew up in."

"I wonder what's the story with his father," I say. "Maybe he grew up in the same area?" I know Jay won't want me searching for him, but I need to know more about his father.

"We could look at yearbooks from the high schools in the area. Maybe Jay's dad went to the same school as his mom," Gracie suggests.

It's not a bad idea, but I hate doing something that could upset Jay, even if it's for his benefit. "Can't hurt. I'll see if they're online. I'll do some digging about her job too. I wish his cousin would talk to us. Did she ever respond to your DM?"

Gracie shakes her head. "She didn't block me, though. I'll try again." When she opens the account on her phone, Manal's art again takes my breath away. I watch Gracie leave her a second message, saying she was Jay's next-door neighbor and has some of Jay's things. She offers to drop them off for her.

It's not a bad strategy. Maybe the rich kids and the Birdwatcher have nothing to do with Jay's death, and we're barking up the wrong tree. I open my notebook and add *Jay's family* to the suspect list.

~

Jay messages me the second I'm back in the room. He's clearly still weirded out by the news that his phone and jacket were found, and he's now presumed to be dead.

Jay: The more I think about it, the more I think Taylor might be the Birdwatcher.

Aleeza: Why? Did you ever get the feeling that she had a thing for you?

Jay: No, not really. When I was with Lance, she was always around. I thought she was kind of mean-girl-ish . . . like she was subtly making fun of me.

Aleeza: She's like that with me too. I'll try and talk to her. Maybe she'll give something away.

Jay: Who else are you looking into now?

I can't tell him that Gracie and I are planning to investigate his family.

Aleeza: Jack. He was so cryptic at the party. And also when I went to get my sweatshirt from him. I get the feeling that he knows a lot more than he lets on. I wouldn't be surprised if he knows who the Birdwatcher is.

Jay: Maybe. But Jack never makes any sense when he's high.

He certainly wasn't making sense at the party. Jack said to *follow the money*. Which brings me back to Taylor's comment about Jay not paying his own tuition. I know I should ask Jay about that, but it feels like money and family are the two things that he is uncomfortable talking about.

Aleeza: Hey, question, at the party Bailey said Taylor told her you don't pay your own tuition. Does your scholarship cover everything?

Jay: Yeah, most of my fees and living expenses. My mom's paying the rest. She never wanted me to take student loans, so she's been saving a long time.

Aleeza: Academic scholarship?

Jay: No. Well, yes and no. They looked at my grades, but the scholarship is also needs based. It's from an organization that my mom's boss is affiliated with. She sponsored my application.

Aleeza: What's the organization?

Jay: Why does that matter?

Aleeza: I have no idea what matters and what doesn't. Who knows? This might be important.

Jay: The Bright-Knowles Award.

I write the name in my notebook.

Aleeza: How would Taylor know about it?

Jay: Lance and I were close first year. I don't tell many people about my scholarship, but I'm almost positive I mentioned it to him.

I don't know what to make of this. Would someone want to kill Jay for a scholarship?

∿

That night, Jay and I watch another time-travel movie. We watched the first *Bill and Ted* last night, which was fun, but I could tell Jay wasn't in the mood for such a silly movie, so tonight we pick *The Time Traveler's Wife*. He doesn't text me nearly as much as he did last week for the *Back to the Future* trilogy, and I don't blame him. He's got a lot on his mind.

Jay: Do you think you'd want to be in Henry and Clare's time anomaly instead of ours? With me showing up at random times in your life instead of this?

I think about it.

Aleeza: It would be strange. I mean, our anomaly is strange too. It would be cool to have more time, though.

And it would be amazing to know for sure that he *could* come back. To know that a goodbye might not be a final goodbye.

Aleeza: And it would be nice to know that there's a possibility we could have a future instead of only a past and a present.

I can't believe I said that. But it's the truth. I don't know if I want a future with Jay, but it would be nice to know it was possible. He doesn't write anything for a few moments, and I'm worried that I scared him off. This is the guy who hates commitment. Then a message appears.

Jay: Yes, I agree. And it would be nice to be able to actually be in each other's lives physically. We were cheated. We signed up for the wrong time anomaly.

Aleeza: I knew I should have ordered a DeLorean instead.

Jay: No, not that one. I am NOT going to the prom with my mother.

After we watch for a bit longer, Jay sends another message.

Jay: Any chance you feel up to sleeping in my bed again? If I know you're there, I might actually get some sleep.

Aleeza: Absolutely. I'd love to.

It's the least I can do for him. I'll sleep better with him near too.

SIXTEEN

At lunch the next day, I spend some more time googling. First, I look up Jay's scholarship, the Bright-Knowles Award. I can't find much about it, though, only it's mention on a few websites that list Canadian scholarships. It's apparently funded by several high-profile donors, and the only way to apply is to be sponsored by one of the members of the board.

The scholarship itself doesn't have a website or a list of board members anywhere, so I can't see who makes the decisions. Maybe Salma Hoque's boss is on the board?

I google Salma Hoque next. Most of the hits from her name are from the press conference two days after Jay disappeared. I watch the clips carefully to see if I missed anything when I first watched them.

Salma Hoque is beautiful. Medium-brown skin about the same tone as my own, and big brown eyes that look like Jay's. She does look younger than my own mother. She's sad in the clips, of course, with bloodshot eyes and hunched shoulders. I don't know the woman, but her emotions look real to me. Not faked.

I can't find any mention of her on the internet after this date, so that means this was the last time she made any statement about Jay's disappearance. I google every combination of *Jay Hoque* + *father* and *Salma Hoque* + *boyfriend* and come up empty. It would have been too easy if a Google search could have found Jay's father. I look up Jay's address on Google Maps. It's a small townhouse in Scarborough. The outside view doesn't tell me much.

Salma Hoque legal assistant gets a hit, though. I find her name on some person's public Instagram post from five years ago about a law office's staff holiday party. Jay mentioned his mother worked at the same place for years. This must be it. On a whim, I call the office and ask for her. The person says she hasn't worked there for months, and they can't tell me where she is now.

I can't find anything telling me if she's working now. Has Salma been unemployed since Jay went missing? I remember Kegan's comment that she hadn't responded to messages from the housing office. But she must have contacted the school to unenroll Jay right before I moved in. Where is she now? Just lying low? Is she depressed? I open a transit map and see that it's only about a fifty-minute ride to Jay's house in Scarborough.

I think I'm going to have to pay a visit to Salma Hoque.

~

That evening I'm in my room editing the second podcast episode when my phone buzzes.

Jay: We don't do the standing eight o'clock dates anymore, do we?

Aleeza: I mean, we can? We usually talk before eight. What are you up to?

Jay: Just lying in a dark room having an existential crisis.

Aleeza: Oh no. Are you okay?

Jay: I mean, finding out I'll be dead in a few months is kind of heavy. I thought about going to the campus drop-in counseling, but what the hell would I tell them?

Shit. Maybe I shouldn't have told Jay about his coat and phone washing up on the beach. I could have investigated it on my own without involving him.

Aleeza: Jay, we will figure this out. I promise. And then you'll know how to avoid it. You'll be okay.

Jay: Okay, let's talk about something else. You posted another octopus on your Instagram today. Why are you so into them?

I check my Instagram, and yes, I posted an octopus mural I saw in early November. He must be checking my feed regularly. He didn't follow me—I'd notice if Jay Hoque followed me on any social media.

Aleeza: I went to an aquarium when I was a kid, and the tour guide went on for a while about what amazing problem solvers they are, and how they're really smart. My brother said I was like an octopus because I was into puzzle games. And it kind of stuck.

Jay: You like them because they're smart?

Aleeza: And I think they're cool looking. Plus, I love that some octopuses can camouflage themselves to blend into their environment.

Jay: I don't think you blend in even though you want to.

Aleeza: What do you mean?

Jay: I mean the few times I've seen you in person you stood out. I noticed you. But that could be because it's hard not to notice the person who told me I'm dead.

I exhale. My heart is breaking for Jay. I wish I knew how to make him feel better—even a little bit.

Aleeza: We will figure out how to prevent it.

Jay: But we haven't yet, have we?

Aleeza: We will. I'm like an octopus, remember? I solve things. I won't let you go.

Jay: I trust you. But . . . I keep thinking about all the things I'll miss out on if I die. I'm only nineteen.

Aleeza: Things like what?

Maybe this is how I can help him. I'm no therapist. But I can listen.

Jay: Like . . . I don't know. I want to travel. Maybe go see Dhaka, where my mom was born. Or Africa, or India. I'd love to see Japan too.

That reminds me of what Jack said that night, that *wanderlust shouldn't hurt someone*. But it seems unlikely that Jay wanting to travel has anything to do with this—he didn't have a trip planned. He was last seen in Toronto, and his things were found in Toronto.

Aleeza: What else?

Jay: I want to work. Like as an engineer. I want to help build sustainable buildings. I want to look at a cityscape and know I had a hand in making them stand there. And I know I'm probably just being a romantic, but I want a family. A wife and kids. A normal nuclear family in a nice house. I want to be a good dad and cook dinner for my wife.

Aleeza: What happened to no commitment?

Jay: I guess my priorities have changed.

Wow. He's not afraid of commitment anymore. This is huge for Jay. It wasn't that long ago that he called me naive for wanting my own family. But I suppose learning about his mortality changed him.

Aleeza: Are there things that you've always wanted to do that you can do now?

Jay: I already have. Today I spent over forty dollars that I really don't have on a burger and fries from this pricey place I read about on a food blog. Because I may never have another chance. But I'm not going to tell you the thing I want to do the most . . .

Aleeza: Why not?

Jay: Because you'll tell me it's impossible.

Aleeza: We're literally texting each other from different times. Nothing's impossible.

Jay: Okay . . . I want to hold you. I want to wrap my arms around you in a big hug, and not let go. I seriously considered going up to past-you today and asking for a hug.

Heat pools through my body. I curl up on my chair.

Aleeza: Just a hug?

Jay: Well . . . no, but I'd be happy to start with that.

I close my eyes for a moment. I want that too. This is torture.

Jay: I have a confession.

Aleeza: Okay . . .

Jay: I did go find you this morning. I went to West Hall and hung out in front for a while to see if you'd come out. You did. I almost approached you. But I couldn't. Then you dropped your bag, and I picked it up and handed it to you.

I swallow.

Aleeza: I remember that. That happened.

This is more proof that this friendship, or whatever it is, between Jay and me is *real*. Jay waited for me outside my old residence because of our relationship. And I remember seeing him there. In fact, I remember seeing him in a lot of places. Now I wonder if all that wasn't random at all.

Jay: LOL, I should probably lay off a bit, or you'll think I'm a stalker.

Aleeza: No. I mean . . . I wouldn't think that. I used to see you everywhere. I noticed you.

Jay: Why did you notice me?

Aleeza: Because I've always liked you.

I can't believe I said that.

Jay: You had the hots for me.

I pause. I really don't know how to answer that. I take a slow breath before responding.

Aleeza: Doesn't everyone at the school?

Jay: I don't care about anyone else at the school. I want to know what YOU thought of me.

Aleeza: Okay, fine. Yes, I had a crush on you. I thought you were cool. Way out of my league, though. I always felt like you weren't like the other students here.

Jay: I'm not out of your league. I think we're in exactly the same league, just not in the same time. Why didn't you think I fit in?

Aleeza: You did fit in. More like . . . you know when you're looking at a Where's Waldo picture and it's so hard to find Waldo because there are so many people with black hair, or with glasses, or with red stripes on? Imagine a Where's Waldo picture where no one else is anything like Waldo . . . he belongs there in that crowd, but he's still so noticeable. Your eyes are drawn straight to him.

Jay: Maybe a part of you knew we'd be close.

Aleeza: Yeah, maybe.

The chat falls silent for a while. I don't know what to make of this whole conversation. Is Jay saying he actually wants to be with me? Maybe I should just ask him.

Aleeza: If things were different . . . if we met because we were maybe rooming near each other or had a class together, what do you think would happen between us?

Jay: I don't know. I think I'd notice how smart you are. And how we're both weirdly obsessive about our favorite foods, and how we both like old movies. I'd like to think I would've asked you out, but . . . I don't know. That's what I should do, in that hypothetical situation. But it's possible I'd be too much of a dumbass to actually do it.

Aleeza: Because you didn't believe in commitment.

Jay: I think I would have realized that you'd be worth so much more than a hookup, and I would have backed away because that wasn't my style. Honestly, I think my whole no-commitment thing is a trauma response. Learning about your ultimate demise in weeks kind of makes you rethink how you've lived your life, you know?

Aleeza: I can imagine. Why a trauma response?

Jay: I went to see my mom again today. She said something that made me think. She said she knows she has a screwed-up view of relationships, and she's afraid she passed it to me. She was in a strange mood . . . kind of melancholy. I kept thinking she might know what's going to happen, too, but of course that's not possible. Maybe my mood was contagious.

Aleeza: Do you think it's her depression?

Jay: No. I mean, this is nothing like when she was really bad five years ago. She kind of closed in on herself then. Yesterday, she was chatty.

I want to ask him more about his mother and where she could be now. This could be my chance to get more information out of him. But . . . it feels so wrong to deceive him after he told me he wants to hold me. Even though it can't happen.

Aleeza: Why does she think she has a screwed-up view of relationships? Because of your father? Or did she have other bad relationships?

Jay: No, she hasn't had a lot of relationships. She goes out on dates sometimes. Nice Bangladeshi men my uncle finds who don't mind that she's a single mother. She once even almost married this divorced man, but it didn't work out. I think I'm portraying her as some tragic fallen woman here, but she's not. Mom's a ton of fun. She's just had some rough things happen to her. My whole family has. They came to Canada with nothing.

Aleeza: How old was she?

Jay: Thirteen. They all had it rough for a long time. My grandparents, aunt and uncle, and mom all lived in a one-bedroom apartment, and they all had to work. Every weekend in high school, Mom waited tables at some posh place near the lake. She still refuses to butter toast from all the brunches she served.

Aleeza: Do you know what happened between her and your father?

Jay: Not much. She was eighteen when I was born. I know she was lucky her family didn't disown her. They're all a lot more religious than she and I are, but they're thankfully not the "disown the sinners" type of religious.

Aleeza: Do you think she still talks to your father? He should have paid child support, right?

There is no response to that. A few minutes ago, he said he wanted to hold me. He said he wanted to do more than hold me. But now I'm pushing too hard. Finally, he responds.

Jay: I don't know. I can't ask her about him.

Aleeza: Is there another way we can find out about him? He might be relevant. Does she have any friends from back then? Yearbooks?

Jay: Don't think so. Her closest friends are people from work.

This is going nowhere.

Aleeza: What high school did she go to?

Jay: East Scarborough Collegiate.

Aleeza: Did you go to the same school?

Jay: No.

This is still going nowhere.

Jay: I'm sorry, but that's all I got. I'm not willing to ask my mother about my father. And I really doubt it's important, anyway. He's not a part of my life. At all.

And I'm not willing to give this up either. Because it's the biggest unanswered question about Jay. But also? I'm not willing to push Jay too hard either. He's having an existential crisis, and facing his mortality head-on, and I'm the only one he can talk to about it. I want to be there for him, not make this harder.

I stop bugging him about his father and ask him about his aunt and uncle instead, but I don't learn anything useful. He doesn't talk about them the same way he talks about his mother.

Aleeza: You all live together. You aren't close?

Jay: No, we are. Sort of. I got the impression from Mom once that my aunt assumed she'd be the one raising me when they took Mom in. But Mom always made sure she was my parent, not them. We saw a lot of them of course, but Mom kept a separate life too. She even got her mail sent to a friend because she suspected my uncle was reading it.

That sounded significant. Could the aunt and uncle have been bitter or resentful about that?

Aleeza: Oh wow. Do you think your aunt and uncle would ever hurt you or your mom?

Jay: No, it wasn't like that at all. They're good people. It's just, you know how intrusive Desi families are.

Yup, I absolutely know what he means. My parents were born in Canada, so they're pretty westernized, but my mom especially can be very intrusive.

Jay: Anyway, I loved living with them because I love my cousins. Manal is one year older than me, and Madhuri is three years older. They're awesome. Like cool big sisters. Manal especially—she's like a best friend and a sister at the same time.

He's quiet again for a while.

Jay: I hope they're okay.

Aleeza: I'll figure this out, Jay. I'm not going to give up on you. Ever.

Jay: I know you're not. I have faith that my octopus will save me.

Later, after we watch another movie, I'm in his bed and have turned off the light. My phone buzzes with a message.

Jay: Why can I feel you here when we're both in this bed?

Aleeza: I don't know. I feel it too.

Jay: Maybe it's the anomaly's consolation gift. I can't kiss you, but I can at least feel you near me.

I squeeze my lips together. He wants to kiss me. I turn so my back is against the wall and clutch Ted close to my heart. And like last time, I feel surrounded . . . enveloped, with warmth, comfort, and belonging. I pick up my phone.

Aleeza: Good night, Jay.

Jay: Good night, Aleeza.

SEVENTEEN

In the morning I have a text waiting for me.

Gracie: Manal agreed to meet me!

Aleeza: Oh my god, yay!

Gracie: I said it's just to give her Jay's stuff. I have no idea if she'll talk. You'll come, won't you? We're going to meet at a coffee shop near her college at four.

Aleeza: I'm absolutely coming. I have somewhere I need to go first, but I can meet you there. I'll bring some of Jay's stuff to give to her.

It looks like I won't be going to class at all today, but I should be done in Scarborough in time to meet Gracie at four. I check ResConnect—Jay isn't there. I know he has an early class. I'm glad he's not here because I don't want to tell him I'm going to be digging up information about his family today.

I reluctantly get up. Even though Jay's not in it anymore, I still love being in his bed. It feels warmer, cozier than mine. Even though it's got my sheets and blanket on it, there's a subtle scent—cologne or deodorant, or laundry detergent—that's not mine. I've never really been close enough to smell Jay, but still, it smells like the most comforting memory.

But now, despite what's happening between Jay and me, I'm keeping something from him, and I feel terrible about it. He would not be happy about me going to his family's house today. But this might be the only way to save him.

Before I leave, I sit on the floor near my closet to pick out some stuff from Jay's box to give to his cousin. There's no way I'm giving everything to Manal—partially because this is a lot to lug around all day, but also, I don't want to give away anything that might be useful evidence. I tried not to look too closely at the stuff when I packed it because it seemed like such an invasion of privacy, but now things are different. I'm getting desperate to solve this.

There are clothes, toiletries, books, and some mail in the box—nothing of value. His mother must have taken his computer and anything important right after he first went missing. I put together a tote bag of things for Manal—some clothes and a few books.

All the mail is postmarked *after* the date he disappeared. The don probably brought it up and left it in the room. Most of it doesn't look important: some junk mail, a holiday postcard from a dental office, a letter from the school registrar. That last one I saw the day I moved in. I put the mail in the bag to give Manal.

I get dressed, shove the tote bag full of Jay's things into my backpack, then head to the subway station. The weather is finally not brutal . . . in fact, the sun is even shining. Most of the snow from the last dregs of winter melted, revealing the mud and dirt of early spring. But it's still cold. I'm glad I have a warm sweater under my puffer jacket.

It takes me two subways and a long bus ride to get to Jay's neighborhood in Scarborough. My grandmother's sister lives in Scarborough, so I've been here a bunch of times before. Scarborough is the farthest east and the biggest of the six districts in Toronto. The whole city is considered to be one of the most multicultural cities in the world, and Scarborough is the most diverse part of Toronto. As I sit on the busy city bus, I wonder what it would have been like to grow up here instead of in Alderville. Here, where there are more nonwhite people than white. Where I would blend into the crowd instead of always being the odd one out. The food would certainly have been better.

Jay's part of Scarborough is very flat, with strip malls and plazas lining the major streets. Most of the housing is old low-rise rental buildings, with some townhouses and small bungalows too. After getting off the bus, it's a five-minute walk to Jay's family house.

Their unit is on the end of a large complex of attached houses clad in faded yellow siding. Instead of a driveway, there's a courtyard in front. The parking lot for the complex is behind the backyards.

It's strange to see where he grew up. It feels so . . . detached from him. The Jay I know belongs in the huge, crumbling mansion-turned-dorm in the middle of the loud and busy downtown Toronto, not in this small townhouse. Short windows at the base of the house suggest a basement—probably where Jay and his mother lived. Or . . . *live*. Steeling my shoulders, I knock on the door.

A woman opens the door—it's not Salma Hoque. This woman is older. She's in a pale-green salwar kameez, and her hair is pulled back. "We don't need fiber internet," she says instead of saying hello. Her South Asian accent is strong—stronger than Jay's mother's in the press conference.

"Oh, no, sorry. I'm not selling anything. My name is Aleeza. I'm looking for Salma Hoque?"

The woman narrows her eyes. I can see inside the house a bit and catch a glimpse of wood floors and pale-pink walls. The faint smell of spices is in the air. "She's not talking to reporters." She starts to close the door.

"I'm not a reporter," I say quickly. "I'm a friend of her son's from school." But the woman, I assume Jay's aunt, continues to close the door.

"Please," I say quickly. "I just want to talk to someone about Jayesh!"

She shakes her head angrily. "No one is talking to anyone. Go away." She slams the door closed.

I have no idea what to do next. If they won't talk to me, then what else can I do here? I walk around to the back of the house and see the fenced backyard, which is empty. Should I knock on a neighbor's door? Try to find out if Salma is even here? I have no idea how close anyone in the family is to their neighbors. And if reporters and media are coming around a lot, maybe the neighbors have been told not to talk to anyone. But I'm not a reporter. I really am Jay's friend.

It occurs to me that I'm in school to be the kind of reporter who's been harassing this family. I sigh. Maybe now's not the right time for me to question the ethics of my chosen career. I'm not here for some clickbait headline, anyway. I am here to *save* Jay. There must be someone nearby who knows Salma. I consider going to her work, but it's back downtown. And it's a law office—they'd be even less likely to speak to me.

Has Jay ever mentioned Salma going somewhere else regularly? A library or nearby café? I didn't see any cafés nearby. Just small takeout restaurants and corner stores. My stomach rumbles then. It's lunchtime.

I smile. I know exactly where to go—a place that both Jay and Salma went to often. A quick Google search on my phone tells me that Shawarma Delight is only a five-minute walk from where I'm standing.

The moment I step into the tiny hole-in-the-wall shop, the smell of fire-roasted meat and garlic hits me. The place looks like it's been recently renovated—or at least recently been slapped with new paint and signage. As it's a bit early for the lunch rush, it isn't too busy—only two people stand in front of me in line.

When I get to the front, the girl at the counter smiles. She looks to be about my age, and she has a cream-colored hijab on, along with a sweatshirt that says SHAWARMA DELIGHT on the corner. There's another woman at the counter making the sandwiches for the people in front of me.

I need to be undercover here, and I'm worried I'm going to mess this up. I smile. "Hi!" I glance up at the menu. "A friend of mine told me to come here! She said it was the best shawarma in town. But I don't remember if the chicken or the beef was her favorite. She comes here all the time. Do you know Salma Hoque?"

The expression on the girl's face changes immediately from friendly to one of sympathy and compassion. "Of course we know Salma. She was our best customer. She even helped paint the restaurant last year. Salma always got beef."

I nod. "Can you make me one like how she used to have it? And I'll have a bottle of mango juice."

The girl nods and calls back to the woman preparing the food. "Beef shawarma with everything on white pita. Extra spicy."

I need to keep this conversation going. While I'm paying with my debit card, I say, "It's so sad what happened to Salma's family. I used to work with her. She came here a lot, didn't she?"

The girl nods. "Yeah, Salma was like family. She hasn't been here for months, though. Not since her son went away."

"I know how much her son meant to her," I say. "I'd love to send her a card—do you know where she is?"

She leans forward and lowers her voice. "She's gone, too, but apparently her family won't report her missing. It's so terrible . . . maybe her brother sent her back to Bangladesh because of the scandal."

My breath hitches. Salma is *gone*? Where?

The other woman behind the counter turns sharply. "Amina! Don't gossip!" She gives me a long stare, like she knows I'm lying.

"It's fine," I say. "It's really so heartbreaking. Salma and Jay were so great. I hope everything ends well for them."

The girl nods. "I pray for them every day."

"Thank you," I say as she gives me my sandwich and drink. I take my lunch to a table, unwrap it, and take a bite. It's amazing. A little spicier than I normally prefer, but so flavorful. Perfect charred meat, perfect garlicky sauce, perfect toppings, and fluffy pita. And for some reason, this perfect sandwich makes my eyes water.

Will Jay ever have this sandwich again? Will Salma? I can't believe she's gone too. Does her family know where she is? Did Salma leave town because she's heartbroken over losing her only child?

The whole thing is so . . . tragic. I feel close to both Jay and his mother here in their favorite restaurant. I have no idea where they are, but I do know that the little family doesn't deserve the pain they're going through. And not just Jay and Salma—so many people are hurting. Jay's aunt and uncle, Jay's cousins, and all their other family. Even the people here in the shawarma shop are mourning them.

I'm not sure I believe that Jay's uncle forced her to go back to Bangladesh, though. Jay did say his aunt and uncle were more religious and traditional than Salma and Jay, but from what Jay told me about his mother, she wouldn't let anyone force her to do anything she didn't want to do.

When I'm about half-done with my shawarma, someone sits down in front of me at my table. It's the older woman from behind the counter—the one who scolded the younger one for gossiping.

She looks to be in her thirties or maybe early forties, and is also wearing a Shawarma Delight sweatshirt, but with a black hijab. She's pretty, with fair skin and kind eyes. "You said you're Salma's friend?"

"Yes."

"My name is Ausma. How well did you know her?"

I'm not sure how I should play this. If I'm honest with her and tell her that I've never met Salma, I'm afraid she won't talk to me. But I can't pretend I do know her because she'll ask questions I can't answer. "I know . . . the family." Maybe since I'm Brown, this woman will believe I'm a friend of the family.

She looks at me curiously. "You're *Jayesh's* friend, right?"

I nod. Is it possible that Jay told this woman to trust me, too? Like he told his mother and cousin?

"He's such a good boy," Ausma says. "He was good to his mother."

"You and Salma were . . . are . . . close?"

The woman nods. She exhales. "I haven't seen or heard from her in a long time. But . . . Jay was here. That day, I mean. When he went missing. I think he *knew*. He told me that if something ever happened to him to make sure I'm there for Salma." Her eyes get a little glassy with tears. She shakes her head. "But I failed her. I wasn't there for her. I'm working so hard. I have my own kids and a busy restaurant. And now Salma's gone too. That day, I asked Jay if he had a girlfriend yet. I haven't forgotten what he told me. He said there was a girl he's close to, and that he hoped one day they could be even closer. He told me she was helping him. And that he hoped his family and friends would help her in the future. That's you, isn't it?"

Jay *did* tell her about me. I can feel my eyes well with tears. He said if something happened to him away from the room, he would get a message to me. Is this that message?

I nod, wiping my eyes. "Did he say anything else? How was he? Did he seem upset?"

She shakes her head. "No, there was nothing else. He was . . . cheerful, in fact. The way he talked about you . . . I remember thinking, *This girl makes him very happy.* I wish I had more to tell you."

I exhale. When he spoke to this woman, he didn't know yet what was going to happen. Or he would have told her more.

"Are you trying to find him? Is that why you are asking questions?" she asks.

I nod. "I'm trying to find them both."

Ausma hands me a plastic bag. I peek inside. It's filled with envelopes. I know what this is. Ausma must be the friend who's been collecting Salma's mail.

"Her mail," I say.

"Can you use this to find them? I didn't want to give it to her brother. I don't know what she was hiding from him . . . but . . ." She sighs.

I peer into the bag. It looks like it's mostly bank statements and junk mail. "I don't know. Maybe . . ."

"I wish I could help more. Salma was private about a lot of things. We were friends, but she never talked about anything big, you know? Not about her past."

I nod. She's telling me she doesn't know who Jay's father is.

"What was . . . is Salma like?" I ask.

The woman smiles sadly. "She was like the sun. I didn't realize how bright she made everything until she was gone. Find them, okay? I put my number down in there, call me if you need any help. Anytime."

I nod and thank Ausma, and she says a prayer for me, Jay, and Salma before going back behind the counter. I'm not sure if what Ausma told me, or this mail, will help at all, but it's clear that Ausma misses Salma. And Jay.

If Jay told Ausma about me the day he disappeared but didn't leave me a significant message, then it's clear that when he was here at lunchtime, he didn't yet know what was going to happen that night. I shove the bag of mail into my backpack. I'll talk to Jay about it before opening any of it.

~

When I get back downtown, I see Gracie waiting for me at the subway station near the College of Art. She's wearing baggy jeans and a bright floral button-up, along with her signature cardigan—this one in yellow. While we walk to the café near the campus, I tell Gracie what the woman at the sandwich shop said.

"Oh wow," Gracie says. "That's *so sad*. His mom is gone too. No wonder she hasn't spoken to the media recently. Do you think she even knows that they found Jay's coat and phone on the weekend?"

"Probably. Unless . . . I don't know. Jay's aunt really, really didn't want to talk to me today."

"Hopefully Manal will be more talkative. What information do you want to get from her?"

"Where Salma is. And what Salma was hiding from her brother and sister-in-law." I exhale. "Anything, really. Mainly, does she know of anyone who would want to hurt Jay or Salma?"

"Are you going to give her that mail the shawarma lady gave you?"

I shake my head. "No, Salma didn't want her brother seeing it. I'm not going to give it to her brother's daughter."

"What's in the mail, anyway?"

I shrug, then grab the plastic bag out of my backpack and look through the envelopes. It's all addressed to the shawarma shop's address, and it looks like mostly bank statements. But . . . there is one interesting envelope here. Interesting, because it's for Jayesh Hoque, not Salma Hoque. And it's from a lawyer's office: Choi, Patel, and Associates, Attorneys. Why would a lawyer write to Jay?

"Didn't Jay's mother work at a law office? Is this the same one?"

I shake my head. "No, that was . . ." I don't remember the whole name of that firm. "Featherington and Grant something."

Gracie looks at the envelope. "It's postmarked after he disappeared. It's a federal offense to open someone's mail. We should give it to someone."

I exhale. I'll ask Jay what to do with it tonight. "I'll figure it out."

When we get to the small café near the Ontario College of Art and Design, it's easy to find Manal Hoque in the crowd of art students. She has the exact huge brown eyes as Jay. Her skin is a bit browner, and she's about as short as I am, but the family resemblance to Jay and Salma is unmistakable.

Manal looks like an art student, though. She's wearing wide-legged white pants and a bulky orange sweater and sits at a table near the back of the café working on an iPad. Behind her hangs a large print of the Toronto skyline painted in bright colors. The whole café has art prints all over the walls—probably because it's so close to the art college.

Gracie goes right up to her. "Manal? I'm Gracie Song. Thank you so much for meeting me. I am so sorry for your loss."

Manal stands and looks at Gracie, suspicion in her eyes, then glances at me. I see then that Manal's sweater is cropped, with a gray shirt underneath.

"I'm Aleeza," I say. I hand her the tote bag filled with Jay's things.

Her expression falls immediately. She takes the bag from me and drops it on her table. "*Aleeza?* You're the one who messaged me on

Instagram. Jay's *friend*?" There is a lot of angry accusation in her voice. The barista glances up at us.

Gracie looks at me, confused.

"Yeah . . . I mean, I didn't know him that well, but—"

Manal raises an annoyed eyebrow. "That's not at all what he told me. He told me you two had become *very* close." She looks me up and down. Lord knows what she's thinking about me. The barista is still watching us, concerned.

Gracie grabs my arm in surprise. Her eyes are wide as saucers. "Jay told you he *knew* Aleeza?"

Fuck, fuck, fuck. I promised Gracie weeks ago that I'd never met Jay. Which was true—then. I look at Gracie, hoping my expression is telling her that I'll explain it all later. I have no idea what I'll tell her, but I can't explain it now, in front of Manal. Or in front of everyone else in the café. It feels like they are all staring at us.

"We weren't that close. I mean . . . not really," I stammer.

"He had a *massive* crush on you," Manal deadpans as she crosses her arms. "Shocking too. You don't seem his type." Her voice is dripping with condescension. Does she think I had something to do with Jay's disappearance? Maybe her mother even told her I was at his house today. Maybe she thinks we had a chaotic relationship that somehow ended with him dead.

Coming here was a bad idea. I should have let Gracie do this alone. Clearly Manal doesn't trust me. And I don't blame her at all.

Gracie is clearly also pissed at me. She lets go of my arm and turns away, giving Manal a sympathetic look. "Can I buy you a coffee? I'm gutted about Jay. If there is anything at all I can do to help."

Manal shakes her head. "My family is *grieving*. There's nothing you can do to help us. Tell your friend you'll never win . . . so stop harassing Jay and my family."

Manal starts packing up her things from the table like she's going to leave.

"Wait," I say. "I'm trying to find out who *hurt* Jay. Don't you want justice?"

She looks at me while putting her iPad into a messenger bag. "There is no justice. Don't you see?" She shakes her head.

"Manal, you *know* Jay trusted me," I say. "This is what he'd want . . . me to find out who hurt him. There's something you're not telling us."

Manal looks up to the ceiling, and I see tears in her eyes. Finally, she looks at me. "He mentioned you only once to me. He said he trusted you more than anyone else at that school." She shakes her head. "He said you were special. And that things felt different with you. I remember thinking, *Wow, he's like a whole new person with her.* It was such a change for him. And then, weeks later, he's gone. So don't blame me for not trusting you. You're like the rest of them—sucking him into their world only to suffocate him."

I want to put my hand on her arm to comfort her, but I know she wouldn't want that. "Manal, if you think I'm one of his wealthy friends, I'm not. I promise, I barely know those people. I really am just a friend who wants to know what happened. Jay would want me to help him. You know that."

She exhales, and the hostility finally leaves her face. "I honestly don't know what happened to him. Nothing makes sense. But I think . . . I *know* it shouldn't be this hard to figure it out. People don't disappear into thin air. Only people with buckets full of privilege can make that happen."

"You think Jay's rich friends are responsible?" Gracie asks.

"Of course, it's obvious they are," Manal says, still cleaning up her table.

"I'm not one of them," I say. "I only want to help you. Jay told me how much you meant to him—he said you were like his best friend and his sister."

Manal finally looks at me with teary eyes. "You are not at all what I expected *Aleeza* to be like. And somehow"—she looks me up and down again—"I'll take you at face value. Honestly, good for Jay for liking someone *real* instead of his revolving plastic door. So I'll tell you this. If I were trying to figure this out, I'd start with who was paying Jay's tuition."

"He had a scholarship," I say.

She shakes her head. "A very strange scholarship, if you ask me. One that usually doesn't go to people who grew up where we did. Or to people who look like us."

Clearly, I need to find out more about the Bright-Knowles Award.

"Have you heard of a law office called Choi, Patel, and Associates?" I ask. I'm grasping at straws here, but she's finally talking, and I don't know how long we have with her.

"No, never heard of it," she says. I believe her.

"Have you seen the police report about his disappearance?" Gracie asks. "We've been trying to figure out who saw him last."

Manal shakes her head. "No, but remember this—some people are so powerful that they can *buy* witnesses. Even buy their own justice. I have nothing else I can tell either of you." She resumes packing up her things.

"Where's your aunt?" I ask quickly before she can leave. "Is Salma missing, too, or did she leave on her own?"

She shakes her head. "Salma Aunty spent her whole life trying to escape her past. And her past still came and took him. I don't blame her at all for escaping this damn city. People like us? We can't ever, ever win here. They own it all. They will never let us forget that."

Somehow, I know she's including me and Gracie when she says *people like us*. She means *us*—newcomers, immigrants, and the children of immigrants.

Manal walks away. And there's nothing I can do to stop her.

EIGHTEEN

The moment Manal is out of the café, Gracie turns to me, eyes full of betrayal. "What the hell, Aleeza? You told me when we met that you didn't know Jay. Don't tell me you actually *did* hook up with him."

I sigh, looking out the window at Manal walking away. "No, I didn't know him . . . then."

"That's not what Manal said."

I turn back to Gracie. She looks furious. Can I tell her the truth? It would honestly be nice to have someone out there who knows what I'm going through. And Gracie is my friend. Friends should be open with each other. I trust her. "I can explain. But . . . back in my room. In private."

Gracie stares at me for a long time before exhaling. "Okay, girl. Let's go home."

On the short subway ride home, Gracie is silent, which is good. I need to think. Will she even believe what I'm about to tell her? Or will she think I'm nuttier than a squirrel in the fall? And if she does believe me, will she tell anyone? I don't want my connection with Jay to turn into a freak show. I don't want people to think I've lost my mind, and I definitely don't want strangers intruding on what we have. Especially now—we're only days away from his disappearance. I can't do anything that could make me lose him before we solve this.

When we get back to my room, Gracie sits on my bed and looks at me pointedly. "Okay. Talk. *Did* you know Jay before you moved in here? Have you been lying to me this whole time?" Her eyes are narrowed with accusation.

I sigh. "Okay, but . . . it's not only my story to tell. I need to ask someone first."

I sit on Jay's bed and check the ResConnect app on my phone, and thankfully, Jay's name is there. He's home. I quickly message him that Gracie found out that he and I know each other, and I want to explain everything to her. I ask him if he's okay with that. I say it might be easier for us to get to the bottom of it all if Gracie has all the cards.

"It's Jay you're texting, isn't it?" Gracie asks, eyes wide. "He's not dead and you know where he is, don't you? Why the hell are we doing all this if you can just text him like that? You need to go to the police!"

I sigh, hoping Jay writes back soon. Thankfully he does.

Jay: Do it. Tell her. I trust Gracie.

I exhale and look up at her.

"Okay. This is really complicated. And I'll tell you all of it, only if you promise to keep this here. What I'm going to tell you can never leave this room . . . okay?"

She looks suspicious. "If what you tell me is illegal or is hurting someone in any way, I'm not going to keep it to myself. If that's Jay you're talking to, I'm telling the police unless you give me a good reason not to."

Fair. This is one of the things I like about Gracie—her ethics. She's going to be an amazing journalist one day. "It's not illegal or hurting anyone, as far as I know. You asked if I know where Jay is right now, and the answer is no. I don't. I don't even know if he's alive. But yes, it's Jay I'm messaging."

"*What?*"

I take a breath. "When I'm in this room, I can text Jay using ResConnect. But it's Jay from five months ago. Before he disappeared."

"You're not making any sense."

"I can't explain it, but that's what's happening. The Jay I am texting is Jay from five months ago."

She looks at me like I've lost my mind, which seems about right. But I plow ahead, sitting next to her on my bed and showing her ResConnect, pointing out Jay's name on the list of occupants in room 225. And I show her the message he just sent me. I even message him again.

Aleeza: Say hi to Gracie.

Jay: Hi, Gracie. I just saw you in the hallway half an hour ago.

Gracie looks at me. "You're being scammed. This can't be real."

"It's real. We've done all sorts of tests." I tell her about the sports scores, Kegan in the housing office, and Jay finding me on campus. Plus, of course, she heard Manal say Jay told her he knew me well. Still, I feel like she doesn't believe me.

Aleeza: Jay, text something only Gracie would know.

The chat is silent for a while. Finally, a message appears.

Jay: Has she admitted that she's in love with Aster yet?

I snort and write back.

Aleeza: No, and she doesn't want to talk about it.

Jay: Okay. Tell her thank you so much for the time she lent me a cardigan after the ketchup dispenser in the Tower food hall squirted on my shirt.

I look at Gracie, who's next to me, reading my phone. Her face turns as white as the walls.

"Shit," she says. "I don't understand how this is possible."

"It's not possible," I say. "But it's happening."

Jay: Does she believe us?

Gracie takes the phone from my hand and writes back to Jay.

Aleeza: This is Gracie. I BARELY believe you . . . what's the date for you right now?

Jay: November 2.

Aleeza: What was I wearing when you saw me in the hallway just now?

Jay: A dark orange sweater and jeans. I remember because I commented on the color of the sweater.

"Is that true?" I ask Gracie. "Is that what you were wearing?"

"How the fuck should I know . . . I don't remember what I was wearing on a random day five months ago." Her shoulders slump. "Actually, I remember that. He said my sweater was the exact shade of the library carpet."

I take the phone back from Gracie.

Aleeza: What did you say when you saw her sweater?

Jay: I said it matched the carpet in the library.

I show the message to Gracie. She stares at it.

"So now do you believe us?" I ask. "And are you going to keep this a secret?"

Gracie's eyes are still wide. "Yeah, I don't get it, but clearly there is something weird going on. November second is only—"

"Four days before Jay disappears. That's why I need to figure out what happened . . . so it doesn't happen to him."

"So you're trying to save him."

I nod.

"You think you can bring him back to life?"

"No." I sigh. "If the Jay from our time is dead, there's nothing I can do about that. Like I explained earlier, we discovered that we're in parallel and almost-the-same universes, not at different points in the same timeline. Things he does don't necessarily always affect this time."

"But sometimes it does. Like what he told his cousin about you."

"Yeah, I don't think I can save Jay from the present, but I am determined to save *this* Jay." I tap my phone with my fingernail. "The Jay from months ago who's still living in this room."

Gracie says nothing for a while, fidgeting with the hem of her sweater. I get it—this is a lot to process. Finally, she looks at me. "But we don't know if current Jay is dead or not. If he's not, then solving this means we *can* find him. Alive."

I nod. It seems like a long shot, but yeah, we could. But each day I'm more and more sure that current-day Jay is gone. Because past Jay and I have become so close. He said he wanted to hold me. He said he wanted to ask me out. He wanted to kiss me. We've both admitted our feelings for each other. Hell, he even admitted it to his cousin. And if all that is true, and if the Jay from this timeline is out there somewhere, why hasn't he tried to contact me? Why hasn't he shown up so he could give me that hug? Or get a message to me somehow?

But maybe he's out there, and he can't. Or maybe he's out there, and he doesn't remember any of it. Because it didn't happen to him. It happened to the Jay I know from five months ago. Not today's Jay.

I get up from my bed and walk over to the bulletin board over Jay's desk, where I pinned that picture of him from the school paper. I doubt I'll ever see Jay again in person. We're doomed. But it's still important for me to *save* him. For Salma, for Manal, for Ausma—even for his aunt and uncle. And most of all, for Jay. And who knows, maybe if I can prevent his disappearance, past Jay—*my* Jay—will ask out past Aleeza like he wants to, and they can be happy.

Lucky past Aleeza.

Gracie looks at Jay's empty bed for a while, then up at me. "Okay. We have four days. Let's find Jay."

~

With Gracie sitting next to me watching our messages, I fill Jay in on everything that happened today. And as expected, he freaks out about his mother being missing.

Jay: Where the hell is my mother?

Aleeza: Good question. I don't know. Ausma at the shawarma shop doesn't know either. And Manal didn't tell us much.

Jay: Let me call them—I'll tell them to talk to you in five months, like I'll tell Ausma in four days.

189

"Don't," Gracie says. She looks at me. "Tell him not to do that. For all we know, the fact that he told Manal about you is why she won't talk to us now."

I type out what Gracie says, and he reluctantly agrees. We are seriously fucking up the timelines. Doc Brown from *Back to the Future* would be so disappointed in us.

Aleeza: Why do you have a letter here from a law office? Choi, Patel, and Associates. Do you recognize the office?

Jay: No, I have no idea what it's about. No clue at all. When am I supposed to get it?

Aleeza: Postmarked for . . . December 13.

About a month after his disappearance. Was Salma gone by then?

Jay: Open it.

I look at Gracie. "Is it a federal offense to open someone's mail if they tell you to open it in the past?"

She shrugs. "No clue. Open it anyway."

I open the letter. Gracie takes the phone from me and quickly types out the letter into the chat. She's a much faster phone typist than me.

The letter is short, and it's from a lawyer named Rebecca Guerre. It states that there's an anonymous trust being held for Jayesh Hoque, which he can access only on, or after, his twentieth birthday. It says he must bring government-issued ID and proof of enrollment in an accredited university (unless extenuating circumstances don't allow him to be in school), as the trust is intended to offset his education expenses. There's an expiry date—the letter says if he doesn't claim the fund within six months of his birthday, he'll forfeit it.

"Here's our motive," I say. Money. I take the phone back from Gracie.

Aleeza: Did you know about this?

Jay: No, not at all. Should I ask my mother? She might know.

Aleeza: You're not supposed to have the letter yet. You can't ask.

"When's his birthday?" Gracie asks.

"April 10." That's less than two weeks away for us. But Jay won't be able to claim this trust because he's gone. He was already gone when this letter was mailed. I wonder if the lawyer was aware of that.

"We should call the law office," Gracie says. "Maybe there's something the lawyer can tell us."

I look at the time. It's past seven now. "Tomorrow?"

Gracie nods. "Shit. I have plans with Aster tonight." She smiles, her eyes full of sympathy. "Should I cancel? Do you need me tonight? Or maybe you want to come with us? We're going for noodles."

I shake my head. "No, you go. I'll grab dinner next door and stay here with Jay."

She chuckles. "Now I get why you never want to leave this room. Tell Jay we got him. We'll figure this out."

I nod. It's been a long day. I'm tired and drained. But more determined than ever to get to the bottom of it. And also, it's a huge relief to have a friend who knows what's going on. I'm feeling a little bit less alone tonight.

NINETEEN

That night, Jay and I don't watch a movie. Instead, we talk about all the things we learned today.

First, the Bright-Knowles Award. There is no website for the award, so it's impossible to see who won the scholarship in years past.

Jay: I don't know why Manal would think there's anything fishy about the award. She can't be jealous. She herself got a huge art award.

Aleeza: She said it doesn't normally go to people who grew up where you did.

Jay: It's a scholarship for people from Toronto. How can we find out who else got it?

Aleeza: Give me a second. I'm looking up the name of the award on LinkedIn. Maybe people put it on their resumes.

Jay: See? This is why you're the research queen.

Bingo. I find four people who list the award on their résumé. I write the names out for Jay.

Aleeza: Andersen Taggart IV, Ashling Weston, Cassidy Preston, Braden Albright.

Jay: Does the guy's resume really say IV?

Aleeza: Yep.

Jay: Those are the whitest names I've ever heard.

Aleeza: Do you think that's what Manal meant when she said people not like us?

Jay: Maybe. But I'm half-white. A fact that my cousin reminds me of often.

It only takes about a minute of googling to know exactly what Manal meant. These people are wealthy. They all come from prominent Toronto families. They are not people raised in a Scarborough basement apartment by their single mother. I tell Jay.

Jay: If they're wealthy, why did they need the scholarship?

Aleeza: That's a great question. You said your mom's boss sponsored you?

Jay: Yeah, she's affiliated with the scholarship somehow.

Aleeza: What's her name? Have you met her? What's she like?

Jay: Helen Grant. I've met her many times. She's awesome. Mom's worked for her for years. She's a lawyer.

I google Helen Grant. She's actually a pretty influential lawyer who's been practicing corporate law for decades. She sits on a bunch of boards and does a lot of mentoring for women in law. I remember Jay telling me they stayed in her cottage once. It's clear Jay and Salma's connection to this woman has given them a small amount of privilege normally reserved for old money.

But I can't see how this is a motive for someone to hurt Jay or Salma. Some rich person was jealous that a half-Bangladeshi kid got the old-money scholarship they wanted?

Aleeza: How much was the scholarship anyway?

I realize this is a personal question, but at this point, hopefully we're close enough to answer personal questions.

Jay: 20K a year. 80 total if I finish my four-year degree.

That's probably a lot of money for Jay's family. Hell, it would be a lot of money for *my* family. But it's a drop in the bucket for these rich people. Despite what Manal thinks, I doubt this scholarship is our motive.

Aleeza: I really don't think this is enough of a reason for some rich person to hurt you. This wouldn't be much money for them. What about this trust from the lawyer's office? Who do you think set it up?

Jay: Honestly, no idea at all. The only thing I can think of is

He doesn't finish his sentence again. I wonder if this is how he talks in real life. With sentences trailing as his mind wanders.

Could the trust have been set up by his father? I'm not going to mention that to Jay, because he doesn't want to talk about him, but it's the only explanation I can think of.

Aleeza: Finish your thought, Jay.

Jay: I think my mother has been secretly stashing away money for me for a while. I don't know where she gets it. She mentioned once that what's mine and hers is only mine and hers. I think she's worried my aunt and uncle would try to take the money from me or her.

Aleeza: Would they do that?

Jay: I doubt it. They're a little strict but not bad people. But honestly, why would my own mother set up a trust for me? Can I think on this for a bit? I don't want to talk about this stuff all night.

Aleeza: Jay, we're days away. We need to figure this out.

Jay: Exactly. We're days away. I don't want to spend what could be my last few days dwelling on the messy bits of my life. Let's talk about you, instead. What did you think of my neighborhood?

I sigh. Maybe he's right. It feels like we're still so far from figuring this out. Which means that I may not be able to save him, and we only have a few days left together.

I tell him more about my trip to Scarborough. About seeing his house, about the playground he played in, and about my impression of the beef shawarma at Shawarma Delight. He makes me describe the sandwich in detail, then tells me he's determined to get one on the weekend. At that I laugh. Of course he's getting one. He talks to Ausma about me in four days.

Eventually we talk more about his family, about my family, about how we grew up in such different places but how similar our mothers are.

But there's one thing we don't talk about—the future. Mine, his, or the possibility of having a future together. Because we know we don't have one. We have the past and the present, but nothing else.

~

In the morning, after breakfast, Gracie calls that law office pretending to be Jay's mother. She gets nowhere. Then she pretends to be Jay, and they say that even with ID, they would tell him nothing. With a little prodding, Gracie finds out that if it's unclaimed, it will pass to the next beneficiary, but they won't tell us who that beneficiary is, or how much money is in the trust.

The law office is located in one of those tall towers downtown. I google every combination of *Choi, Patel, and Associates* with *Jayesh Hoque, Salma Hoque,* and even *Helen Grant,* and come up with nothing.

"I don't get it," I say to Gracie in her room that evening. I'm sitting on her unmade bed, and she's on her desk chair. "It says the trust is intended to offset education costs, so it's probably about the same amount as the scholarship, right? Maybe $80,000 to $100,000. Not a huge amount for rich people."

"But the next beneficiary might not be wealthy," Gracie says. "I know Manal thinks this is a rich-people-going-after-regular-folks thing, but we have no reason to know that's what's happening. People have certainly killed for $100,000."

"Yeah, I guess so." A thought comes to me. "I *do* think the trust is the motive. Birdwatcher proves that."

Gracie lifts one brow. "What? How?"

"Think about it," I say. "Jay can only claim the trust if he's enrolled in postsecondary education. The smear campaign against him in the Birdwatcher Tumblr and on Instagram—the bullying, the academic cheating accusations—that could all be to get him to either drop out or get kicked out of school. And then he wouldn't be able to claim the trust."

Gracie smiles, nodding. "Yeah, that totally makes sense. So someone from the trust-fund group, right?"

"Yeah, maybe one of them isn't as rich as we thought they were."

With no leads at all as to who opened the trust, or who the next beneficiary is, we have no idea how to proceed. We decide to go back to the Birdwatcher and hopefully figure out who that is. But we're hitting a dead end there too.

"I need to ask Jay," I say. "He has a late water polo match tonight, so I'll have to talk to him tomorrow. He must know something that can help us get through all these dead ends."

～

On Friday after my classes, I bring my dinner up to the room so Jay and I can talk while I eat.

Aleeza: We should have set up voice-to-text on ResConnect so we could feel like we're having a real conversation.

Jay: Then you'd sound like a robot. I don't mind texting. Hey, did you end up finding my mother's yearbooks?

Aleeza: I looked online but couldn't find any. Did your mother ever mention going to school with your father?

Jay: No.

Aleeza: I think you're going to have to ask her about him.

There's no answer for a while. This is the biggest loose end. We need to know more about Jay's birth father. Finally, he responds.

Jay: Yeah, I think you're right. But I'm not going to do this on the phone. I'll ask her when I see her this weekend.

Tomorrow is Saturday, and he's supposed to disappear on Sunday.

Aleeza: Maybe you should just go there now and stay until Monday after you're supposed to disappear. In fact, you could just go into hiding for a few months until your birthday so no one hurts you before you can claim the money.

Jay: I can't. I wouldn't be able to talk to you.

Aleeza: But it could keep you out of danger!

Jay: We don't know that. We still don't even know if this trust is the reason I'm missing. I'm not going to hide for five months without even knowing if I'm actually in danger.

He's right. The only way to prevent this is to find out if someone did something to him. And stop them. I look over at Tentacle Ted, willing him to help me find the right angle to solve this puzzle. I remember Manal's comments about the kind of people who get away with everything.

Someone knocks on my door then. It's Gracie, her eyes twinkling with excitement. "Aleeza! I figured out how Jay got downstairs that night!"

"What? How?"

"Come, lemme show you." She motions me to come with her.

I quickly text Jay that I'll be right back and leave the room with Gracie. She explains while we're walking down the stairs. "I had a meeting with my psych professor today. Her office is on the second floor. While in there, I heard a noise next door, like someone running downstairs."

"So?" I ask. She gets off the stairs on the second floor. I follow her as she walks down the hallway of professor offices.

"Her office isn't anywhere near the stairs. The main stairs, that is. So, once all the profs had left for the day, I came here and snooped around. Look," she says, pointing at a door that looks different from the others. There's no name or window on it. And no lock. Gracie opens the door.

I'm not sure what I'm expecting, but inside is just a janitor's closet. I see a mop and bucket, a broom, and some shelves full of cleaning supplies. But one thing that's strange is that the room has wood paneling on the walls.

"The rooms on this level have more details from the original mansion. Look." She goes to the left wall of the small room and slides open a wood panel.

"It's a pocket door!" I've seen these in some old houses in Alderville.

"Yes, and hidden stairs." She motions me to join her on the narrow wood staircase. I only hesitate a moment—I really don't want to get in trouble for being here—but I want to figure out this mystery, so I follow her.

"Why are there stairs here?" I ask.

"They're servant stairs. I guess the maids had to get to the second-floor bedrooms without anyone seeing them. And since the camera is on the main stairs between the first and second floor, it wouldn't catch Jay that night if he came down from the third floor and went down these stairs."

At the bottom of the stairs, there's a door. When Gracie opens it, we're in a little hall with three doors. The walls are covered with the cheap-looking white paint of the rest of the building.

"Where are we?"

"That"—Gracie points to the door on one side—"leads to the back common room, which I assume used to be the kitchen of this house. And that"—she points to the other door—"leads outside."

"But I thought there were only the two doors out of the building?"

She nods. "Exactly. This *is* the back door. Don't touch it; it's alarmed."

Huh. I have never used the back door, so I didn't notice this mystery door next to it. I frown. "How did he get outside from here? The alarm would have gone off."

She shrugs. "That part I don't know. He could have gone out through the common room to the front door."

"Yeah, but the front-door camera didn't see him leave."

She shrugs. "I've figured out how he got downstairs."

She's right. This is something. I exhale. "Thanks, Gracie. This does actually help."

After we head back up to the third floor, she tells me she's going for drinks with Aster. I give her a meaningful look.

"Don't," she says, shaking her head. "It means nothing. We're friends, that's it."

I chuckle. "Sure. Just friends."

"You go," she says, pushing me to my room. "Go talk to your *just a friend.*"

I'm smiling as I head back into my room. I immediately tell Jay what Gracie found.

Jay: Cool! A hidden stairwell! This place really is a haunted mansion. You even have a ghost you talk to every night.

Aleeza: You're not a ghost. We'll solve this. I'm going to see if campus security will tell me anything about that back alarm. Maybe there is a way to disarm it.

Jay: It reminds me of Travis's family cottage. We all went up there last year. His dad had all these secret passages built into it for fun.

Aleeza: What else did you do with Jack and his friends?

Jay: Regular stuff. Parties, clubs, hanging out.

Aleeza: Did you leave town with them a lot?

Jay: Just Travis's cottage, that's in Muskoka. Wild place. And we went on Jack's boat a few times, but that's in Toronto harbor. Not out of town.

Oh. Jay's things were found washed up on Lake Ontario. Maybe he was on Jack's boat.

Aleeza: Is that the boat Jack lives on?

Jay: Yep. It's a sailboat. His family has several, but this one was his twentieth birthday present. Once we went on a midnight cruise—we didn't even get back to the marina until 3:00 a.m. There were at least a dozen of us. It's a big boat, but still, that's a lot of people.

Aleeza: Which marina?

Jay: North Toronto Yacht Club. Stupidly named because it's in the south end of the city. Bunch of others also had family boats there.

Aleeza: The marina is open until 3:00 a.m.?

When Jack was high, I remember him mentioning swamps and water lilies. Clearly water is important. I look up the yacht club on Google, and it's about ten kilometers from Woodbine Beach, where Jay's things were found.

Jay: No, but security took one look at Jack and just waved him in. He stays overnight there a lot. Jack took us out to see the most amazing view of the Toronto skyline at night.

Aleeza: Did anything strange happen to you there? Maybe you went on Jack's boat again that night.

Jay: I guess it's possible. Nothing strange happened last time. It was nice. I really got to know Jack that night . . . he wasn't drinking. He said he always stays sober while sailing.

Aleeza: What's Jack's sailboat called?

Jay: Wanderlust. I remember the name clearly because Jack and I talked about it that night. I told him all about the traveling I want to do, and he said the same. It's why he named the boat that.

Shit. There it is.

Aleeza: That's it.

Jay: What?

Aleeza: That night at Jack's party . . . he said "Wanderlust shouldn't kill anyone. It's a gift." I thought he was talking about traveling . . . but he was talking about his boat.

Jay: Holy shit. Maybe I'm going to be on his boat Sunday night.

Aleeza: The more I think about it, the more I think Jack knows a lot that he's not saying. He's probably the Birdwatcher. He was so cryptic at that party. Aster told me he used to have a secret Instagram where he aired dirty laundry about his wealthy peers.

Jay: Yep. He got into a lot of trouble for that. Did you know the old Birdwatcher Tumblr claimed I was the one who exposed Jack as being the person behind that secret Instagram? Of course, I didn't do it. A few days ago, Birdwatcher Instagram repeated the accusation.

Aleeza: Wow. Why did the Birdwatcher think it was you?

Jay: No clue. I told Jack that it wasn't me. I've never even seen his secret Instagram. He said he believed me. All the trouble slid off him, anyway. Rich people get away with everything.

Maybe with murder. If Jack thought Jay exposed his secret Instagram, that could be motive.

Aleeza: If Jack is behind the Birdwatcher Instagram, then him reposting that accusation a few days ago tells us that he hasn't really forgiven you. This grudge has been festering for a year now. It's ready to blow. Someone said he's been drinking since Halloween, and he said after that. You disappeared a few days after Halloween. Maybe he was so traumatized by what he did that he's been on a bender since then. I need to talk to him.

Jay: Be careful.

Aleeza: Yeah, I know. I will. Let's hope Jack has some answers for me.

TWENTY

The next day, after I tell Gracie about Jack's boat, *Wanderlust*, she agrees to come with me to talk to him. But that proves harder than we expected. The Instagram account he messaged me from about my sweatshirt strangely no longer exists. And neither Gracie nor I have his phone number. We can't exactly show up at his mom and dad's house asking for his number because we think he murdered his classmate. Gracie finally asks Aster to call him, but he doesn't answer his phone or texts from her. Aster even calls Nat, and she doesn't know where he is. Nat laughs it off and says Jack always turns up eventually.

"Perfect," I say, curling my legs under me on Jay's bed. We just finished recording the third episode of the podcast, and I admit, we both kind of half-assed it. We're a little too preoccupied with the actual mystery to put enough attention on the mystery podcast. "People I want to talk to keep dropping off the face of the earth," I say. First Salma, and now Jack.

"He's probably on another bender," Gracie says, unplugging the microphone from my computer.

"He's apparently been on a bender since fall." The more I think about it, the more I'm sure Jack is our culprit. Jay even said he didn't trust him. I decide to see what else Jay knows about his so-called friend. It's strange to be able to text Jay with Gracie here, but it certainly makes things easier.

Aleeza: What do you know about Jack's family?

Jay: Not much. I've never met them. They're rich.

I google the Gormley name and end up finding a lot. Gracie sits next to me on the bed and takes my phone to type out what I find for Jay.

Jack's father, Victor Gormley, is in real estate. He apparently owns a company that manages several commercial buildings. His mother's name is Kate, and as far as I can tell, her job is to be a professional wealthy person. She sits on boards and goes to galas, and she looks like she should be on *Real Housewives of Toronto*. I find an older picture of Victor and Kate together, and it mentions Kate's maiden name.

"His mother's last name was Tanner. Why do I know that name?" I ask Gracie.

She shrugs. "I dunno. It's a common name."

"It might be relevant." I take my phone back from her.

Aleeza: What's significant about the name Tanner?

Jay: No idea. I don't know any Tanners.

I know the name has been mentioned at some point. I go through my black notebook and can't find the name Tanner anywhere. Finally, I search through the screenshots of all my conversations with Jay, and I find it.

Aleeza: You DID tell me the name Tanner! It's the name of the architect who designed three identical mansions.

Jay: Yes! Ernest Tanner designed East House. But how is that relevant to this case?

After a few more moments of googling, I have an answer. Gracie looks over my shoulder as I explain it to Jay.

Aleeza: Ernest Tanner was Jack's great grandfather. His grandfather and his mother both grew up in a mansion identical to East House. And I assume Jack spent a lot of time in that house. Which means Jack would know all the secret doorways and hidden stairwells. Including the one that leads from the second floor to the back door.

Jay: Brilliant. Yes, Jack would know the layout of this house, even if he's never been in it.

We had the motive. And now we have the opportunity. We have our guy.

Gracie looks up at me. "But if Jack got Jay out of East House through the secret stairs, why? Why not bring him down the main stairs? Was Jay unconscious?"

I shake my head. "I have no idea. Jack's not a big guy—he couldn't have carried Jay down the stairs. Jay must have gone willingly."

Aleeza: When Jack gave me back my sweatshirt, I asked him when he last spoke to you, he said it started with a text and a picture. Maybe he texts you a picture of his boat?

Jay: Maybe. But now that I know I'm probably going to be thrown overboard, I'll just ignore whatever picture he sends me to entice me out of the dorm. Should I go to the police?

"Great question," Gracie says. "Also, should *we* go to the police?"

I think for a moment, then shake my head. "We should get some proof first. Let's see if he turns up. And now Jay knows not to get on Jack's boat." Jay knows how to stay safe.

~

Saturday night after Gracie leaves, Jay and I watch *Everything Everywhere All at Once*. It's not technically a time-travel movie, but it's a movie we both love.

Jay: If I could drop into different universes, I'd find the one with you and me sitting alone on a beach staring at the waves with no memory of all this shit.

Aleeza: That sounds like heaven. Let's manifest it.

We both know it's not possible. But dreams are all we have. When the movie is over, we keep talking. Tomorrow is disappearance day, and neither of us knows for sure what will happen.

Aleeza: So, what's your game plan for the morning?

Jay: I'll go to my mom's. Did any of those news articles say I was at my mom's that day?

Aleeza: No, they all say you came back to East House at six, were seen in the lobby at eight, and then were never seen or heard from again. They don't say where you were before six.

Jay: Okay. I guess I'll be back here at six. Will you be here?

Aleeza: Yes, I promise. I'll be here all day. Message me the second you're in the room. And then stay with me.

I swallow. I wish we had more answers, but what we have has to be enough. I can't lose Jay tomorrow. I absolutely can't.

Jay: I'll message you the moment I'm back.

Aleeza: And then I won't let you go.

Jay: Okay. What happens if I don't show up at six?

Aleeza: You will show up. The camera saw you. You're not going to go with Jack.

He doesn't answer for a while.

Aleeza: This isn't a goodbye, Jay. You will be back here at six. Then just stay with me. Don't go down to the second floor. Don't take the hidden stairs to the back door. Don't get on Jack's boat. Stay here. We got this. We figured it out.

Jay: You're right.

Aleeza: Of course I am. I'm as smart as an octopus.

Jay: Ha ha. Hey one thing, if

I wait for him to finish his sentence.

Jay: I'm really glad I met you. I hate everything that's happened or going to maybe happen, but I got you out of it. I hope we can see each other in person one day.

I wipe the tears that are falling. He's saying goodbye. But this can't be a goodbye.

Aleeza: We will talk tomorrow! This isn't a goodbye.

Jay: No, it's not a goodbye. But if it were, I'd be saying thank you, and I'm going to miss you more than I can say.

Aleeza: Tell me that tomorrow, Jay.

Jay: Okay. And I'll tell you now too. Thank you. I'm going to miss you. Good night Aleeza.

TWENTY-ONE

Jay leaves for his mother's early on Sunday, but I wake up to text him another *not a goodbye* before he leaves. I don't want him to go to Scarborough all day. I want him to stay right here with me, so I know he'll be fine. Still, I understand why he needs to go. If we can't save him from whatever will happen tonight, then he might not see his family again.

He seems more optimistic now than last night, at least.

Jay: Talk to you around six.

Aleeza: Okay. I'll be here waiting. Make sure you come back.

Jay: Don't worry. I'll always come back for you.

In the afternoon, I'm working on the script for the next podcast episode when there's a knock on my door.

I open it to find Gracie and Aster. Gracie grins at me with excitement. "Nat spotted Jack at the Laundromat."

"He's doing laundry?" Does Jack really do his own laundry?

"He's not really doing *laundry*," Aster explains as she walks into my room and sits on my desk chair. She's in workout pants and soccer shirt. "Laundromat is a secret bar. Like a speakeasy."

I laugh. "Seriously?" We are not in the 1920s . . . why are there speakeasies in the city?

"It's not a real speakeasy," Gracie explains. "Just a secret place."

"You know the Laundromat near the park?" Aster asks. "There's a beaded curtain in the back. Through there is a dive bar. Well, not really a dive bar—it's expensive as sin."

"It's where rich people go to pretend they're slumming," Gracie adds.

"That's nuts."

Aster nods. "My people are weird. We should go now, before he leaves."

I'm supposed to stay in all day in case Jay shows up, but I also need to talk to Jack. I give Gracie a pointed look. "I need to be back here at six."

She nods. "*I know.* I'll make sure of that."

"Here," Aster says, pulling something out of her backpack and handing it to me. "Put this on. It's a voice recorder. Ontario only requires single-party consent for voice recording, so you can record any conversation you're participating in—just in case he says anything useful."

It's a silver chain with a large black crystal pendant. I put it around my neck. "Why do you have this?"

"I bought all sorts of spy gadgets when we started." Aster's grinning like a kid telling me what she got for her birthday. "I'm excited we're finally using something. I have a burner phone, too, if you need it."

After she shows me how to turn the pendant on, we head out of the building. It's a fifteen-minute walk to the bar. Thankfully, it's not very cold out, so I'm okay with just my bulky sweater. I really hope winter is finally over. When we get to the Laundromat, I realize I *have* seen this place many times before, but since I do my laundry in the residence, I never thought twice about it. I had no idea it was really a rich students' hangout.

Inside, the Laundromat looks like . . . a Laundromat. And smells like one too. A wall of stainless-steel heavy-duty washers and dryers runs along one side, and a counter lines the other. There's even a person loading clothes into a dryer, and someone else folding. Aster guides us to the back, where a pink plastic beaded curtain covers a doorway. After passing through the beads, we head down a flight of stairs and through another hallway. Eventually we reach a door that looks like an old-timey saloon door from cowboy movies.

The space beyond it looks exactly like Mia's grandmother's basement. Fake wood paneling. A makeshift bar on one side. Old video game systems. And a pool table. All in all, not the kind of place I thought I'd end up in on a Sunday afternoon. There are about fifteen people down here, all around our age, and it smells like fabric softener and weed.

"Seriously?" I ask. "This is where the other half hangs out?"

"Not me," Aster says. "I don't believe in enjoying things ironically." She looks around, frowning. "Weirdly empty today."

It's a Sunday afternoon. How many people are normally in a bar? Again, I'm reminded of how enormously I don't fit in with this crowd.

"There," Aster says, pointing to the back of the room. Jack is alone in a booth, a bottle of beer next to him. It's strange—I thought he was extremely good-looking the first time I saw him. But now? He looks . . . deflated. Defeated too. His hair isn't gelled back, and he has circles under his eyes. He's in a suit again, this one pale gray, with a paisley shirt underneath. He looks up and sees us coming toward him. I can't tell if his expression is full of disappointment or if he was expecting us. I wonder how much of his drug use is guilt because of what he did to Jay. At least he's feeling remorse, I guess. I discreetly turn on the voice recorder before we approach him.

"Aster, you brought these two to the Laundromat? Seriously? You *must* find a hobby other than corrupting young minds."

"I'm surprised you remember us," Gracie says. "You were pretty out of it at your party."

He looks up at me. "I would never forget *you*. My little octopus girl. Apologies if I was inappropriate at my party."

"Can we talk for a second?" I ask. "About something you said to me that night."

He sighs. Loudly. "I knew this was coming. Yeah, sit." He looks at Gracie and Aster. "Do you mind if I talk to her alone? I'd rather not have an unnecessary audience for my potential downfall."

I frown. Gracie looks like she doesn't want to leave me, but with others around, I'm not sure Jack will be honest. At his party he was way more open when it was just the two of us. This is why I'm the one wearing the voice recorder.

"C'mon," Aster says, pulling Gracie by the arm. "They have an old Super Nintendo here. Let me smoke your ass at *Super Mario Bros.*"

I slide into the seat opposite Jack. "Why did you know this was coming?"

He shrugs. "Gut instinct. I talked to you a lot that night—I'm sure I said something I shouldn't have."

I frown. "Do you often have *gut instincts*?"

"All the time. They can be eerily accurate. My mom calls me a fortune teller." He runs his hand over his hair.

My eyebrows raise. I remember back to the cryptic things he said that night. Was Jack seeing the future?

"I don't know how you remember your party so well," I say. "You were drunk. And stoned."

"I usually am."

"Are you now?"

"Am I what?"

"Under the influence of anything?"

He holds up the dark-brown bottle of beer. "No, it's taken me almost an hour to drink about a quarter of this. I doubt I'll finish it."

"So, where've you been for the last few days, then? We've been looking for you."

"The siren call of *Wanderlust*." He takes a sip of beer, makes a face, then pushes it away.

"That's your boat, right?"

He nods. He's not looking at me. He's looking at the table instead.

I take a deep breath. "Jack, why do you think you talked too much at your party?"

"I shouldn't be trusting anyone." His eyes still don't meet mine.

There is something so sad, so broken about Jack today. I remember what Jay said—that Jack has his own demons.

But then I remember that he may be responsible for Jay's death. He may not deserve my sympathy. I'm only here to get answers.

"You did trust me," I say. "I mean, I was drunk and stoned that night, too, but the one thing I do remember is you saying 'Wanderlust shouldn't kill anyone.' I thought you meant Jay had wanderlust, like he wanted to travel or something, but now I know you meant your boat. I also know that once last year you took Jay and a bunch of others on a midnight cruise on the *Wanderlust*." I pause, leaning forward, trying to put a trusting look on my face. "Jack, did you take Jay on another cruise in the fall? The night he went missing?"

Jack doesn't say anything. Instead, he picks up his beer and takes a long sip. So much for not finishing it.

Finally, he looks at me. "Are you going to turn me in to the police?" he asks.

"I want to know what happened first."

"You have such a trusting face . . . You should do this for a living." He exhales. "The truth might be a bit blurry."

"You were high, weren't you? The night Jay disappeared."

He shakes his head. "Not intentionally. I don't drink and sail. Or do anything at all and sail. But for some reason, it's still blurry."

"So you *were* on something."

He shrugs. "I practically grew up on boats . . . I may be a reckless dick in every other part of my life, but I take water safety seriously. When they called asking if we could have a little boat tour that night, I told them no. My boat couldn't leave the club because I was too wasted. But I said they were welcome to come *hang out* on the boat—we just wouldn't be sailing. I switched to Gatorade anyway just in case because safety first. But . . . something happened that night. Things got weird.

Foggy. I blacked out on the boat. I don't remember much until the screams woke me up."

Screams? My fist clenches. "You were at the marina?"

"No. On the lake. Open water."

"Who called you? Who was on the boat with you?"

He exhales. "Lance called me. It was Lance and Jay."

I exhale. *Lance.* Mia's boyfriend. Fuck.

"Why did you pass out? What did you take?"

He shakes his head. "I told you I didn't take anything. I think someone spiked my Gatorade."

I narrow my eyes. "That's awfully convenient. Did you *see* either of them tamper with your drink?"

He shakes his head. "I can't tell you how it happened. I just remember feeling . . . strange. Not drunk, but really gone."

I'm not sure I should believe Jack. "When did Lance call you? What did he say?"

"I don't know. Maybe around six that night? Lance said he and Jay were looking for something to do, and would I be interested in taking them for a little boat ride? His dad has a boat at the club, too, but Lance's dad's an asshole."

I'm still having trouble wrapping my head around Lance being there. "Did you actually *see* Jay get on the boat? How did he look? Was anyone else with them?" There is no way Jay would have willingly climbed into that boat. Maybe he was drugged too?

"I . . . only remember them." He looks up with a distant look in his eyes. "I remember Jay's coat and Lance's douchey backward hat. It's there, but foggy."

"So, Jay might not have been on the boat, the—"

Jack shakes his head. "He *was* there. I found his boots on my deck the next day. Doc Martens. I tossed them in the water."

I inhale. The boots Jay told me he always wears. "Why didn't you tell the police this?"

"Lance told me not to. Said we'd both get into a world of trouble. Told me if I said something, he'd turn me in for boating under the influence."

"Was it Jay who screamed?"

His voice is small. "I don't know."

I squeeze my eyes shut. *Lance.* Mia's boyfriend is the one. He threw Jay overboard on Jack's boat. Jay even screamed.

But why?

I now know what happened to the Jay from my timeline. The one who hasn't been seen for months. But have I done enough to prevent it from happening in Jay's timeline?

"What exactly did Lance say happened?"

"He said it was an accident. We were all drinking vodka and I passed out. He and Jay were fooling around, and Jay fell overboard. There were empty bottles on the deck. A lot."

I inhale sharply. Maybe that's exactly what happened. Just boys being dumbasses.

"Why would Jay have taken his boots off?" I ask. I remember Jay telling me he wouldn't be able to swim in them.

He shrugs, looking down at his hands. "I wouldn't have let someone on my boat with boots. She's new."

That made sense. And it was cold that night, so Jay would have kept his wool coat on.

"You *should* have done something when you sobered up," I say. "Told the police. Maybe they could have rescued him from the water."

He shakes his head. "It was November. The water was pitch black. No one could have survived in it very long. Even a good swimmer. But . . ."

"But what?"

His face falls. "I *did* want to report it the next day. But Lance said he would ruin my life. He's got a lot on me. He was so sure we'd never be caught. I'm on thin ice with my parents. I'd get kicked out of school.

And he said everyone would be fine." He looks up at me. "But Jay's not fine, is he?"

"Lance was blackmailing you. I thought you were friends."

Jack snorts. "Known Lance *forever*. Wouldn't trust him with my pet hamster. There are no friends. Not really." He looks down at his now-empty beer bottle. "So much for nursing this drink. I want another."

"You should quit drinking."

He glares at me. "Yeah, I am well aware of what I *should* do."

I exhale. This is a lot to take in, and so much of it doesn't add up. "Do you think it was an accident?" I ask. "Or did Lance *intentionally* throw Jay overboard?"

He shrugs, but he doesn't defend Lance.

"Jack, do you know if Lance was behind that whole Birdwatcher stuff?"

He shrugs again. "I honestly have no idea who that was."

Could it have been Lance? I wonder who else knows that Lance was with Jay on a boat that night. Bailey Cressman? His sister, Taylor?

Or maybe even Lance's own girlfriend, my oldest friend in the world, Mia?

"So what now?" Jack asks. He points to my necklace. "You recorded that whole conversation. You going to report me to the police now?"

I exhale and turn off the voice recorder. Of course he knew what I was doing. I *should* go straight to the police with this information. Jay was on Jack's boat and went overboard. And Lance brought him there.

But I don't know if I should trust Jack. He's admitted that he's drunk more than sober. And his memories of the night are foggy. I look at the time. It's past four. Jay will be back in the room soon. I need to be there when he gets home so I can tell him it's Lance. I'll make sure he doesn't go anywhere with Lance tonight.

But also . . . I need Lance's motive. I need to find if this was a random dumbass accident, or if Lance killed Jay on purpose. Because if it was on purpose, if it was for that trust or for another reason, Lance will only try again if Jay doesn't go with him tonight.

"Two days," I say. That'll give me time to investigate Lance to see if this was intentional. "You report it to the police, or I will. I'll even come with you if you want, but let's wait until Tuesday. In the meantime, say nothing to anyone about this conversation. Deal?"

He looks up at me, eyes wide. "You'll seriously come with me?"

I nod. I don't trust Jack, but I remember what Jay said—Jack has his demons, but Jay trusted him. "Yeah, I got you." I reach toward him with my right hand, my smallest finger out. "Pinkie swear."

He curls his finger around mine. "Okay," he says.

We will get justice for present Jay. But before that, I need to make sure past Jay stays safe and *alive*.

~

It's five by the time we get back to East House. Jay isn't on ResConnect yet. I put on sweatpants and my octopus sweatshirt, grab my computer to watch a movie, and sit on Jay's bed, now my favorite place to sit in the room. I don't want to investigate Lance yet—I need to talk to Jay first. So, I wait.

But Jay doesn't turn up at five thirty.

He's not here at six either. Maybe there was traffic on the subway? Or maybe he's here, in the building, but not in the room yet.

He's not here at six thirty. By six forty-five, my heart is pounding heavily in my chest. At seven, my hands are shaking.

At seven thirty, I squeeze Tentacle Ted, begging my octopus to tell me where Jay is. But Ted knows nothing.

With tears falling down onto my chest, I text Gracie.

Aleeza: He's not here. He's gone, Gracie. We didn't save him.

TWENTY-TWO

Gracie comes straight to my room and immediately wraps her arms around me in a hug. Her yellow cardigan is soft and comforting on my cheek.

"We're too late . . . ," I say. My voice is cracking. "I don't know what happened. Why isn't he here? I should have stayed in the room all day."

Gracie rubs my back, then lets me go to look at me. "He's not supposed to go missing for another half hour . . . remember . . . someone saw him in the lobby at eight."

"But we don't know who saw him! Lance could have paid someone to say that!" I sit back on Jay's bed, hugging Tentacle Ted close.

"Maybe he's still at his mother's?" Gracie suggests.

I shrug. I have no way of finding out. No way to know if we saved him, or if he'll die tonight. I feel a tear run down my cheek.

Gracie sits next to me and puts her hand on my leg. "He *would* have protected himself, Aleeza. He knows not to go to the yacht club. Or anywhere near the lake."

"Maybe Lance forced him," I say. "Maybe he drugged him like he drugged Jack."

"People would have noticed Lance bringing an unconscious guy to the marina."

I shrug.

Gracie takes my hand and squeezes. "Aleeza, we've done everything we could. He knows something bad will happen, which is way more than the Jay in our timeline knew. We saved him. I can feel it."

But I can't feel it. I'm on Jay's bed, and I can't *feel* him here with me. And that's what's scaring me. But she's right. There's nothing I can do for *my* Jay now, the one I've talked to every day for weeks now.

The one I fell in love with.

Because yeah, that's what happened. I fell in love with him. Talk about falling for an impossible guy. He's not even in my fucking universe.

Jay from *this* time, the only one on the same plane of existence with me, is *gone*. He's been gone since before I even met him. I was never going to bring him back for his mother, his cousins, or anyone else. Or bring him back for me. The Jay I know, the one from the past—he and I could never be together anyway. Our connection was only in this crappy dorm room. And as hard as I tried, I couldn't save him. Everyone in his timeline will hurt all over again. I rub my hand over my face, wiping away my tears. I won't know what happened to him. I will never know if I helped him at all.

"Why don't you get some rest," Gracie says softly. "I'll stay here in your bed if you want. Maybe he'll be here in the morning."

I sniffle, then nod. Maybe he'll be here in the morning. Maybe he decided to stay away tonight so Lance won't find him. Maybe, maybe, maybe.

I'm so tired of maybes. I need a definite answer. *Where is Jay?*

∼

I didn't think I'd be able to sleep. But somehow I did. I wake up way too early, though, and the first thing I do when my eyes open is check ResConnect.

He's still not here.

I guess I make a sound, because Gracie stirs, then gives me a sad look. "Still nothing?"

I shake my head. "No."

She sighs. "I'm sorry, Aleeza. I don't even know what to say."

What could she say? That I'm ridiculous to try to change the fate of someone I don't even know? That I'm an idiot for falling in love with a ghost?

I sit up in bed. "I guess I should give up on the podcast?" I ask. The irony is that my media project—the reason I did all this in the first place—is also a failure. I've made a complete mess of everything.

Gracie gives me an annoyed look as she sits up. "We're not giving up, Aleeza! We have to keep fighting! We know *who* he was with and *where* he was on the night he disappeared. We almost have this. We need to bring justice for Jay and give his family some closure!"

I sit up and rub my eyes. She's right. His family . . . the family of present Jay . . . deserves justice.

But this might not be as easy. "So we just go to the police tomorrow with Jack? And hope they actually do something? Don't you remember what Manal said? These are the kind of people who get away with *murder*. We know *who*, and *where*, but without a *why*, they're just going to *boys will be boys* the whole thing and Lance will get a slap on the wrist. Guys like that get away with this shit all the time."

Gracie suddenly gets out of bed. "Let me get my computer. We have a few hours before politics. I'm positive we can find out the why."

Ten minutes later we're sitting across from each other—me on Jay's bed and Gracie on mine—with energy drinks, bananas, and our computers on our laps.

"Lance is a douche," Gracie says. I assume she's looking at the same thing I am—his Instagram account. *Douche* doesn't seem quite a strong enough description for the person I am seeing.

TCU doesn't have fraternities, but if they did, I'd expect some of these pictures to come from frat houses—Lance and his boys drinking and partying and surrounded by skinny, conventionally attractive girls.

Lance's light-brown hair was longer last year, and I can't find any pictures where he's not wearing a backward hat. It's actually weird. I met Lance in October, only a few months after these frat-boy pictures. Now he wears chinos and polos (except on Halloween, when he was wearing a terrible Spider-Man costume) and his hair's shorter. It's like he's trying to appear more respectable.

But also, I can't wrap my head around the fact that he and Jay were such good friends last year. Jay's socials from that year are so different. His grid is almost completely pictures of buildings and bridges, or art and food—no open beer bottles to be seen. And I know that Jay's family income level was nowhere near Lance's and his friends'.

Why were they friends?

Jay said that Lance initiated their friendship, and they played water polo together. Maybe the friendship itself wasn't random.

But maybe I'm making assumptions.

"I can't find anything about Lance's family," Gracie says. "His last name, Murray, is too common. Can you ask Mia for Lance's parents' first names?"

I shrug. I'm really not interested in getting in touch with Mia right now.

"Never mind, found something," Gracie says. "Taylor has a picture with her mother on her Instagram at an International Women's Day event, and she linked back to her account. Her mother's name is Denise. A lawyer. So, maybe not old money like Jack's family?"

I google Denise Murray, and it doesn't take long to find pictures of her at charity events. "Oh, here's an interview with her from her law school," I say. I skim it. "She's apparently a third-generation lawyer. So that's pretty old money. She also mentions she's divorced."

"I'm looking at it now. Hey, this is cool—Denise's *mother* is a lawyer, not her father. Have you found Denise's ex-husband's name? I assume that's Taylor and Lance's father."

I shake my head. I google every combination of *Denise Murray* + *husband* or *ex-husband* that I can think of, but I can't find it.

"Jack said Lance's *father* has a boat at the yacht club. Maybe he's listed somewhere?" I ask while I google *North Toronto Yacht Club + Murray*. Eventually I find something. In an old copy of a club newsletter, there's a picture of an Andrew Murray.

"Bingo. Denise's ex-husband's name is Andrew Murray." I frown. "Probably should have looked up the yacht club and Murray first."

"Ah," Gracie says. "But then we wouldn't have learned that Lance's maternal grandmother, Denise's mother, is a kick-ass trailblazer in corporate law. Seriously. I wonder if she'd agree to an interview. She *pioneered* corporate ethics in Canada."

"Can we first figure out if her grandson had a reason to kill our friend?" It takes me about thirty seconds of googling Andrew Murray to see he doesn't hold the same high regard for ethics as his former mother-in-law.

"Wow, Andrew seems like a dick," Gracie says.

"Yeah, I think I'm reading the same news story."

It's from some business newspaper. The gist is that, about twenty years ago, Andrew Murray went into business with Stephen Everett, Denise's brother. They started a tech company, but it struggled in the early 2000s, when all the other tech companies were booming. Andrew wanted out and sold his half to Stephen. Stephen kept the business, and it finally started to do well. He sold a decade later for an undisclosed but presumably ridiculous amount of money. Andrew Murray promptly sued Stephen, claiming he was entitled to half the proceeds. He lost the case and probably lost a lot in legal fees. Five years later, Stephen died in a boating accident.

Shit. I think I know the name Stephen Everett. I grab the notebook where I've been taking notes on my media project.

"Maybe Lance's father isn't all that wealthy anymore," Gracie says. "I can't imagine suing my own family. Like . . . it's beyond my frame of understanding. Asian families would never . . ."

Finally, I find my notes, and yes, I see the name Stephen Everett.

"I knew it!" I say, pointing at my notes. "I've read about Stephen Everett. He's the Toronto mystery that Mia and I were about to cover in our web series before we stopped. This wealthy Toronto bachelor went sailing in the Caribbean and disappeared off the face of the earth. No one knows what happened. It was a calm day, and he was a very experienced sailor. Locals saw nothing out of the ordinary."

Gracie whistles low. "And Jay also disappeared in a boating accident, just like Taylor and Lance's uncle. Do you think it's a coincidence that Taylor convinced Mia to change the topic of your web series right before you started working on an episode about her uncle?"

I shake my head. "I don't think there are any coincidences."

"Wasn't your web series supposed to be about mysteries associated with the school?"

On my laptop, I open the folder of preliminary research I did on the case months ago. "Stephen Everett did his MBA at Toronto City University and donated a bunch to the school right before he died. Probably with that tech money." As I scan the article, I find a nugget of information that makes me gasp out loud. "Oh my god, he won the Bright-Knowles scholarship. Gracie, what's the name of the kick-ass lawyer? Denise Murray and Stephen Everett's mother?"

"Helen Grant. She must use her maiden name professionally. Her kids have a different surname."

My hand goes to my mouth, shocked. "Holy shit," I say quietly. "There's the link to Jay."

"What?" Gracie asks, eyes wide.

"Helen Grant is Salma Hoque's boss," I say. "Jay's mother has worked for Lance's grandmother for years."

Gracie looks up at me. "That's some coincidence."

"It's not a coincidence! The motive was the *scholarship*, not the trust. Lance's dad doesn't have much money anymore because of Lance's uncle, Stephen. I assume Grandma, Helen Grant, took her son Stephen's side. Maybe helped get great lawyers. So when Lance's new friend Jay tells him about his mom's boss, who sponsored him for a scholarship,

Lance was angry, because Jay took what he thought was his birthright. Angry enough to hurt Jay."

Gracie whistles low. "Wow. That's got to be it. Which means . . ."

"It means Lance killed him intentionally. It wasn't an accident."

We sit with that information for a while. I can't believe it's Lance. Mia's boyfriend. I shake my head. All this happened a few weeks after Mia and Lance met. They were "talking" then, not exclusively dating. Did he tell her about the late-night boat ride? Did he tell her that he drugged one friend, and threw another overboard?

Has Mia been covering for Lance this whole time?

"How do we let past Jay know this?" Gracie asks. "We need to tell him, because if he was able to save himself last night, Lance might still want to hurt him."

"We can't. Not unless he comes back into the room while I'm here."

"Well, I hope he does."

I exhale. "Me too, Gracie."

TWENTY-THREE

Monday night, before going to sleep, I text Jack.

Aleeza: How are you feeling tonight?

Jack: I'm sober, if that's what you're asking. I fucking hate it. You're still coming with me to the police station tomorrow, right?

Aleeza: Yeah, absolutely. I'm doing some digging. We'll have more to tell them tomorrow.

Jack: Okay. I'm bringing my family's lawyer. Just in case.

Aleeza: Good idea. And Jack? You know you can call or text me anytime, right? Just to talk.

Jack: Thanks. Question: there's more to you and Jay than what everyone sees, right?

I chuckle. I have no doubt there's more to Jack than everyone sees too. Who knows? One day we may even be friends.

Aleeza: You're perceptive. It's not something I can explain, though. Go to sleep—I'll see you tomorrow.

Jack: Yeah, night.

With my arms around Tentacle Ted, I finally get some sleep. It's lonely without Jay here. All I can do now is try to get him some justice.

~

The visit to the police station in the morning is . . . anticlimactic. Jack clearly expects the worst, which is why he brought the lawyer in the power suit. The police keep us waiting for a long time. When someone finally sits down with us, the detective barely seems interested. She eyes us suspiciously when Jack says he was high—she clearly doesn't believe him when he says he had to have been drugged. She even calls him an unreliable witness, which, fair.

When I tell her about Lance's connection to Jay through the scholarship and Helen Grant, she nods and writes it down but still doesn't look interested. She says she'll ask the yacht club for its video surveillance and will look into the Grant/Murray family. Mostly, she looks bored and annoyed that we bothered her. And she clearly isn't willing to let go of the suicide theory.

Once we leave the police station, Jack's lawyer takes off, and the rest of us—Gracie, Jack, and I—go to a local café that specializes in crepes and fancy hot chocolates for lunch. Aster meets us there. I don't really feel like socializing, but I get the impression that Gracie's trying to cheer me up—and maybe keep Jack with us so he doesn't go home and drink to celebrate the fact that the police didn't arrest him. We grab a table near the back with plush pink velvet seats, and order hot drinks. I get a hazelnut hot chocolate, but honestly, it tastes bitter to me. I'm just not in the mood for tasty things.

Aster shakes her head in awe after we fill her in on what happened at the police station. She's in her soccer clothes again, and sits next to Gracie across from me. Jack lounges next to me and is, of course, wearing a suit. But this one is different from his others, the dark gray and the conservative cut much more subdued than normal.

"I've never trusted Lance," Aster says, "but this is *wild*."

"You'll keep it all on the down-low, right, Aster?" Gracie asks. "The police said they don't want us to say anything to Lance until they investigate."

Aster nods. "Yeah, of course. Can't say I'm all that surprised it was him."

"How well do you know Lance?" Gracie asks her.

Aster shrugs. "Not that well. Bit of a himbo, isn't he? Fucked his way through first year."

Jack nods. "He made *me* seem like a nun last year. Surprised he settled down, actually. Doubt he's faithful." He looks at me, maybe remembering that it's my former friend who Lance is likely cheating on.

Seems Lance is an *actual* player. Not like Jay, a player only by reputation.

I shake my head. "It's so weird. I still can't get over the fact that I lost my oldest friend because of him." And lost Jay because of him too. I may not have known Jay as long as I knew Mia, but he meant just as much to me. More. I look down at my hot chocolate. The whipped cream is melting into an oily puddle.

What do I have now? No Mia. No Jay.

Gracie looks at me, head tilted. She knows exactly what I'm thinking. I smile at her. I do have new friends now.

"To be honest, none of this surprises me," Jack says. "Lance is a dick. Lance's dad is a bigger dick."

"Yeah, you said on Saturday that his dad's an asshole," I say. "Have you had issues with him before?"

"Yeah, lots. When he found out I was the one behind that Instagram account, he tried to get my family kicked out of the club." Jack snorts. "As if they'd ever kick my father out. All because I posted a picture that's literally hanging on the wall of the club restaurant. It's from, like, twenty years ago, from the club's fiftieth-anniversary thing. I guess he didn't like my caption."

Gracie raises a brow. "What was the caption?"

Jack shrugs. "I don't even remember." He takes out his phone. "I archived all the posts, though." After a few seconds, he chuckles, then reads his caption: *"I wonder if Andrew Murray attached himself to this prominent family of lawyers because he knew he'd one day need his future ex-mother-in-law to help cover up that GHB possession charge. Doubtful—Andrew isn't smart enough to be that strategic."* Jack laughs. "Honestly, not my best work, but wow, Andrew looks *exactly* like Lance in the picture—the *idiot* genes are strong in that male lineage." He slides his phone in front of me to show me the picture.

I frown at Jack before looking at it. "What's GHB?"

Jack snorts. "You really are an innocent, aren't you?"

"It's a drug, Aleeza," Gracie says. She looks at the picture. "Wow, sea of white people."

"It *is* a yacht club twenty years ago," Jack says.

I look. The picture is of about a dozen teenagers standing beside a huge sailboat. It takes me all of three seconds to find Andrew and Denise with their arms around each other. I chuckle. It must be so awkward to have a picture of you with your ex-husband forever hanging on the wall of your yacht club.

"Wow," Gracie says. "Lance looks *exactly* like his father. It's uncanny, really."

And then I see it. Gracie is right—the picture *is* a sea of white people. But there is an exception that catches my eye.

"Holy shit. *Salma Hoque*," I say, pointing to the screen.

It's from twenty years ago, but one of the girls looks exactly like the woman I saw in the press conference, except younger. I zoom in. She's kind of small, with really pretty, big eyes and brown skin. She's standing with a tall, dark-haired teenager, who has his arm around her shoulders. He's *beaming*. In fact, his smile seems borderline too big for his face.

I've seen him before. It's Stephen Everett.

"Oh my god. She's with Stephen Everett," Gracie says, eyes wide. "That's totally her. Do you think—"

I don't know how I didn't see it before. The resemblance is so strong. I lean closer to the screen, scanning the lines on the familiar face. "Stephen Everett is Jay's father."

TWENTY-FOUR

J ack leans over to look at the picture. "That girl is Jay's *mother*?"

I nod, still not really believing it. But the picture is right there . . . that's Jay's smile, right on this man's face. "Yup. Did Stephen get her pregnant back then? Do you remember Stephen Everett having scandals?" Getting a teenage immigrant girl pregnant would have been a major scandal, wouldn't it?

Jack snorts. "People like us don't have scandals. We pay to make them go away."

"Did Jay ever see this picture when he was at the yacht club?" Gracie asks.

Jack shakes his head. "I don't think so. I never took him into the restaurant."

And I remember him telling me that he'd never seen Jack's secret Instagram. I google Stephen Everett, finding a picture of the guy not long before he died. Stephen Everett looked like any other rich white guy. Nothing stands out. Brown hair, brown eyes, and a big smile.

"That would make Jay Lance and Taylor's first cousin, wouldn't it?" Aster asks, forehead furrowed. She's clearly trying to make sense of the relationships here. I don't blame her for being confused.

Gracie nods. "Yep. Their mother and Jay's father are siblings."

I exhale, staring at the picture. This is *huge*. This is Jay's *father*. "I can't even imagine." I look up at Gracie. "Do you think Stephen knew about Jay?"

Gracie shrugs. "*Someone* knew. This is all connected. Andrew thought he was entitled to Stephen's money. And now Andrew's son thinks he's entitled to Stephen's son's money."

"The trust," I say. "*Stephen* set it up for Jay."

Gracie nods. "Maybe it's an inheritance. And who would be next of kin if Jay doesn't claim it?"

"Maybe Stephen's nephew. Or niece."

Relationships and money. Pretty much the only reasons why anyone wants to hurt anyone.

Jack frowns. "Wait. How do you know Stephen set up a trust for Jay?"

Um, good question. We can't exactly say Jay told us. Or that we opened his mail.

"His cousin told us," Gracie says quickly. "His cousin on his mom's side. She said he had a trust that he could claim when he turned twenty, but no one knew who set it up."

I'm impressed by Gracie's quick thinking. I wonder if she's thinking the same thing I'm thinking that if past Jay is safe and avoided getting on that boat with Lance, then Lance has a motive to keep trying to kill Jay until Jay claims the trust.

"Should you give the police this new information?" Aster asks.

Jack shakes his head. "I need to speak to my lawyer first. He was adamant that we can't go back to them without checking with him. I'll give him a call this afternoon."

The person I wish I could tell is Jay. "Better question is, should I tell Mia?"

"Lance's girlfriend," Jack says.

I nod. "Yeah, and supposedly, my oldest friend."

Aster shakes her head. "You seem so different from that girl. How long did you know her, anyway?"

I exhale. "Mia? Forever. We were best friends since I was seven. That's when I moved to Alderville. But . . . I don't think I was *her* best friend." I exhale. "I was a sidekick. She was only happy with me when I was doing what she wanted."

"Ugh. So . . . basic," Jack says. "You're no one's sidekick. You're way better than her."

I exhale. "Yeah, I should have dropped her on Halloween. That was the beginning of the end. Ironically, the day she met Lance."

Gracie frowns. "What happened on Halloween?"

That night was the first moment that I realized maybe I wasn't going to fit in here. That I was a weird, octopus-loving book nerd, and everyone knew how to make friends but me.

"It was stupid," I say. "We were supposed to have matching costumes. It was the first time in forever that I had a non-octopus costume."

Aster raises a brow.

"Aleeza has this weird thing for octopuses," Gracie explains.

I nod, counting on my fingers. "I've been Davy Jones from *Pirates of the Caribbean*, Ursula from *Little Mermaid*, Squidward—"

"Squidward is a *squid*, not octopus," Jack says.

I shrug. "He's still a cephalopod. Anyway, she was supposed to be Sherlock Holmes and I was going to be Watson. So I showed up to the student center Halloween party in a tweed jacket, mustache, and a bowler hat, and all of Lance's friends laughed and mocked me. And Mia pretended she didn't even know me."

"Holy shit," Jack says, looking at me with awe. "I was there, in a Joker costume!"

I blink. It makes sense—Jack was friends with Lance, so of course he'd be there. I remember the Joker, actually. He was drunk out of his mind. Did he laugh at me that night?

Aster nods, grinning. "Oh my god, I remember you! Personally, I thought you looked *hot* . . . I *loved* that jacket." She shakes her head. "The tailoring! It fit you so well!"

Huh. Realizing that these people, my new friends, saw me at my most embarrassing was . . . well, embarrassing. But these two probably weren't laughing at me. Maybe my perceptions of the night are off? *Everyone* wasn't laughing.

And of course, the night wasn't all bad. That guy in the cheap Cthulhu mask didn't laugh at me and said those things that made me feel better. I was drinking, so I don't remember much, but he also said I'm no one's sidekick.

I chuckle to myself. I remember thinking meeting that guy was a *sign*. It was such a coincidence that the guy trying to pick me up had a freaking Cthulhu mask on—a mythical creature depicted with an octopus face. I'm not sure I would've ever walked away from Mia, ever stood on my own two feet, if it weren't for that little pep talk from the octopus-faced guy.

But . . . there are no coincidences. My skin tingles with goose bumps.

"Was Jay at that party?" I ask slowly.

Aster frowns. "I don't think so."

"No, he was. He came with me," Jack says. "He was Cthulhu."

It was *Jay*. My heart beats heavily in my chest. The whole time, the guy who was kind and made me feel better that night was *Jay*. I open the calendar on my phone, where I marked the dates in Jay's timeline so I could remember how much time we had until his disappearance. That Halloween party on Jay's October 29 would have been my March 25—the night of Jack's party. I remember getting home that night from Jack's house sad and drunk, and Jay made me feel better. Again. He told me he'd been out and would tell me later where he'd gone. And we slept in each other's arms across time. But the next day they found Jay's coat and phone, and he never ended up telling me where he went.

It was all on purpose. I told Jay I'd gone to a Halloween party dressed as Dr. Watson, and he went so he could find me. He wore a mask so I wouldn't recognize him. But he got an octopus-related mask so I'd pay attention to him.

"You okay?" Gracie asks.

I nod. I, of course, can't let on to Aster and Jack why this hurts so much. But Gracie has to understand. "I wish I could have known him," I say as I wipe away a tear. "I feel like I do, after investigating his disappearances for so long." I chuckle. "He liked Cthulhu, and I like octopuses."

"I have a bunch of pictures and videos from that party," Aster says. "I think you might be in one of them." She searches on her phone.

Aster finally holds out her phone to show me a picture. It's definitely from that party. There are a lot of people around, but on the side of the picture, I'm there on a couch. I have that ridiculous hat on my lap.

And Cthulhu is next to me. My head is resting on his shoulder.

I don't remember this, but I was quite out of it that night. I look closely at the picture. It's the most ridiculous image I've ever seen. Dr. John H. Watson, sitting deep in her feelings, with Cthulhu.

But it was us. Me and Jay. Why didn't he tell me about this? This happened, both in his timeline and in mine.

I wipe another tear falling down my cheek.

"You did meet him," Gracie says softly. She, of course, knows that I fell in love with him too.

Jack smiles. "Jay was a great judge of people. He saw through phony crap better than any of us. I wish I remembered you from Halloween when we met at my party."

I stare at Jack, realizing something. "You did."

He raises a brow.

I nod. "Jack, you *did* remember me! When I got to your party, you said, 'Oh, it's you. You looked better in a suit.' And you said all this cryptic shit, calling me a water lily and saying Jay danced with the water lily. You also knew about Jay's father. You said the swamp flows through Jay's veins. I thought you were just stoned, but you actually *knew* all of this."

Jack frowns. "I don't remember that."

"You've always said weird shit when you're baked," Aster says.

"Jack," I say. "You told me on Sunday that your gut instincts are so good your mom calls you a fortune teller, right?"

He nods, but I can see that he's embarrassed.

"What if . . ." I'm about to sound like a complete idiot. This is so implausible that it's almost laughable. But me and Jay talking daily for the last month is also implausible. And so is Jay in a Cthulhu mask finding me at a Halloween party. Yet it all happened. "What if you can tell your past self things? Just now, you said that you wished that back at your party you knew that it was me in the Dr. Watson costume at the Halloween party. What if that's why you knew who I was back then? People always say they wish they could tell their past self things . . . What if you actually *can*?"

Everyone at the table stares at me like I've lost my mind. Which, fair. But at least Gracie should know that the impossible is actually possible.

Jack blinks at me. "I can."

"Can what?"

His eyes are still, like he can't believe what he's saying either. "I feel like I've always known I can do that. When I'm really drunk, I talk to my future self."

Gracie exhales. "This is wild shit."

Aster nods. "I've heard of this! This lady on Etsy does future-self readings! Jack, you can make a fortune if you sell this ability."

Jack rolls his eyes. "I don't need a fortune—I have several waiting for me. Plus, I can't control it. It just . . . *happens*."

I shake my head, excited. "No, I think you *can* control it. But you control it on the future side. Like, right now, you said you wished your past self knew something. And your past self *did* know it. I think . . ." I exhale. "Tell your past self all about Jay."

He turns and looks at me like I've lost my mind. I don't blame him. "What?"

"Tell your past self," I say again. "On that night on your boat when you drank spiked Gatorade. Or before that. You said you were drunk in the afternoon, then sobered up. Tell that Jack that Stephen Everett is Jay's father, and that Lance wants to kill Jay. Maybe Jay can . . . I don't know. Run away or something. Save himself."

Everyone is looking at me like I'm nuts again, but I have to make Jack try. I'm grasping at straws here, but this is the only way I can get a message back to Jay. Jack is the only one who can do this.

Jack shakes his head. "I don't even know how to do that," he says. He doesn't look as skeptical of me anymore, at least.

"Like you just did," Gracie says. "Wish that you knew back then that Stephen is Jay's father. Actually, wish that you'd shown Jay that picture of his mother with Stephen, and Lance and Taylor's parents."

I snort. *This* is the picture that Jack sent Jay. "You did! Remember when we met on the library steps after your party, you said it started with a picture on a text."

Jack raises a brow, then finally sighs. "Fine. What could it hurt? The day Jay disappeared, I really wish I knew that he was Stephen Everett's son. I wish I'd texted him the picture from the yacht club so he could save himself." He exhales. "Who knows, maybe even a fuckup like me can help someone."

I shake my head. "You're not a fuckup." Jay said Jack was weirdly the most trustworthy person in that group. "I . . . I don't think Jay thought you were a fuckup either."

He's quiet for a while before smiling small. "What did he say to you that night? In the Cthulhu mask?"

I shrug. "He gave me some advice about stepping away from people who were holding me back. And he said . . ." I pause, remembering how his words made me feel like I could break free of Mia's influence one day. "He said when things don't go as planned, *friends never forget friends.*"

Gracie frowns at me. "Jay said that?"

I nod. He said that. And now I know he was talking about him disappearing. Telling me he wasn't going to forget me.

And here we are now, and things didn't go as planned. He didn't get back to the room at six on Sunday like he was supposed to. But he wouldn't have forgotten me. In fact, he promised me once that if something went wrong, he would leave me a message somehow.

I may not have a way to talk to the past (other than a long shot with an inebriated trust-fund kid), but Jay is *in* the past. He *had* to have left me a message.

I just have to find it.

~

After my last afternoon class on Tuesday, I rush back to my room to find any message Jay may have left me, but when I get there, I don't know where to start.

I check the whole closet, especially the tiny space behind the shelf where he tried to leave me a message last time. Nothing. I check the beds and under the mattresses. I inspect every wall. Every drawer. Under every drawer. There is nothing. Anywhere.

This is ridiculous. Of course there's nothing.

I sit on Jay's bed. I'm making too many assumptions here. Assuming the timelines match up enough that the message would be here for me. Assuming the cleaners missed the message when they cleaned the room over the Christmas break. And most of all, assuming he would have had the ability to leave me a message at all.

If he made it back to this room, he wouldn't have left it again of his own free will. He could have been drugged, knocked out, or whatever. Maybe he didn't even come back from his mother's. Maybe the cameras were wrong, and he wasn't here. Maybe he took my advice and stayed away, hiding until he could claim the trust. Maybe, maybe, maybe.

I sigh. I'm all out of ideas. If he left me a message, I would have seen it five months ago, long before I knew what I was looking at.

I look at Ted, and Ted gives me nothing. Because he's a stuffed animal, and I'm losing my mind.

I can't sleep at all that night. I want to, because I'm exhausted, but my mind keeps replaying everything I learned this morning. I get out of bed at 2:00 a.m. and turn on my computer, looking for more confirmation that Stephen Everett *is* Jay's father, and Lance and Taylor's uncle. After looking at Taylor's and her mother's socials going way, way back, I find old pictures of family events that include Stephen. I even find some pictures of their grandmother, the kick-ass lawyer Helen Grant, at a birthday party at her cottage. A huge crowd of beautiful white people, with young Lance and young Taylor in the middle.

Jay should have been in that picture.

I google *Stephen Everett* and *Salma Hoque* together and find no hits at all. I find that picture in the yacht club's newsletter online, and Stephen's name is in the caption, but Salma's is not. It doesn't make sense. Why was she there at the yacht club at all? Stephen apparently grew up in north Toronto and went to private schools, while Salma grew up in Scarborough in an immigrant community. They did not go to the same high school. Their paths should never have crossed.

I think back to the things Jay told me about his mother. She moved to Canada with her brother, sister-in-law, and parents when she was thirteen. She, like the rest of the family, had to work. *Mom waited tables at some posh place near the lake. She still refuses to butter toast from all the brunches she served.*

Could the place by the lake be the yacht club? If she worked there, I could see the club not bothering to label her in the picture, even if she had a relationship with the son of a member. She was just a waitress.

I couldn't save my Jay, but getting justice for his mother, the smiling young girl who worked at a yacht club, is enough of a reason to keep going.

~

After breakfast, I'm on my way to class when someone taps my arm. When I turn to see who it is, it takes me a few moments to remember the face.

"Kegan!" I finally say. "You work at campus housing."

He smiles. "That's me. And you're Aleeza from East House. I've been meaning to call you all week—I fixed the glitch in your room."

I frown. "What glitch?"

"Remember you came into the housing office last month saying your ResConnect was glitching? Last week, I happened to see a duplicate record in the backend. Just like you said, the former resident wasn't completely removed from the room. It's all tech jargon, but I deleted the duplicate record. It's backend systems, so it may take a few days to reflect in the app, but you shouldn't see anyone else in your room anymore."

All the air seems to leave my lungs at once. I have to lean on the nearby wall so I don't fall over.

He *deleted* Jay from my room.

"Are you okay?" Kegan asks, concerned.

I manage to speak. "When did you do this?"

"Friday, I think. I was cleaning up the database. It was a tangled mess back there."

"So . . . would it have been fixed by Sunday?"

"Yeah, could have. You probably noticed the student wasn't there anymore and thought it was magic or something. Not magic, just complicated tech! See you later!"

Kegan walks away, and I stand there with my head resting on the wall. Our connection was *deleted*. If Jay was safe that day, he wouldn't have been able to tell me. And I'll never know because he'll never be on my ResConnect again.

I close my eyes. *I'll never speak to him again.*

I exhale. If the ResConnect glitch was fixed, then it's possible he came back to the room on Sunday but couldn't see me in the app even though I was in the room. Did he think I abandoned him when I promised I'd be there?

What would he have done if he came back to the room to tell me he was fine, that he got Jack's message, that he knew to stay away from Lance . . . but I wasn't there?

I push myself off the wall. He would have left the message somewhere else, that's what he would have done. He said so many times that he'd never forget me. I think back to the facts I know from that night. He came back into the building at six and was seen climbing the stairs. Then seen going down them at eight. An eyewitness saw him in the mailroom then. Then he went back up the stairs, and he wasn't seen again. I assume he came downstairs again at some point using the secret staircase, but I don't know when.

What was he doing in the mailroom at eight o'clock on a Sunday? There is no mail on weekends. And he couldn't have been leaving me a message in my mailbox because I would have seen it a long time ago.

Wait. There's a bulletin board in the mailroom, one that hasn't been emptied in months. Screw my media class. I rush back to East House and go straight to the mailroom.

The bulletin board is about five layers deep of paper. I have no idea why no one ever cleans it. How can I find a note from Jay in all this? I don't even know what I'm looking for.

After about three minutes of searching the board, a red-and-orange image draws my eyes. I push aside the ad for tutoring that's half covering it.

It's an abstract watercolor painting of a flame, done in fiery shades of orange, yellow, and red, with some wisps of blue around it. The style is unmistakable. This is Manal Hoque's art.

I take the painting down and inspect it. It's painted on a small postcard-size sheet of watercolor paper, and up close, I realize it's not a flame at all. The swirling lines are tentacles.

It's an octopus. This is the painting that Jay asked Manal to make for me. The one that he said he'd find a way to get to me one day. Did he pin this to the board right after Manal made it?

Or did he leave it here on Sunday when he realized he couldn't leave me a message in our room because he thought I wasn't there?

I turn the small card over.

In small, messy writing, it says, *I LOVE YOU. Follow me on Instagram for updates.*

I blink. He loves me? The picture blurs with tears, but I've cried enough in the last few days. I wipe my eyes and read it again. What does he mean by *follow me on Instagram*? Follow who?

I take the painting and rush up to my room. I check ResConnect first, but of course he's not there. I look back through the screenshots to what he said when Manal painted this. *I'll give it to you in person when I am safe and sound.*

This painting is the message. He's safe and sound. But where? I check Jay's Instagram account, but he hasn't posted in months. Not since long before he disappeared. I try to check Manal's next, but she still has me blocked. If the message is on her account, I won't see it.

I almost call Gracie and ask her to check Manal's account, when I wonder: Did Jay have another Instagram account? I suddenly remember . . . the fake one he set up to follow the TCU Birdwatcher account! But he never told me the name of his fake account. I open the Birdwatcher Instagram and look at the followers. There are more than a hundred of them. One of them is Jay.

I start scrolling through the names. Now that I know more people in the school, I do recognize some of the accounts following the Birdwatcher. Or more like, I recognize the pictures. I see Bailey Cressman, Tamara from Jack's party, even Taylor and Lance. Also, a lot of birdwatching accounts follow it, too, maybe not realizing that the account isn't actually for watching birds. I have no idea how to find Jay, though. I know the account, or the picture, won't have his name, or even have anything connected to him, or the Birdwatcher would have known who it was.

Finally, I see an account. @Keanu58008. The picture is a nineties-era one of Keanu Reeves. And it follows my account.

Could this be Jay? Maybe he named it this as a nod to that Keanu Reeves movie *The Lake House*? But what about the numbers . . .

I go back and look at the chat logs, and yes, that note he tried to leave me in the closet said 100458008. I now know that 1004 is his birthday, but I never did find out the significance of 58008. But here's that number again.

I open the account, and there is only one post, uploaded on November 6—the day Jay disappeared, at 8:07 p.m. It's a picture of the bulletin board with Manal's art visible on the bottom right corner.

The caption says: *Wednesday's taking me home. I'll be fine with her.*

I blink. What does that even mean? I can't be certain that this account really is Jay—but the Keanu reference, plus the number, and of course the picture on the East House bulletin board tell me this is him. And if it is him, then as of 8:07 p.m. that night, he was fine. He saved himself and thought he would be fine in the future. But if he's fine, if he's alive, why isn't he talking to me? It's been five months—why didn't he pick up the phone and call me? And what does *Wednesday's taking me home* mean? Today is Wednesday. But it was a Sunday when he disappeared. Was it a Wednesday when he had Manal make the painting?

Does *I'll be fine with her* mean he's still alive?

I try to DM the account, but it's closed to DMs. I add a comment on the post from my own account. **DM me if you're alive.** I turn notifications on for Instagram DMs, so I'll know immediately if he responds.

I suddenly remember something. He doesn't mean Wednesday the day; he means Wednesday the *person*.

Taylor. She was sexy Wednesday Addams for Halloween.

If Taylor took him, then I need to talk to her.

TWENTY-FIVE

I text Jack right away, asking him if Taylor was there that night at the marina or if Jay or Lance mentioned at any point that she would be joining them for this night cruise. Jack doesn't write back. I don't know why I didn't think of Taylor being involved before now. She is literally Lance's sister. If this was all for the trust money, she'd also get part of it if Jay doesn't claim it. I don't know if this means Taylor killed Jay, or lured him onto the boat, or anything, really. Or maybe she helped him somehow. Jay wrote that he'd be fine, which means at the moment he posted that Instagram post, he thought Taylor would keep him safe. But it's been five months since then, and no one knows where he is. Clearly Taylor did not keep him safe.

Jack finally writes back that he doesn't remember seeing Taylor or anyone mentioning her, but he doesn't really remember a lot.

Should I go see Taylor? There is no way she would talk to me. The girl hates me. Maybe Mia can help? But then, I'm pretty sure Mia hates me too. I sigh and grab my bag, hoping that maybe some shred of our friendship still exists.

~

I call Gracie and ask her to meet me outside West Hall. When we get there, we follow another student into the building and take the elevator to the fourth floor. I knock on the dorm room that was mine only a month ago. It feels weird. I lived in this room longer than my room in East House, but this building now looks like a distant memory. It feels like a lifetime ago that I left Mia. I'm not the same person I was then.

Mia opens the door, and her face falls when she sees me. Maybe she is expecting . . . *hoping* for someone else?

"Aleeza . . . *what* are you doing here?" She glances at Gracie, and frowns. Gracie is wearing her black-framed glasses, a dress printed with multicolored cats, and a purple cardigan. I think she looks adorable. Mia's wearing sweats and a T-shirt. Her hair is flat-ironed straight again.

"We need to talk to you," I say. "Is Lance here?" I hope he's not.

Mia's face falls a little. I detect it because I know her. But she's trying to hide her disappointment. "No," she says.

"What about Taylor?"

Mia shakes her head. "No."

"Okay, then, can we come in?"

She looks like she doesn't want to let us in. It suddenly occurs to me that as strange as it feels for me to see her like this, it must be even stranger for Mia. I'm the one who walked away from her and never once tried to come back to the familiar place under her wing. I'm the one with new friends, with a new passion, with a new life.

Mia finally steps aside and puts her hand out to let us in. Walking into the room is like going back in time. It looks the same, because of course it does. All the K-pop posters, all the decor—it was always Mia's choice. I was the afterthought. Only Ted was mine.

I'm not an afterthought anymore.

But wait. Kegan told me someone else moved in here. I look over to the door that used to be mine. "Did you get a new roommate?"

Mia frowns. "Yeah, that's Taylor's room."

Oh. How did I not know *Taylor* moved into my old room? And a better question . . . why?

Mia sighs and sits on the small sofa in the room. I don't want to sit next to her, so I sit on one of the wood kitchen chairs. Gracie takes the other.

"Did you and Lance have a fight or something?" I ask.

She doesn't say anything.

"Okay, we'll skip the small talk," I say. "You know we've been looking into Jay Hoque's death, right?"

She nods.

"Did Lance know?" Gracie asks.

Mia nods. "He and Taylor both knew. Taylor said you were pathetic, chasing a ghost."

Were Taylor and Jay two steps ahead of me the whole time? It was only two days ago that I figured out that Lance and Taylor were involved.

"Are you and Lance still together?" Gracie asks.

Mia shrugs again. I see something there. Mia looks . . . a little lost. I can't decide if it's because of the loss of her boyfriend, the loss of her wealthy new friend group . . . or something else. I want to ask her . . . the muscle memory of supporting Mia through yet another breakup is kicking in.

But I can't get sucked into her orbit again. "Okay, I'm glad you're not hanging out with them anymore," I say. "I need to warn you . . . I suspect Taylor and Lance have something to do with Jay's disappearance. We've already gone to the police. We have a witness."

She looks at me, blinking. "Who?"

"Jack Gormley. He saw Jay with Lance that night at their yacht club." My only evidence that Taylor was also involved came from Jay himself, so I don't mention it.

"Jack." Mia snorts. "Doubt he was sober enough to remember anything."

"He *remembers* seeing Lance."

"Lance's father has a boat at that club. Actually, his whole extended family has boats there. Of course he was at the club that night."

"We found a motive too."

Mia crosses her arms in front of her. "So you're here to get information about Lance?"

I shake my head. "No, actually. I'm looking for Taylor. Do you know where she is?"

Mia shakes her head. "I don't understand why you're so *obsessed* with Jay Hoque. Is it because I didn't want to do your little mystery show anymore?"

"No, believe it or not, I'm doing something that has absolutely nothing to do with you. Something bad happened to Jay, and your friends have something to do with it."

"You didn't even know him!"

"But *I* did know him," Gracie says. "He deserves justice."

Mia narrows her eyes at us. "Lance said he was a dick, anyway. You should have stayed here and done the web series with Taylor and me . . . it's going to be huge. She's already lined up sponsors."

I roll my eyes. "No, thank you."

"So you're still doing the weird mystery show with your weird new friends? Taylor says true crime is stupid, and people should leave solving shit to the police."

I smile. "A funny thing happens in a big city, Mia. You were a big fish in Alderville, but there are bigger fish here. And in Alderville, there were no fishes like me, but here in the city, there are lots and lots of fishes like me. I'm not weird here . . . I'm just me."

She snorts. "I don't understand your whole fish obsession."

"You don't have to."

"Octopuses aren't fish," Gracie adds. "They're cephalopods."

Mia crosses her arms, clearly annoyed. She's not used to me talking to her like this.

I sigh. Despite everything, the fact is I'm here because her boyfriend and his sister are my prime suspects in a murder. Mia may not be my favorite person, but I don't want something bad to happen to her.

"Have you ever heard Taylor say anything . . . strange about Jay?"

Mia sighs. "She hated him. She said he didn't belong with her friends. She even showed me this Instagram account the night I met her that was, like, exposing him for cheating or something."

"The Birdwatcher," I say. "Did she say who wrote it?"

"It was anonymous. She said he should drop out of school."

"Why didn't you tell anyone this?" Gracie asks. "Taylor was bullying him, and then he disappeared."

She shrugs again. "Lots of people hated him."

I roll my eyes. Despite what Jay may have thought at the time, I don't trust Taylor at all. There is no way she ever had any intention of keeping Jay safe. "Has she said anything about him recently? Like, when his coat was found, did she say anything about that?"

Mia shakes her head.

The Instagram post said Taylor was taking him home. "Mia, where is *home* for Taylor?" I look around my old dorm room. "Is this the only place where she's living?"

Mia blinks at me, silent.

"What aren't you telling us, Mia?" I know she's hiding something.

She sighs. "I've barely seen Taylor since she moved here. Like . . . she's with her boyfriend all the time."

I snort. Tables have been turned.

"Who's her boyfriend?" Gracie asks.

"He's from out of town or something. She said he's been staying on her family's boat. He sounds like bad news."

I frown. The same way Jack lives on his boat?

"Mia, are you and Lance even together anymore?" I ask.

She looks right at me, then shrugs. "Don't see much of him either. He's not answering my calls."

Gracie chuckles. "He's *ghosting* you?"

Mia glares at Gracie.

"What marina is Taylor's boat at? Same one as Jack's, right?"

She shrugs again.

What if . . . what if there is no boyfriend? What if she's been hiding *Jay* on that boat, holding him captive until it's too late for him to claim his trust money?

Wednesday took me. But I'll be fine with her. Who knows what Taylor told him to lure him to the yacht club that night.

"Mia," I say slowly. "Have you ever *met* Taylor's boyfriend?"

Mia shakes her head. "No. Why?"

I pause, thinking. Is it possible that Jay is alive?

I look at Gracie. She is clearly thinking the same thing. "We need to get to the yacht club," she says.

~

We rush back to East House to grab Aster's voice-recorder necklace. I have no idea what we'll find at the yacht club, but we may need recorded evidence. Once we have the necklace, Gracie calls an Uber to take us to the North Toronto Yacht Club. While we're in the car, it occurs to me that we have no way of getting into this private club. I doubt very much they'll let two teenagers in to check if a member is hiding a missing nineteen-year-old on their sailboat. I text Jack and tell him we need to get into the yacht club to find Taylor and Lance's father's boat right now. He says he's already at the club and will meet us at the entrance.

I piece together a theory on the way there. On that night, maybe Taylor went to see Jay in East House and somehow convinced him to come with her to the yacht club. She promised that they meant him no harm. Since our ResConnect link was deleted, Jay couldn't tell me he was going with Taylor, so he left me the painting and the Instagram post to tell me he'd be fine.

But when they got to the marina, Taylor and Lance did something to Jay. Maybe drugged him like they drugged Jack. And they've been holding him on their father's boat until . . . maybe until he could claim the trust? Or until he could no longer claim the trust . . . six months after his birthday.

Are Lance and Taylor even capable of that? And if Jay has been held against his will at the yacht club all winter, wouldn't someone have noticed? The whole theory seems like such a long shot, but it's worth it to check. Jay might be alive.

When the car drops us off, Jack is talking to a guy in a security booth. He's wearing flannel pants and a T-shirt, with an oversize parka over it. And he has a ball cap on. After seeing him always dressed to the nines, Jack looks a little strange to me. More real.

This isn't my first time at a marina—Alderville is literally on a bay. But the marinas I'm used to are nothing like the North Toronto Yacht Club. Namely, the boats here are bigger and much more expensive. Also? Even though it's only early April, most of the boats are *in* the water, albeit almost all shrink-wrapped in plastic. I'm used to people dry-docking their boats in the winter. This marina has bubblers to keep the water from freezing around the boats. Also, instead of an old club-house, this yacht club has a restaurant overlooking a stunning view of Lake Ontario.

"So what's the deal?" Jack asks once we're through the gate. He guides us over to a bridge toward the docks and slips.

"Mia said Taylor has been spending a lot of time on her dad's boat with a mysterious boyfriend," I say. "Have you seen her here?"

Jack shrugs. "Nah, but their boat is on the other side of the club. Far from mine." He points to a bunch of boats to the left of the club-house. "I got Andrew Murray's slip number from Roger, the security guard."

"Do you think it's possible that Taylor's boyfriend has been living there all winter?" Gracie asks.

Or maybe possible that *Jay* has been living there?

Jack frowns, then looks at the boats around us. "Yeah, it's possible. This club technically doesn't allow winter liveaboard, but I've been here most nights anyway. Security looks the other way for a lot of shit here. There aren't a ton of people around this time of year, so it'd be easy to hide someone." He raises his brows suddenly, probably realizing it's Jay who I believe has been here all winter, not Taylor's mysterious boyfriend.

But the more I think about it, the more I know it's incredibly unlikely that Jay has been hiding out on a boat all winter. Right here—in downtown Toronto the whole time?

But I need to know. Even if he's not *my* Jay . . . the one from the five-months-ago timeline, even if he has no idea who I am or why I'm here, I need to know that he's okay.

I glance over at the boats with the opaque white plastic around them. "Where is Andrew Murray's boat?"

Jack points. "It's over—"

"Shit," Gracie interrupts, looking in the direction of the club entrance. Taylor is coming down the gangplank. She's talking to a man behind her. Maybe there really *is* a secret boyfriend?

We rush off the bridge and duck behind a sailboat, but I peek to watch them. The guy is tall and very well dressed—not in a suit, but the pants and dress shirt he's wearing fit perfectly. He's Black with medium-brown skin and close-cropped hair. Very good-looking, but clearly a lot older than Taylor. He's carrying reusable grocery bags from a gourmet store.

Jack motions us over to a sailboat a few slips away from the one we're behind. It's enormous. Seriously. Like, bigger than my house. "Is this what your boat looks like?" I ask Jack when we get to it.

He shakes his head. "Nah. Mine's a bit bigger."

Gracie peeks out from behind the boat. "They're headed left from the bridge. Should we follow?"

"They'll see us," I say.

"Give them five minutes or so, then we go snoop."

I exhale. This guy must be the mysterious boyfriend, which means . . . Jay isn't here. But still. Something *is* going on with Taylor. I'm sure of it. Jay's message to me was clear: *Wednesday took him home.* And Taylor is Wednesday. But where is home? Her dad's boat? Her mother's house?

I don't know what yet, but my gut is telling me that something is going to happen here today.

TWENTY-SIX

After giving Taylor and her companion a healthy head start, we quietly make our way over to the slip where Lance and Taylor's father keeps his boat. The boats on this part of the club are older than the ones we were hiding behind. Some are in bad shape . . . but most are well maintained. Following Jack, we turn at the end of a dock to an even more secluded area. This would be a great place to hide. Jack motions us to squeeze in beside a wooden sailboat covered with clear wrap, and quietly points to the boat next to it, mouthing, "It's that one."

I nod.

Unlike the other boats, Andrew Murray's sailboat isn't covered with shrink wrap. It's not huge, at least compared to some of the others we've seen, but it's big enough for someone to live on. I can see an open window to the cabin below deck. Very quietly, Jack moves closer to the boat and crouches near the window. I follow him. Gracie wordlessly stays where she is, closer to the main docks, keeping watch. Voices bleed from the window. It's Taylor and, I assume, her mystery man. I turn on the voice recorder, but I'm not sure I'll get a clear recording from outside.

"Why is he still sleeping?" Taylor asks, annoyed. "Fuck. He's driving me up the wall. How much longer do I have to coddle him?"

"Another few weeks, tops," a man's voice says, I assume the boyfriend.

"I can't even stand the sight of him," Taylor says. "Lance should have thrown *him* overboard . . ." Her spoiled voice is so distinctive. Even if I didn't see her, I'd know it was her.

"Shhh. We're so close, Taylor. This is bigger than you and Lance."

"You all owe me. I can't even believe I'm related to *that*."

Does this mean she *does* have Jay on the boat? I start to get up, intending to burst in and get to him, but Jack holds me back, pressing his finger to his lips to quiet me.

"Sounds like he's awake," the man says.

I open a text with Gracie on my phone.

Aleeza: It sounds like Jay might be on the boat. I'm going in.

Gracie: Shit. Don't . . . I'll call the police. Wait for them.

I don't want to wait. I want to get Jay out of there before another moment passes. And I want to throw Taylor overboard into the cold water. She clearly lured Jay here somehow and betrayed him.

"What the fuck are you two doing here . . . ?" a loud male voice behind me says. Shit. I turn. It's Lance. He's alone.

"Hey, Lance," Jack says, scrambling to get up. "Was showing Aleeza around the club, and we thought we saw your sister come onto this boat."

Lance looks confused and angry. And at that, the door to the cabin of the boat bursts open, and Taylor's boyfriend, the well-dressed man I saw earlier, comes out.

"What's going on here?" the boyfriend asks, climbing off the boat and onto the narrow dock between the two slips. Taylor emerges from the cabin behind him.

"They were listening at the window," Lance says.

Taylor's eyes widen. "What the hell?" She looks right at me. "Why is it always *you*? Mind your own fucking business!" She steps toward us, clearly furious.

Jack steps in front of me, but Taylor keeps talking. "First your damn web series, then you move into his room! And now, sneaking around—"

"Taylor . . . ," the boyfriend says, voice full of warning.

"Who were you talking about in the cabin?" I ask. "Who's sleeping on the boat?"

She glances at her boyfriend. "No one."

"Do you have Jay hidden on there?" Jack asks.

At that, a noise bangs below deck. Loud footsteps follow, and a door opens.

My heart picks up speed when I hear the thumping of the person's feet on the deck. Then I see him.

It's not Jay.

It's an older man. Blond hair, backward cap, and bloodshot blue eyes. And a very familiar face. If Lance weren't standing next to me, I would think it was him. This must be his father, Andrew Murray.

He points at me. "Who the fuck are you?" he growls, passing Taylor and her boyfriend to stand directly in front of me and Jack.

"Dad," Taylor says. "She's nobody. Just a friend from school."

"Bullshit she's nobody." Andrew looks at Lance, who's behind me on the narrow dock. "She's one of them, isn't she? Salma's family. They'll fucking haunt me until I die."

"Dad, she's not. She's *nobody*," Taylor says again. "You're drunk—go back to bed." Her boyfriend looks at her nervously.

Does this guy—Andrew Murray—think I'm related to Salma Hoque because we're both Brown?

Jack glances at Andrew and snorts. He's turned back into the Jack I first met—that bored, world-weary expression on his face. "You look like shit, Andy. You've been living on this boat? Oh, how the mighty have fallen. My father always said you'd never live up to the family you married into. Not surprised they took out the trash, honestly."

"You little shit," Andrew says to Jack. "This is *your* fault. I told Lance to never trust a Gormley. You're as useless as your father."

"Don't you dare talk about my father like that, you snake," Jack hisses. "You can only dream to be half the man he is. But you're dirt. Idiotic, trashy dirt."

Andrew lunges at us. I jump out of the way, and Jack tries to duck, but Andrew lands a punch right to the side of Jack's face. Andrew isn't a small man, and he punches like he's done it many times. Jack crumples to the ground, hitting his head on the old wood boat on the way down. Taylor's boyfriend pulls Andrew off Jack as I rush to Jack's side.

"I'm okay, I'm okay," Jack says, holding on to his face. He doesn't look okay. He's kneeling on the dock and his eyes are watering. Blood drips from his lip.

Andrew's still being held back by Taylor's boyfriend. "Take a picture of *that*, Taylor," Andrew spits out. "Tell that bitch that's what her precious boy looked like right before he went over."

"Dad . . . *shut up*," Lance warns.

Who is Andrew talking about? Was he there when Jay went overboard? Or is *that bitch* Helen Grant, and he's talking about the look on Stephen's face when he went overboard in the Caribbean?

"You killed Stephen Everett, didn't you?" I ask.

Andrew lunges at me, but Taylor's boyfriend holds him back.

Taylor narrows her eyes at me. "I hope you know the mess you've made. I still don't get why you're so obsessed with Jay."

I shake my head. That's exactly what Mia said. "No, *you're* obsessed with Jay," I say. "He was just living his life, happy with his mom, until you all came into it. All because you wanted something that was supposed to be his. I *know* he was here that night. What did you do to him?"

"He *wasn't* here," Lance says. "You have no proof."

"Bro, I *know* he was here," Jack says, holding on to his face. "I *saw* him."

"No one would believe a burnout like you, Jack," Lance says.

"*Nothing* was supposed to be his," Andrew says. I don't think he's even listening to his son. "He wasn't supposed to be here! *You* aren't supposed to be here either." He looks at Jack. "As much as you're a troublemaking punk, *you* belong in this fucking place. But Salma didn't belong here, and neither did her bastard kid. Stephen shouldn't have polluted the waters. Knocking up some foreigner . . . a fucking waitress . . . an *immigrant* . . ." He says *immigrant* like it's a slur. "He shouldn't have severed a family legacy! All of it should belong to *my* son. It should all be Lance's!"

"Racist piece of shit," Jack says, which makes Andrew lunge again, but Taylor's boyfriend has him. The guy is strong.

"Way to forget I exist again, Dad," Taylor deadpans.

"Yeah, what about Taylor?" I ask. "Especially since *she's* the one who brought Jay here to the marina for you. Are you sexist as well as racist? And too cowardly to do your own dirty work, so you have your kids do it for you?"

Lance's eyes go wide and shoot to Taylor. Of course, he doesn't know that Jay told me that *Wednesday* was taking him. I almost think Lance is going to admit something, but instead he snarls at me.

"Jay belonged in this world a hell of a lot more than any of you," I spit out. Clearly Jay is not here, and he's not alive. One of the three of them threw Jay off Jack's boat—I just need to get them to admit it while my necklace records them. A thought occurs to me. "Hey, Jack?" I ask. "Do you think maybe Lance *and* his father were on your boat that night with Jay? With that douchey hat on, they look mighty similar. Maybe we should turn them both over to the police."

Jack is still crouched on the dock, holding his eye. He nods, then wipes a trickle of blood dripping from his nose. "I don't know why I didn't think of it before," Jack says. "Andy, you drugged me that night, didn't you? With your favorite drug, GHB. Then you told Lance to toss Jay overboard. Just like you did to Stephen years ago. All of you are a complete waste of space. I'll see that you are removed from the club forever—so better find some trailer park where you can fit in."

No one says anything at that. I take their silence to mean Jack is right. Andrew was here, and one of them pushed Jay off the boat, but I still need one of them to say it.

I roll my eyes at Lance. "And of course you needed *Taylor's* help to get Jay here. Mia told me you were the most useless boyfriend she'd ever had and you could never *rise to the occasion*."

All hell breaks loose. Lance screams that I don't fucking know what I'm talking about, and Andrew lunges at Jack again. Lance comes at me, and I come very close to falling in the water trying to get away from him before Taylor grabs Lance. Taylor's boyfriend is the only thing keeping Andrew from hitting Jack again.

Lance eventually gives up on me and screams at Jack, "I should have thrown you *both* off your boat that night!"

Bingo. And I had that on the voice recorder.

The dock shakes with new footsteps. I turn to see two police officers. Even more chaos erupts. Lance is still screaming at Jack, Taylor is screaming at her boyfriend, and the boyfriend is still holding Andrew back. Other club members have come out to see what's going on. And the cops are trying to shut it all down.

I don't hear any of it, though. All I can think is that Andrew killed Stephen. And Lance killed Jay. Like fathers, like sons. Lance threw Jay into the water on that cold November night, just like his father did to Jay's father five years ago. Jay isn't alive. His father isn't alive. My breath catches in my throat. We didn't save anyone.

"Everyone stop shouting!" the woman officer says. Then she notices Taylor's boyfriend holding Andrew's hands behind him. "Cameron. What are *you* doing here?"

Taylor's boyfriend sighs. "Failing miserably at a sting operation, apparently. This is Andrew Murray. Cuff him. I saw him assault that boy, Jack Gormley. I've been investigating Andrew for a fraud and money-laundering ring for months, and I was this close to getting him to give me the names of his associates. Doubt he'll talk now."

Wait, what? Taylor's boyfriend is with the *police*?

Andrew looks back and forth between the two cops, his kids, me, and Jack, and realizes there's nowhere to run. He snarls at Taylor.

"Your boyfriend's a *fucking cop*? My own daughter . . ."

Taylor looks at her father with disgust, then anger. "You don't care about your children," she says angrily. "You only want our fucking money. Or Mom's money."

I blink repeatedly. Is this really happening? Why is everyone caring about *money* more than murder? I point to Andrew Murray. "He practically *admitted* to killing Stephen Everett. And Lance admitted he killed Jay Hoque. He threw him off Jack's boat. Taylor lured Jay here. I have it all on audio," I say, pointing to my necklace. "You should arrest Lance and Taylor too."

Cameron, the undercover cop/boyfriend, shrugs. "Yep, may as well take Lance in too. We'll sort it out at the station."

Lance gives Cameron an angry look before chaos erupts again. Andrew starts shouting at Lance. Lance and Taylor shout at their father. Gracie appears next to me and wipes the blood from Jack's nose with a napkin. Eventually the cops lead Andrew Murray and his son out of the yacht club. I have no idea why Taylor isn't taken too—maybe because she's dating the cop? I remember Mia telling me Taylor has a cop fetish. It figures. I want to throw up.

The police make the rest of us stick around to answer questions. I tell them we were investigating Jay's disappearance for a school project, and that when we came here to talk to Jack about Jay, we noticed Taylor acting strange, so we followed her.

Cameron shakes his head. "Amateur sleuths. It's always amateur sleuths. You should have left this to the police."

Gracie shakes her head. "Considering now you have two possible murder suspects in custody, you should be grateful."

Cameron puts his hands in the air. "Who cares about Stephen's murder! That's not even in this jurisdiction! It happened in Grand Cayman! But now we'll never find out who Andrew is working with." He rubs his face. "He's probably already called his lawyer. Months of work, down the drain."

"So money is more important than people?" Gracie asks.

"Yeah," I say. I can't believe I'm hearing this. Why does no one care about *Jay's* murder? "Does no one care about getting justice for Jay?"

Cameron looks at me a moment, then snorts. "Jay doesn't need justice anymore. And believe me, Andrew's going to pay for *all* his crimes. But we're not going to get more than him now."

I frown. "What does that mean, Jay doesn't need justice?"

"It means nothing," Taylor says. "Are we free to go? I want to be there when you tell my mom and grandma what happened here."

The cops ask some more questions, take down everyone's contact information, and let us go. As we walk out of the yacht club, I stop Taylor.

"What's your role in this?" I ask her. "Were you here that night when Jay went overboard?" I still don't know why Jay left me that message that *Taylor* had him. Or maybe he didn't. I could have misinterpreted his note.

Taylor puts her hands on her hips and gives me such a mean-girlish look that I wonder if this is all some candid-camera prank. "*You* are the biggest mystery in all this, Azalea."

"It's *Aleeza*."

"Whatever," she says, waving a hand. "Showing up at the weirdest times. Asking the most inconvenient questions. I've never trusted you. You and your Nancy Drew Crew should mind your own business."

"Why? Because we're not rich like the rest of you?"

"I'm rich enough to make up for it," Jack says, putting his hand on my arm.

Taylor shakes her head. "No." She looks at Gracie a moment, then back to me. "Look, right now I need to focus on my family. Mom and Grandma are going to flip out. Word of advice, though—don't publish that podcast of yours yet. This story isn't done."

She doesn't say anything else and leaves with Cameron.

I spend the rest of the day with Jack and Gracie in the hospital emergency room holding an ice pack on Jack's red and swollen nose.

His left eye is darkening, and although he's clearly in pain, he turns down painkillers.

"My dad's going to murder me," he says. "He's going to have to smooth a lot of ruffled feathers at the club."

"Seriously?" Gracie asks. "You didn't do anything wrong. Lance and his dad literally *killed people.*"

He snorts, then winces in pain. "It's an old boys' club. I broke onto another member's boat. Brought someone in who called the police on a member. We protect our own. We don't air our own's dirty laundry."

"And you brought in some Asians who disrupted their peace," Gracie says.

He nods. Then winces again. "Whatever happens, happens."

"Would your father stop supporting you?" I ask.

He shrugs. "Nah. Believe it or not, my parents *do* love me. And people like us protect our own, remember? It's the worst club to be in, but they'll have my back."

I'm not so sure. Look what happened to Stephen and Jay.

I take Jack's arm. "You can be in our club instead. The Nancy Drew Crew." I frown. "I'm not sold on Taylor's name for us."

He smiles and rests his head on my shoulder. "Careful, let me in and you'll never get rid of me."

I don't want to. After losing Jay, I want to keep the friends I have close.

TWENTY-SEVEN

After an entire night spent in the emergency room, Jack is released with a fresh ice pack and a list of instructions, but no prescriptions—when asked again, he turned down painkillers. His nose is broken, and he has a mild concussion. Since I don't think he should be alone, I offer to take him back to East House, but he insists he can't take away his mother's opportunity to dote on him. He calls an Uber to take him to his parents' house.

Gracie and I take the streetcar back to campus. I'm physically exhausted, but more than that, I'm emotionally wrung out. After the ups and downs of the day, I now have to accept that Jay's gone. Forever. And it hurts so much to go back to our room knowing I'll never talk to him or feel him there again. Somehow, within minutes of getting to my room, I manage to fall asleep.

That evening, after I've napped, I try to catch up on the piles of coursework I missed in the last few weeks. A text from Jack interrupts me before I've read even one article for politics.

Jack: If I go to rehab and go clean, will my powers go away?

Aleeza: I don't know. Do you want to keep your powers?

Jack: Great question. It feels a bit like a curse. Why would I want to know the future? The present is hard enough.

Aleeza: True. How are things at home?

Jack: Surviving my mother's babying without chemical armor is the hardest thing I've ever done.

Aleeza: So it's your parents who want to send you to rehab?

Jack: It's always been an option. I'm thinking of accepting the offer this time. If I give all this up, will I still be me? How much of this shit has shaped who I am?

Aleeza: I have no idea. I do know that I've seen you both drunk and sober, and I like sober Jack just fine.

Jack: You're a real gem, you know that? You don't need me unloading this on you. I should talk to my therapist.

Aleeza: You can talk to your therapist, but we're friends. You can talk to me too. I don't mind the unloading.

Jack: No, let's talk about you. One day I'll get you to explain what's the actual situation between you and Jay Hoque, but for now, why are you so obsessed with octopuses?

We continue to text for a while. I tell him about growing up in Alderville and being the weird one in my school. He tells me about private schools and European holidays and sailing trips he still wants to take. I suspect he's talking so much so he won't be tempted to drink, but I don't mind. To be honest, I need the distraction too. And . . . after everything, I like Jack. Getting to know him and seeing beyond his rich-kid mask, I can tell there's something real and genuinely *kind* about Jack Gormley. I completely understand why Jay kept him as a friend after drifting apart from the others in the group.

The next few days are pretty . . . normal. I go to all my classes. Have lunch with Gracie. I start reading a new mystery series—a gender-swapped Sherlock Holmes retelling that I'm now obsessed with. I talk to my mother for longer than normal. She tells me she can help get me a summer job in the library in Alderville if I want it, and I say yes.

I feel numb, though, like I'm just going through the motions. Actually, it feels like none of it happened, and this is how my life has always been. Since I sent the police my audio recording of the fight at Andrew's sailboat, I haven't heard anything about Lance, Taylor, or their father. Which is fine. Right now, I don't want to think about them, or about what they did to Jay and his family. It hurts too much. But eventually I am going to have to think about it. My media project is due in two weeks, and I know I need to finish it. I need to document the justice we tried to get for Jay.

To be honest, any justice feels pretty hollow. Nothing will bring him back. And I doubt I'll ever learn what actually happened that night. I have no doubt that the three of them—Andrew, Lance, and Taylor—won't suffer any consequences for any of it. But now that I've seen the underbelly of the privileged life, and what some people will do—and get away with—for money, for *entitlement*, I wonder if not knowing would make my life easier.

Mostly I'm just sad. For Salma, who I've never even met. For Manal. For everyone who loved Jay and lost him because one rich man decided he was entitled to what another rich man had.

And I *miss* Jay. In just barely a month, he became the best friend I ever had. More than a friend, actually. All I have to show for it now are the screenshots of our conversations. I printed them all out in the library so I can reread them easily. Pages and pages of conversations. Our entire relationship is now in a stack of paper on my desk, and a picture on my phone of Dr. John Watson cozied up with Cthulhu. Oh, and a beautiful watercolor octopus that says *I love you* on the back.

On Tuesday, five days after the chaos at the yacht club, I have dinner with Gracie and Aster at a noodle place near campus. Gracie insisted I come—she said I need a change of scenery, and she's probably right.

"Are you going to stay in East House?" Gracie asks once our noodles arrive. I ordered cold sesame noodles, and they look amazing. I wish I could tell Jay about this place.

I frown. "Yeah, why wouldn't I stay?"

"I dunno. Too many memories."

"You could go back to Mia's now that Taylor moved out," Aster suggests. I know she's kidding. Aster came straight from soccer practice today, so she's in sweats and her hair is pulled back. Gracie's in her yellow cardigan, and she's wearing red lipstick.

I cringe, shaking my head. "Mia and I are not going to be friends again." I pause. I've barely thought about Mia in the last few days. "Has Taylor moved out?"

Aster nods. "Word is she is going to finish the school year remotely because of her *family crisis*."

Of course, the school is bending over backward to accommodate her. It all still infuriates me. Taylor should also be in jail. She may not have been the one to push Jay off the boat, but she was an accessory to it. She knew what her brother and father did. I don't know how she lured Jay to the yacht club, but Jay left East House thinking he was safe with Taylor.

But I have no doubt Taylor will walk away from this without a blemish on her record, thanks to her powerful lawyer mother and grandmother. Hell, Lance may also get off scot-free.

"I think it would be weird to live in Jay's room," Aster says. "After learning what happened to him. So sad."

I shrug. That room is the last tangible thing I have of Jay's. When I have to leave at the end of the term in a month, all I'll have is the stack of printouts and that painting.

"I'll be fine." I smile at Gracie. "I want to be next door to you. I should probably think about finishing the podcast too. It's due soon."

"What do you think Taylor meant when she said to wait? That the story isn't finished yet?" Gracie asks.

I shrug. "I dunno. Probably some self-serving bullshit about her family being innocent in this. Or about her thinking she should get Jay's money. I honestly don't even care anymore. None of it can bring Jay back." I take a bite of my noodles. The chewy noodles with the creamy sesame sauce and crisp cucumber almost make me feel better.

After dinner, Gracie goes with Aster to her apartment. I'm again not sure what's going on between them, but hope Gracie figured out how to get out of her own way with Aster. Someone in East House deserves to be happy. I walk back to campus alone and take the stairs up to the third floor.

It's unseasonably warm—a huge change from when I first moved here, but I shiver the moment I get to the third floor. In fact, my stomach falls with dread. I exhale. Maybe Gracie is right and I *should* look into leaving this building. There are too many memories here. Not all of them are welcome anymore.

As I walk to my door, my phone buzzes with a notification. Assuming it's a text from Jack, I check my phone, but I don't have any new texts. Or ResConnect messages. It's an Instagram DM on my screen.

While opening my door, I read the message.

@KEANU58008: Hi. Long time no chat.

I stare at the message. Is this—

"Hey, Roomie," a deep voice inside my room says.

I drop my phone. It lands on the linoleum in my doorway with a thud.

Jay Hoque is in my room. The real Jay. Not an illusion, not a message on my phone. And he's not wearing a Cthulhu mask. It's Jay, alive and well, sitting on his bed with a computer on his lap and a stack of paper and Tentacle Ted next to him.

My bag drops to the ground, landing on top of my phone.

Jay isn't dead. He's safe. He's *here*.

TWENTY-EIGHT

D o you mind closing the door before someone sees me?" Jay says. "I need to lay low for a bit."

I stare at him, mouth agape. This is a dream, right? Should I pinch myself? How is Jay here?

"Aleeza? The door?" he says again.

I'm not used to hearing his voice . . . but when he says my name, it sounds like he says it all the time. It sounds so *normal* that it snaps me out of my daze. I kick my things fully into the room, hoping my laptop and phone are okay, and close the door. Then I latch the chain lock so no one can come in.

I turn back around and he's still there. It's really him. I haven't seen Jay in person for months . . . since that party two days before Halloween. I didn't see his face then, but I still know it well. From all those newspaper articles. And from seeing him all over campus before he disappeared. Bumping into him at the library, seeing him outside West Hall, and all those random encounters that turned out to be not so random after all.

But because I know his face so well, I can see that he's changed in the last five months. He's thinner. Skin a bit paler. His chest isn't as broad, and the wavy black hair pushed behind his ears is almost to his shoulders. He's wearing glasses I didn't know he had. There's a scruff on his chin and dark circles under his eyes.

He looks tired. But he looks beautiful too. *Alive.*

"Are you going to say anything, or just look at me like a shocked walleye?" Jay asks, the hint of a smirk on his face. It's the same one I imagined when he teased me in texts. "I met Ted. He's bigger than I expected. And . . . oranger."

"You're supposed to be dead," I say. It's the only thing I can think of to say.

He chuckles, and the small laugh on his face makes him look . . . well, *hot*. Really, really good-looking. Jay's here. *My* Jay. "Yeah, about that," he says, "I can explain everything . . . but first." He holds up the papers. It's my printed-out screenshots of our conversations. Pages and pages of it. "You printed our chats?"

I still have no idea what to say, so I nod, then slowly walk closer until I'm standing right in front of my bed. We're only a few feet apart. My heart races in my chest.

"Why didn't you message me on Instagram earlier?" I ask.

"It's a long story. Partly because the password was saved on my phone, which, if you'll recall, spent a few months at the bottom of Lake Ontario. I got it back from the cops, but it's dead."

"*You're* supposed to be at the bottom of Lake Ontario."

He laughs, then motions for me to sit. I do, on my own bed, directly across from him.

"I've been waiting here for you for an hour," he says, "so I cross-checked your chats against my screenshots. Guess the percentage in common?"

"Eighty-five percent?" I ask. Every test we did showed about 85 percent similarities between our timelines. All those sporting events and news stories. Our universes were 85 percent the same.

He shakes his head. "No, 100 percent."

"Really?" But when I think about it, it makes sense, because the Jay I'm looking at now is the Jay from *my* timeline. From my universe. Not the Jay I talked to from the five-months-ago universe.

But it doesn't make sense because the Jay from my timeline and I didn't know each other before he disappeared. Didn't have all those conversations for the last few weeks. But if he's here now, and he knows me, doesn't that mean that the two Jays are the same person?

Maybe there's no point in looking for the logic here. Kegan is wrong—it's not a tech glitch. It *is* magic.

Jay's still smiling at me—that smile that looks too big for his face. We stare at each other like that, just smiling. I wonder if he's thinking the same thing, that this is amazing, and exceptional, and miraculous, and it feels so right to be here on the same plane of existence for the first time. It feels . . . normal.

He shakes his head. "You're not what I was expecting in person. I thought you'd talk more. Look how much you talked in our chat." He holds up the papers again. "And you were talkative at the Halloween party too."

I frown, remembering that party. "Why didn't you tell me that was you in the mask?"

He shrugs. "I was going to. But then you told me I was dead, and that kind of, I don't know. Screwed up the vibe. By the way, you looked *adorable* in that suit. I didn't realize I had a thing for girls in Victorian menswear, but that might be my origin story. Do you still have it?" He wags his brows suggestively.

My eyes widen. This isn't happening. Now he's flirting? He just came back from the dead, and now he's flirting?

I take a breath. "Jay, what the *hell* are you even doing here? How is this possible? Lance was *arrested* for your murder last week, and his dad practically admitted to killing your father. He was being investigated for money laundering or fraud or something, and Taylor's boyfriend turned out to be an undercover cop, and there was a big fight at a yacht club and your uncle punched Jack and he has a concussion, and you're here talking about my Dr. Watson suit? Do you even know that Lance and Taylor are your cousins? Their mom is your father's sister. Their father had a long-standing beef with your father and probably killed him in the Cayman Islands five years ago . . . Wait, I'm sorry, if you didn't know, that's a lot to spring on you at once, and—"

"There you are." He smiles.

I tilt my head. "Jay, you're *dead*. You're supposed to be dead."

He shakes his head, still smiling. "But I'm not. I'm here because of you, my little octopus. You and your ragtag group of friends figured it all out and saved me. I have no doubt I *would* be dead if you hadn't got that message to me."

I frown. "What are you talking about? What message?"

He hands me a phone, which has an open text on the screen. It's a picture—a screenshot of Jack's Instagram post of the photograph of Andrew, Denise, Stephen, and Salma at the yacht club more than two decades ago.

"When Jack sent it," Jay explains, "I called him asking where he got the picture and why he was sending it to me now. He was drunk out of his mind. But he said John told him to send it."

"Who's John?" I ask. There's no John in all this, is there?

"*You're John*, Roomie. Dr. John Watson. I knew right away the message was from you." Jay shakes his head. "Did you really ask him to send it?"

I nod. "Yes, last Monday."

Jay looks confused. I don't blame him. Jack said it started with a text and a picture . . . and it did. A text that I asked him to send. I want to call Jack and tell him it worked, but I don't want to stop looking at the person sitting in front of me.

I take a breath. "Okay, Jay. Tell me *everything*. What happened when you went to your mother's that day? And where have you been for the last five months?"

He nods. And then explains what happened. Basically, when he got to Scarborough that Sunday, the first thing he did was get shawarma, which was when he talked to Ausma about me. Then he went home. But soon after he got there, he got the text from Jack. Jay had no idea why his mother was in that picture, but he recognized some of the other people—Denise Murray and Stephen Everett. He knew them as the children of his mother's boss, Helen Grant. He did not know that his mother knew Denise and Stephen that long ago. He showed it to his mother, and Salma finally admitted that Stephen Everett was Jay's father.

"So your mother knew who her boss really was?"

"Yeah, apparently way back, Helen arranged for a big lump-sum payment to Mom—basically prepaying for eighteen years of child support at once. Mom planned to have no contact with the family after that. But Helen kept in touch, checking on her every once in a while when I was a baby. Eventually she offered to pay for Mom to go to college and then hired her to work in her law firm."

"But your mother never saw Stephen? Your father?"

Jay shakes his head. "Barely. She never wanted to. I still don't know what happened between them. But Helen, I don't know, she actually *liked* Mom. It wasn't just that she felt obligated to help the woman her son knocked up. She even helped me get that scholarship. Anyway, when I showed Mom the picture, I also told her that I thought I might be in danger—that someone had been following me and could be trying to hurt me, and that this picture had something to do with it. Mom turned white as a ghost and called Helen. Soon a car showed up and took us to Helen's house." He chuckles, shaking his head. "It was *wild*. The house is as big as Jack's. Couldn't believe that was my family. Taylor showed up soon with Cameron, an undercover cop."

"Wait, what? Taylor was *helping* you? I thought she kidnapped you! Why didn't she say she was on your side? She was being *terrible* at the yacht club."

"Yeah, Taylor's technically a good guy here, but that's debatable. Anyway, they all explained that it's true: I was in danger because Taylor's dad was, like, *obsessed* with me. Apparently, years ago, when they set up a company together, my father and Andrew Murray each set up trusts for their kids—or future kids—to pay for school. They put in clauses that if they didn't have children, the money would go to each other's kids. When Andrew sold his half of the company to Stephen, he dissolved his kids' trusts because he wanted to keep the money for himself, and he figured his kids would get Stephen's trust since Stephen didn't have kids."

"Andrew didn't know about you?"

Jay shakes his head. "Nope. Only Stephen and Helen knew about me. Until Stephen and Andrew were arguing in the Caribbean, and Stephen told Andrew that his trust would go to me. Salma's son."

"And Stephen was killed for it."

"Andrew thought he deserved *all* of Stephen's money—not just the trust—since he started the company with him. But yeah, learning that I would be getting the trust instead of Lance and Taylor pissed him off. Apparently, Andrew *hated* that Stephen was dating a Brown girl all those years ago. Anyway, when Helen explained it all to me, I didn't tell anyone that I already knew about the trust. I *did* say I thought someone was going to do something to me that night at the yacht club. I assume they thought Jack tipped me off. Cameron was concerned that even if they were able to keep me safe that night, I would continue to be in danger. Andrew was the one following me in the Corolla, by the way."

This is ridiculous. "For the love of god, if they *knew* you were in danger, why didn't anyone tell you until then?"

He nods, also annoyed. "I *know*. My mother let them have it about that. Mostly Cameron was afraid of doing anything that could sabotage his fraud and money-laundering case. Andrew was the linchpin, but they really needed to get the names of the others involved. They thought I'd be fine. The police were following Andrew when he was following me."

"He really wanted to *kill* you so his kids could get your trust fund?"

"Yup. Their original plan was to bully me until I dropped out of school. Because then I couldn't claim the money since the trust required me to be enrolled. But that plan failed because I didn't care about the gossip."

"Oh my god, Lance was the Birdwatcher?"

"Lance and Taylor did that together."

I shake my head. "I don't get it. I thought Taylor was on your side?"

He chuckles. "Lance and Taylor are on Lance and Taylor's side. Their dad told them for years that Andrew's trust would go to them. They were also pissed when they discovered I existed."

"So they figured they'd get you to drop out of school so they could have your money."

"Yep. It's why they befriended me in first year. But their grand-mother discovered what they were doing when my mom had a law-yer from her firm write that cease-and-desist letter to the Birdwatcher. Lance and Taylor's mother apparently tore them a new one and threat-ened to cut them off financially if they didn't stop bullying me. And when their father became obsessed with *killing* me instead for the trust, Lance and Taylor told their mother what Daddy was planning. When they went to the police, they found out about the fraud investigation, and the kids officially joined the sting operation against their own father so their mother wouldn't cut off their gravy train."

I snort. "That's wild."

"I know." He shakes his head. "These people are *messed up*. You wouldn't believe the drama. Helen's cool, but the rest . . . I cannot *believe* I'm related to them."

I cringe. "It had to suck to discover you have a whole other family at the same time as learning they want to either bully you out of school or kill you to steal your trust fund. And then learn your father died before you knew him."

Jay shrugs. "It did suck. But it was five months ago. I've come to terms with it. Besides, he *wasn't* my father. Just a sperm donor. He never *wanted* to be my father. He figured giving me his money was enough."

I shake my head. "But why does Andrew Murray think *Lance* killed you?"

"That was my idea. See, I knew what was supposed to happen that night—I was supposed to end up in the lake. So I made the suggestion to Cameron: What if we let Andrew *think* his son killed me in the same way he killed my father? Then he'll stop trying to murder me, and the cops could concentrate on the fraud case. So Lance called Jack and snagged an invite to his boat that night. Lance told his father he was going to take the opportunity to do to me what Andrew did to my father. I boarded the boat wearing an inflatable life jacket under my coat, and I deleted anything I didn't want anyone to see on my phone. Should have written down my Instagram password, though. I'd been saving our screenshots to a cloud drive by then anyway. I had a submersible GPS tracker pinned to my pants. Cameron trailed me in a dinghy after I went over."

"Why do it on Jack's boat, then? Why didn't Lance just tell his dad he was taking you out on the water and not actually do it?"

"Andrew is a paranoid ass. He insisted on being on the boat too."

I snort. "Ha! I knew Andrew was on the boat! He drugged Jack with GHB!"

He frowns. "Holy shit, seriously? I thought it was strange Jack was so tanked. I'll bet Andrew drugs girls in bars with that." He cringes. "Anyway, when we reached open water, I discreetly took off my boots, then Lance picked a fake fight with me and pushed me off the boat. He pushed me hard . . . I think he really wanted to hurt me. I don't think he would have been the slightest bit upset if he actually did kill me.

"As soon as I hit the water, I pulled my coat off and inflated my life jacket. Lance sped away so Andrew wouldn't see me. I can tread water forever because of water polo, but the water was fucking cold. Cameron showed up after about three minutes, and I thought I was going to die. Once we got back to shore, Helen and my mom were waiting with dry clothes and all the stuff I was able to get out of my dorm room using the secret stairs. Cameron drove me straight to Helen's cottage that night. They said I wouldn't be there long—just until they wrapped up the fraud case and arrested Andrew. They said a week or two, max. But I knew I'd be there at least five months because, well, I wasn't back in your time." He exhales.

"Holy shit. You've been *in hiding* for five months?"

He nods. "I was lonely as fuck."

"Who knew you were there?"

"Only Helen and my mom. Mom moved in with me three months ago to keep me company. Oh, and of course Taylor and Lance knew. It's a miracle they didn't say anything. We couldn't even tell my aunt, uncle, or cousins."

I shake my head, amazed. "What have you been doing this whole time?"

"Netflix, mostly. I saved anything time travel related for us to watch together, though. I also read *a lot*. I did leave the cottage sometimes, just not often. I stayed in the area and wore a face mask and hat."

I laugh when I realize something. "Wait, you told me your mother's boss's cottage is near Alderville! You've been *twenty minutes* from my hometown this whole time?"

He nods, grinning. "I mean, the Instagram post I left you did say Wednesday was taking me *home*."

I laugh. "I didn't think you meant *my* home!" I realize something else. "Holy shit, you went to the Alderville library, didn't you? My mother told me about you."

He chuckles, turning a little bit pink. It's adorable. "*Busted*. It wasn't hard to find the science fiction–obsessed Indian librarian. What did she tell you about me?"

"She was delighted with you. She wanted to set me up with you."

He laughs. "Really?" He lowers his eyes with a smoldering yet playful look. "So that means your mom would already approve of me asking you out?"

I can't believe this is happening. I raise one brow. "Do you think I need my mother's approval?"

He chuckles again, then slowly moves the computer and papers aside and stands. He's taller than I remember. And so *real*. Seeing him standing so close to me, I'm now *sure* that he's the same person who made me feel like less of a disaster at the Halloween party. I remember that picture of us sitting together—me with my head on his shoulder. I want to be that close again.

He takes one step toward my bed and stops. I know this guy. I'm an expert on Jay Hoque. But I'm not an expert on his body language yet. So I wait for him to speak.

"Can I sit with you?" He indicates the bed I'm on.

I nod.

He sits. I can feel the warmth of his body. Smell his scent. It's what sleeping in his bed smelled like. I'm aching to touch him, feel him really here instead of the ghostly sensation I felt sleeping in his bed. I lean toward him.

"So?" he says, looking into my eyes.

I squeeze my lips together. "So what?"

"Will you go out with me?"

"After everything, that's all you want? Just a date?" I move closer to him. I can't help it. He's like a magnet. I decide this is my favorite moment *ever*. Right now beats everything else.

He chuckles and leans even closer, and I can feel his breath on my face. "Well, no. I want a lot more than just a date. How about we start with this." He puts a hand on my cheek, and my whole body tingles with the touch. I slip my hand in his hair, wanting to feel those dark waves between my fingers.

And finally, our lips touch. And it's . . . amazing. His lips are soft, and his arms wrap around me. I move closer, and it's complete magic.

We fit here, in this physical space, as well as we fit together on ResConnect. He pulls me closer, and soon we're half reclining on my bed. Soft kisses. Getting to know each other's lips. I clutch him tight. This is Jay. *My* Jay that I'm kissing.

I could kiss him like this forever.

~

We almost do kiss like that forever, but eventually slow down. We end up lying on my bed with my head resting on his chest and his arm around me. My T-shirt is riding up a bit, and his fingers trail lightly across my skin, giving me goose bumps.

"Does that mean you *will* go out with me?" he says. I can feel his voice through me louder than I can actually hear it.

I smile. "Of course I will. I'm delighted you're not dead." I scoot up so I can lean into his neck and inhale. "I can't believe this is real," I whisper.

His hand moves to rub my back. "For five months, all I wanted was to talk to you," he says softly. "Watch movies with you. Laugh with you. But mostly, I wanted to hold you. Like I used to when you were sleeping."

He shifts so we're face-to-face, and reaches out and puts his hand on my cheek. It's warm, real, and alive. "Me too," I say. "Except . . . not the five-months part. The part I still don't get is . . . why are you here now? Why are you out of hiding?"

"Yesterday was my birthday. I'm twenty."

"I know. Happy birthday." I give him a happy-birthday kiss.

"Thank you," he says, smiling. "And because of you, Roomie, I'm not in danger anymore. Andrew is behind bars. I came out of hiding, and we went to the lawyer to claim my trust. I suspect Lance and Taylor were secretly sabotaging the fraud case so I'd have to stay in hiding until it was too late to claim it, because the deal I made with them was to pretend I was dead until Andrew was arrested. You sped up the process a bit. So I got my money, and I'm free."

I laugh. "These people are all loaded, though. Why do they care about an education savings account?"

He shakes his head. "Because that's not all it is. This was set up when their company was just incorporated, and it included some shares in the company. Shares that have since exploded. Also, Stephen's will left a bunch of money to the trust too. It's a lot more than an education savings account."

My eyes widen. "Holy shit. Seriously?"

He nods. "I know you said that you have no interest in rich people, but . . . would you date a millionaire?"

I pretend to think about it. "Maybe. Lance and Mia broke up. Is he available?"

He laughs and clutches me tighter. And it all feels so good. Just laughing and being myself with him. This could be the beginning of something. But . . . I still have questions.

"Why did you leave Manal's painting on the bulletin board?"

"Taylor and Cameron were driving me to the yacht club, but I insisted we come here first. I told them it was to collect stuff I'd need while in hiding, but really it was so I could message you and tell you the plan. But you weren't here. I stalled them and waited two hours for you, but you never came. I knew you wouldn't abandon me because you had Jack send me that message, so something must have happened. What's that about, anyway? How did you tell Jack last Monday to send me a picture five months ago?"

"Oh, Jack can talk to his future self when he's high," I explain. That might be the most believable part of this story.

Jay snorts. "Of course he can. Anyway, when you didn't show up, I put the painting on the bulletin board. I thought I was so slick to use the anonymous Instagram account, but then I was a dumbass and forgot to get the password off my phone. Why weren't you here that day?"

I shake my head. "I *was* here. I was freaking out that you didn't show up. I found out later that Kegan severed the link between us on ResConnect."

That makes Jay laugh. "Damn it, Kegan!"

"I mean, you can't be that mad at Kegan. He's the one who placed me in your room in the first place."

"Yeah, but only because I had my mom call the school and unenroll me that morning so my room would be vacant when you went to Kegan looking for a room."

I frown. So Jay is the one who masterminded me ending up in his room in the first place? "None of this makes sense."

Grinning, he shakes his head. "Not a lick of sense. But here we are."

"I'm realizing that almost everything that's happened to me since I started school was because of *you*."

"No. Only since October 29. The day we met. And you can't be mad. I masterminded all those things so you could *save* my life."

I shake my head. "Oh, I'm not mad. Okay another question . . . what's 58008? From the note you left me, and your secret Keanu Instagram account?"

He looks at me like I should know this. "58008 is *boobs* upside down on a calculator."

I snort. Jay always seemed wise and mature, but he's still a teenage boy. Or he was . . . until yesterday. "Why didn't you find another way to tell me you were okay? You let me think you were dead."

"I couldn't tell you. You didn't know me when I went into hiding, remember? And I was practically in witness protection—the cops were monitoring all my communication. But I did intend to convince them to let me contact you once we passed the day we met on your timeline. But . . ." His voice trails off. He has an intense look in his eyes. Is he always like this in person? Like . . . there's more *Jay* in this person than should be possible. He's filling all my senses. He's *here*.

"But what?" I ask.

He runs his hand over my skin. "Remember all those movies, with all those time anomalies? Like time machines, and time loops, and all that other stuff. I had months to think, and I decided that our anomaly was the best one. I didn't want to do anything that could mess up what we had. I had to wait for you. Just like Keanu Reeves had to wait for the lady from *Speed* in that bonkers *Lake House* movie."

I smile. "Sandra Bullock. Keanu Reeves was also in *Speed*. Why don't we call him 'the guy from *Speed*'?"

"Because he's Keanu Reeves."

Good point. "So, what happens now?"

He sighs, staring up at the ceiling. "A lot happens. Helen found me a lawyer to help me officially come out of hiding. Technically, I may be charged with mischief for faking my death, but since some police were aware of it, that seems unlikely. I was able to claim my trust even though I'm not technically enrolled in the school anymore, because they agreed being afraid for my life was a good extenuating circumstance. I am going to reenroll, though, and figure out what to do about the months I missed. I'll have to figure out how to be around people again. And I really want a burrito. And good pizza. I love my mom's cooking, but I'm ready for something other than desi food." He looks back at me. "Why is there no shawarma in Alderville? I did try that roast beef and gouda sandwich on sourdough from that tea shop you told me about. Life changing."

"Bennington's," I say. It's my favorite restaurant in Alderville. This is all so . . . strange. And amazing.

He nods. "We should go together one day."

I don't say anything to that. I don't know what to say. Can we just . . . fall into a relationship? I mean, now he's here with me, and I know without a doubt that I'm in love with him. But . . . we've been apart so long—for him, at least. He needs to adjust to living in the world again.

We stare at each other for several long seconds. There are only inches between us, and I have so much more I want to say, but I don't know how.

"I thought about you a lot while I was waiting," he says quietly. "First a week went by . . . then a month, then a few months . . . it was . . . surreal. I felt like maybe I imagined it all. Like I imagined you. I reread those chats so many times. Then, to feel closer to you, I started reading all those mystery books you love. Ironically, with your mother's help, I didn't let myself forget you. But it's been a long time."

It had been about a week and a half for me. But *five months* for him.

"University has, as a whole, been hell for me," he continues. "Now I realize it's because people were trying to kill me. And others were trying to bully me to make me drop out. I expected to make amazing friends and connect with cool people. But I never felt really happy, really *comfortable*, until you showed up on my ResConnect. You were like . . . this illusion. This weird, brilliant, octopus-obsessed mirage."

"Weird?"

He leans forward and kisses me briefly. "Weird in the best possible way. But you were always ahead of me. Always out of reach. I didn't mind waiting to catch up to you."

"I'm not out of reach anymore."

He hugs me tighter to him. "No, you're not. We're both here now."

"And I don't even have a fake mustache like I did the last time you saw me."

"Which is good," he says. "Because I don't want to kiss mustache glue." He leans forward and kisses me, and then his lips trail down my neck. "Wow, you taste delicious. You should know . . . I think I'm in love with you, Aleeza."

"That's what you wrote on the watercolor octopus," I say. His lips are still on my neck.

He chuckles. "So I did. It's true."

"How can you be in love with someone you've never met?"

"We *have* met. Many, many times." He kisses my lips again, like he can't stop.

"Just so you know," I say when he pulls away, "I'm definitely in love with you. I'm so glad you caught up with me."

"Me too." He kisses me again. And I feel like I always knew that this is how it would end.

EPILOGUE

Of course, Jay and I can't hide out in room 225 deliriously happy forever. But we do stay there a long time. We even fall asleep in each other's arms—for real this time. But eventually, we have to face the world again.

The first few days after Jay's return are very intense for him, with police interviews and meetings with various lawyers. Plus, the media hounds him and his mother nonstop, asking for a statement. I support him when I can, but I can't be with him all the time. He holds up pretty well, but I know that things are harder for him than he's letting on.

Three weeks after he comes back, it finally starts to feel like the dust has settled on his legal issues. And the media inquiries trickle to almost nothing. To celebrate, Gracie and I take him to the hand-pulled-noodle-bowl place for some sesame noodles.

"Oh my god, this is good," Jay says while twirling the thick sesame noodles around his chopsticks.

"Are you finally moving from team sandwich to team bowl?" I ask. Of course, he's already had every Toronto sandwich he missed while he was gone. Since he's living back at his mother's in Scarborough, he's had Shawarma Delight several times.

He shakes his head. "Nope. Honestly, what these noodles need is maybe . . . a tortilla? A Greek pita? Maybe shove them in a baguette?"

I pretend to stab him with my chopsticks.

"Children, children. *Behave*," Gracie says, laughing. "I understand Jay forgetting his manners after he was in hiding so long, but Aleeza is . . ."

"Aleeza is *what*?" I ask.

"Aleeza is adorable," Jay says, kissing me on the cheek. He does that a lot. We're still in the can't-get-enough-of-each-other phase of our relationship. We laugh a lot. We kiss even more. And we do a lot more than just kissing.

But everything hasn't been all rosy and perfect since Jay's return. It's weird—I didn't know him before all the trauma he went through, but I can still tell that the moments of quiet that sometimes come over him are not his normal self. He doesn't talk much about his father, or what his uncle and cousins wanted to do to him. He's happy to be back in the world, and we're happy together, but it will take him time to heal from it all. All I can do is be here to listen when he wants to talk. He has a therapist, too, but of course he can't tell her everything—like the truth about how he and I met. Or how he's alive. But she's still helping.

When we're alone, we both admit that this is the best relationship either of us has ever had. And the closest. Strangely, it doesn't feel that different from how we were when we could only talk on ResConnect. We can still watch movies and talk for hours and never get bored—except now we sometimes do it in person. We still text a lot, though, since I'm still on campus in East House. Jay is planning to stay at his mother's and commute from there when he starts school again in September. I'll be moving into an off-campus apartment with Gracie.

Jay doesn't end up having any legal ramifications from faking his death. Andrew Murray was charged with assault for punching Jack, and the fraud or money-laundering or whatever charges are pending. There's some talk about extradition to the Cayman Islands so he can be charged with Stephen's death, but I doubt that will happen, which sucks. Another thing that sucks is that Andrew is out on bail. But there is a no-contact order that prevents him from seeing or contacting Jay, Jay's family, me, Gracie, or Jack. As expected, Taylor and Lance didn't face any consequences for anything. I think they should have at least been thrown out of the school for the lies and bullying in the Birdwatcher Tumblr and Instagram. But instead, the media has been portraying them as *heroes*. Because those all-Canadian good looks and old-money wealth mean *they* are the ones who saved the poor Brown kid from Scarborough. And of course, Taylor and Lance are eating up the attention. They haven't once contacted Jay, their *cousin*, to see how he's doing. I would bet that they're pissed they didn't end up getting his money.

The paperwork for Jay to access the trust is still being sorted, but Jay says the first big thing he's going to do with it is get a larger house for his mom, aunt, uncle, and cousins. And get his mom a new car. His mother won't let him spend more than that on her—but he wants to take her on a vacation too.

I've met Salma a few times now, and I really like her. She's a lot like Jay—super easy to talk to and gets really enthusiastic about the things she loves. She seems to like me, but that could be because Jay told her that I'm the one who saved his life, not Lance, Taylor, or Jack. She doesn't fully understand how. I don't fully understand how either.

Of course, Jay and I can't tell anyone the real way we met. Gracie is still the only one who knows the truth. We've been telling others we initially met at that Halloween party and were talking up until he disappeared. When I randomly moved into his old dorm room months later, I started investigating his disappearance for my media project. We told people that when I interviewed him for the final episode of my podcast (which I really did—mine was the only podcast he spoke to), we hit it off again and started dating.

A lot of people think he's with me only because he's grateful I helped solve the case, and they think I'm with him only for his money.

But we know it's not true. My mother thinks *she* manifested our relationship after she got to know him at the library, like some kind of psychic matchmaker. Jack suspects we knew each other in a past life or something, but we haven't told him the truth.

Jack is still in the sixty-day rehab program where his parents sent him after he healed from his injury. At first, he could only email us, so I would get these long, anxious, rambling emails about how he's afraid getting clean will change who he is and that no one will care about him if he isn't the same Jack Gormley anymore. He's allowed to text now, and his mood and anxiety already seem better. He texts Jay and Gracie regularly too. I think he'll still be *Jack* when he gets out, even if he can't talk to his past self anymore. He'll still be the center of his group of friends—it will just be a new group.

Speaking of Gracie, she finally admitted that she won't date Aster because she's afraid Aster will grow bored of her and leave her for someone rich like Nat, which is ridiculous, of course. Aster is crazy about Gracie. But at least Gracie isn't pushing Aster away anymore. They're not officially a couple, but Jay and I think they will be within a few weeks.

"Oh shit, look who's here," Gracie says, looking at the door of the noodle shop. This place is near campus, so a lot of students come here. From Gracie's face, I expect it to be Taylor or Lance, two people neither Jay nor I want to see.

But it's not. It's Mia. She's with someone I remember from West Hall who's in her program. It seems Mia ditched the trust-fund crew too. Or they ditched her.

When Mia sees us, she freezes, like she's not sure what to do. Eventually, she comes over to our table. I wonder if she's going to make a snarky comment about me or Gracie.

"Hi, Aleeza," she says. I can't read her expression. I think I must be out of practice with her. But she doesn't seem . . . angry at least. Or phony.

"Hey, Mia," I say. "You remember Gracie. And this is my boyfriend, Jay."

She introduces me to the girl she's with. Jay just nods to them, not saying anything. He's guarded for a reason—because he's been in the news so much, people he barely knows have been constantly coming up to him or contacting him since he's been back. He's not interested in being a celebrity or being in any spotlight. Plus, he's a loyal boyfriend, so he doesn't like Mia.

But Mia doesn't seem to be here for Jay. She gives me a hopeful smile. "Aleeza, will you . . . I mean, are you going to be in Alderville this summer?"

"That's the plan," I say. "I got a job at the library with my mother." And I'll be visiting Jay in Toronto whenever I can. He's planning to visit me in Alderville too. Sometimes he'll stay at my place, and sometimes he'll go to his grandmother's cottage. After being near Alderville for so long, he says it feels like his second home.

"Oh, okay," Mia says. "I thought maybe we could move home together. Like, my dad could drive us. No reason for both our parents to come get us. And maybe we can hang out this summer?"

I look at her, confused. She looks genuine, like she's actually trying to be my friend again. Does she really think I'd want to hang out with her after everything?

"Why?" I ask.

She frowns.

"Mia," Gracie asks, "I heard Taylor moved out of your room. Did she drop your web series?"

She shakes her head. "No, we're cool. I mean"—she looks awkwardly at the person she's with—"I'm sure I'll see her soon."

I snort. "I don't think Lance or Taylor will be back." I look at Mia. I wonder if she's going to say anything about her ex-boyfriend's dad trying to kill my boyfriend. Or mention how strange it is that her ex and my current are actually long-lost cousins. I wonder if she's going to ask how Jay is doing after what Lance's father put him through. Or how I'm doing.

But she doesn't. Because she doesn't really care. She's only here because she feels like she lost whatever fight we were having, and Mia is not used to coming in second after me.

"It's fine," I say. "Jay's driving me home. And I doubt I'll have time to hang out," I say. I smile at Jay. "We're going to be really busy together."

Jay takes that opportunity to kiss my cheek again. I love him for it.

"And she'll be busy with me," Gracie says. "Aster and I are planning to come up for a beach trip to Alderville. Plus"—she looks at me—"Jack will be back by then. You know you'll be seeing a ton of him this summer too. He's talking about finding a marina for his boat there."

I nod. "Yeah, I'm going to be *so* busy this summer. But I'll probably see you around town or something." I turn away from her and pick up some noodles with my chopsticks.

"Fine," Mia says. She starts to walk away from the table, then turns back and looks right at Jay. "I don't know what she told you, but Aleeza was, like, *stalking* you for weeks. She was *obsessed*. It's so creepy you're together now."

Jay shrugs. "Actually, it's not creepy; it's convenient. Because I was stalking her too. I'm even more obsessed with Aleeza."

Mia rolls her eyes and walks right out of the restaurant. Her friend trails behind her, a confused expression on her face.

Gracie snorts a laugh. "She didn't even get food."

I shake my head. "Nah. She's not going to stay and watch me be happier than her."

Jay rests his chin on my shoulder. "Were you really *obsessed* with me?"

"Yep," I say. "Still am."

"Good. Me too." He leans into my neck and plants a kiss there. And then another.

"Ugh, you two. Go get a room!" Gracie says, stabbing a chopstick into each of us. We dissolve into laughter again.

We had a room. And getting that room is the best thing that's ever happened to me.

ACKNOWLEDGMENTS

This book is a little bonkers. As my first mystery, and my first book that doesn't adhere to the rules of time and space, it was both an enormous challenge and the most fun to write. I couldn't have done it without a ton of help, though, and I am so grateful to everyone who supported me while I was working on this story.

First, my daughter, Anissa, who helped me brainstorm possible book ideas for a story that's grounded in the real world but with a touch of magic. My author friends, specifically Roselle Lim, Mona Shroff, Nisha Sharma, and Namrata Patel, who helped me tweak the synopsis to make it *almost* make sense. And to my husband, Tony, who helped me iron out two timelines worth of plot wrinkles, and who helped me with boating terminology that somehow never stuck in my head despite the boat on my driveway.

To my agent, Rachel Brooks, who is always amazing, and who supported me branching out into a new direction. And my editor, Carmen Johnson, at Skyscape—I love that she gave me the opportunity to *play* with this book, and she always had faith that I could pull off a mystery. Thanks to Leslie Lutz for the excellent and insightful developmental and line edits, and to Kellie Osborne for the copyedit that reminded me how commas work and who made me wonder how I should spell *mindfuck*. Huge thanks to the Skyscape team, including production editors Patricia Callahan and Nicole Burns-Ascue; and the entire sales, publicity, marketing, and art teams. I always have confidence that my books are in excellent hands at Skyscape.

Gratitude (again) goes to my family, Tony, Anissa, and Khalil, for all your patience and support for this weird career of mine. And finally, to Darcy and Matcha for their support, their purrs, and for mostly keeping off my keyboard while I was typing this book.

ABOUT THE AUTHOR

Photo © 2021 James Heron

Farah Heron is the author of *How to Win a Breakup*, *Tahira in Bloom*, *Accidentally Engaged*, and *Jana Goes Wild*. After a childhood filled with Bollywood, Monty Python, and Jane Austen, Farah constantly wove uplifting happily ever afters in her head while pursuing careers in human resources and psychology. She started writing her stories down a few years ago and is thrilled to see her daydreams become books. Her romantic comedies for adults and teens are full of huge South Asian families, delectable food, and most importantly, Brown people falling stupidly in love. Farah lives in Toronto with her husband and two kids, plus two cats who rule the house. For more information, visit www.farahheron.com.